PRAISE FOR
SQUIRE OF TRUTH

"Simply amazing. A murder mystery novel set in a fantasy. I loved every second of it, and having Cole as the main character was thrilling"

—**FELL SKYHAWK**, GOODREADS

"I love this return to the fantasy world of the Blood of Kings. I love that Jill Williamson has allowed us to see what has happened to some minor characters from the original series. Williamson doesn't disappoint in this mix of fantasy and murder investigation. It is great to see characters who have struggles that people can relate to. What a great read. I can't wait for more."

—**JAMES NICHOLS**, GOODREADS

"Such a great addition to the Blood of Kings: Legends!"

—**DUNCAN**, GOODREADS

"I loved slipping back into this world and visiting these characters again and getting to know new ones. It's like attending a family reunion! I loved Cole so much. His quiet and inwardly-very-flappable-but-outwardly-stoic nature just made me want to hug him."

—**JESSICA DOWELL**, GOODREADS

SQUIRE OF TRUTH

←BLOOD OF KINGS: LEGENDS→

SQUIRE OF TRUTH

←Blood of Kings: Legends→

JILL WILLIAMSON

sunrise PUBLISHING

Squire of Truth
Blood of Kings: Legends Book 1

Blood of Kings: Legends

Squire of Truth
Lord of Winter
Lady of Shadows
Heir of Light

Blood of Kings

By Darkness Hid
To Darkness Fled
From Darkness Won

20
18
17
12
11
4
15
7
16
6
1
8
2
10
3

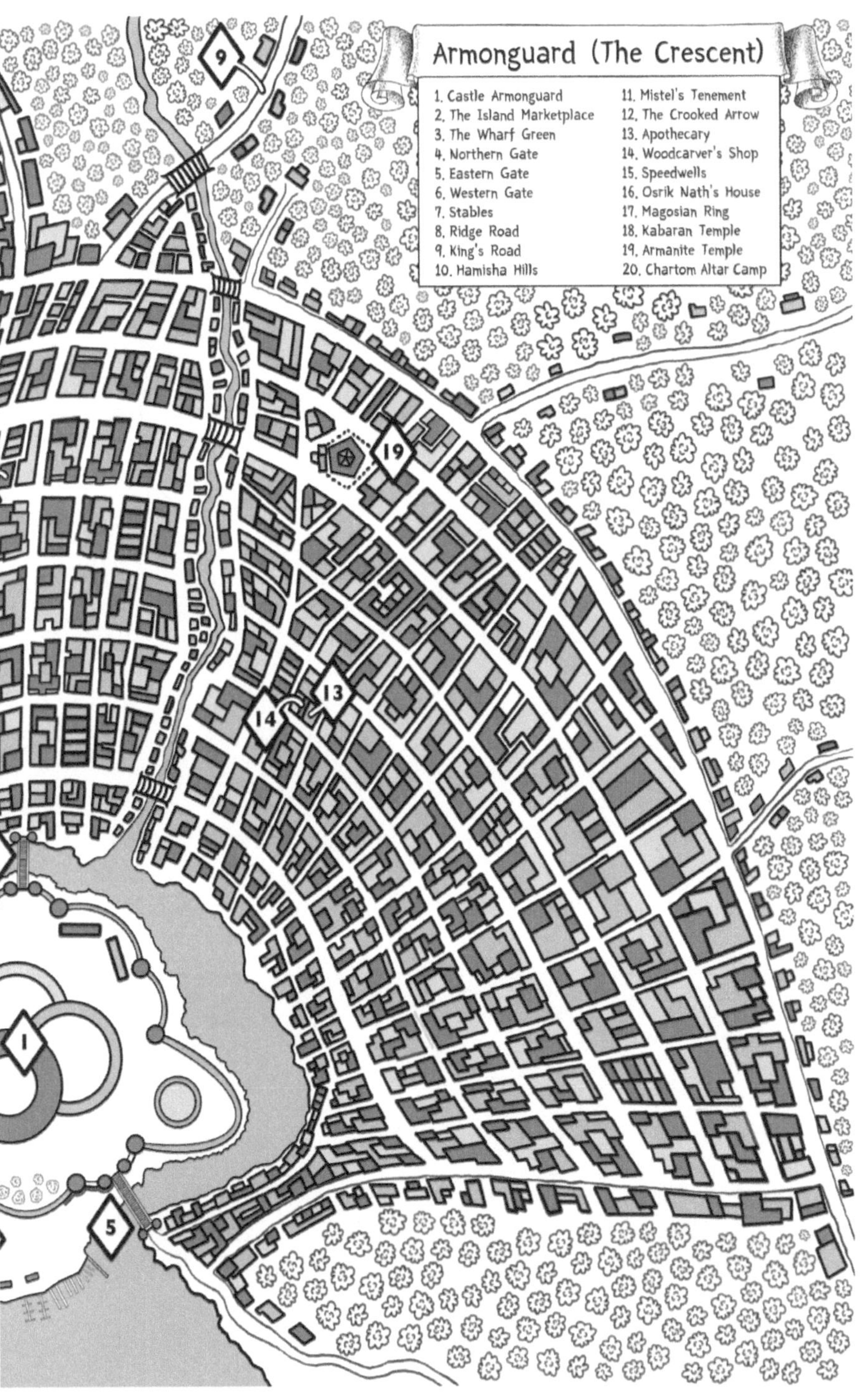

Armonguard (The Crescent)

1. Castle Armonguard
2. The Island Marketplace
3. The Wharf Green
4. Northern Gate
5. Eastern Gate
6. Western Gate
7. Stables
8. Ridge Road
9. King's Road
10. Hamisha Hills
11. Mistel's Tenement
12. The Crooked Arrow
13. Apothecary
14. Woodcarver's Shop
15. Speedwells
16. Osrik Nath's House
17. Magosian Ring
18. Kabaran Temple
19. Armanite Temple
20. Chartom Altar Camp

To Susan May Warren.
Thanks for suggesting I write a story about Cole.
That was an excellent idea!

CHAPTER ONE
COLE

MUSIC SPOKE TO THE SOUL. IT DIDN'T quarrel or judge. It lifted and soothed and roused and comforted. It spoke where words failed, and liberated captives from the prisons of their own minds.

Cole needed it. Had missed it desperately in his positions as stableboy then squire to the Crown Prince. Now that he owned his own lute, he could make music again. Maybe even find others to play with. A place he might finally belong.

He threaded his way through the crowd in the wharf green just outside the walls of Castle Armonguard. The island marketplace ran through the grassy area between the western and eastern castle piers and followed along the scalloped whitestone half wall that overlooked the northern shore of Lake Arman.

The majority of the vendors and shoppers came from the Crescent by ferry, though Cole and anyone from the castle reached the wharf green by taking one of two long staircases down the scalloped walls from the eastern or western castle gates.

Cole glanced out at the glassy water, so still compared to the raucous waterfall back home in Mitspah.

But no. Mitspah hadn't been Cole's home ever since the king-to-be had plucked him from that prison and given him a new life.

In the distance, the thrum of a tabor drum melded with the pure, crystalline tones of a flute. It sounded like it was coming from the waterfront. He altered his course through the market and headed across the green in the direction of the lively sound.

That there had been a vicious battle here five days ago seemed impossible but for the sounds of carpenters and masons working to repair the damage done to the castle. And for the occasional patches of brown grass, stained with sun-dried blood.

As Cole stared at an overly large section of bloodstained grass, someone bumped him, which jostled the lute he was carrying under one arm. Cole quickly cradled the instrument where it would be safe.

The island market was much smaller than those in the Crescent—the greater city of Armonguard, where the vast majority of people lived. Yet many vendors and artists chose to come to the wharf green, hoping that—while most of their sales went to the soldiers and castle employees—they might someday sell to royalty.

Despite its small size, the island market boasted a stunning variety of goods such as handcrafted tapestries, candles, jewelry, leathercrafts, fabrics, weapons, and so much food. Breads and pastries, fruits and vegetables, every kind of meat, and jars of jellies, sauces, and spices.

An old woman approached Cole from a stall filled with figurines of gods, goddesses, and demons. She gripped in her gnarled hands a clay statue of Yobatha, the goddess of pleasure.

"I sense a hostile spirit of dissatisfaction in you, young man," she said. "Let Yobatha help you drive it away for good."

"How much?" Cole asked, curious what people paid for such scams.

Deep-set eyes, ringed in creases, fixed on his. "Can you put a price on freedom and happiness?"

"Not a monetary one," Cole said, continuing on.

It amused him how many vendors already displayed the Crown Prince's likeness. His face graced paintings, tapestries, quilts, dolls, and statues in a variety of mediums.

A puppeteer stepped in front of Cole, working a marionette of Achan, which was the name by which only close friends knew the Crown Prince. "Bow before your sovereign, man," the puppeteer said. "Don't you know who I am? I'm the great bloodvoicer mantic, come to read your mind."

Cole bristled at such mockery of his prince, yet he couldn't help but be impressed by the likeness painted onto the tiny wooden face. The way the artist had drawn Achan's eyebrows, facial scars, and satisfied smirk in meticulous detail in addition to the dark-brown hair styled into a ponytail, the stark blue paint of the eyes, and the walnut-brown color of the puppet's skin made an uncannily accurate imitation. Whoever had made it must have seen the prince up close at some point—or perhaps only one of these vendors had, and the rest had simply crafted copies.

The man maneuvered the puppet's limbs out to the side, its tiny hands extended to convey regal authority. "Don't just stand there!" the puppeteer said. "I demand you bow before the true prince of Er'Rets."

Cole chuckled and moved on. How Achan would hate seeing himself as a puppet, the very title he had given Esek Nathak, the impostor who had for so many years stolen his life—a life Cole knew the prince still wasn't certain he wanted.

The flute's airy timbre intensified with a rapid crescendo. As Cole kept his gaze peeled on the waterfront where performers tended to congregate, a man in the crowd caught his attention. Stringy hair the color of dirt and a short beard. Ice slid down Cole's spine and sent a chill over his entire body.

Atul Shakran? Here? The villain had not been seen since the

prince killed the cham bear in the forest outside Mitspah. All thought him dead.

Cole's eyes said otherwise. He increased his speed to get a better look, but this time *he* knocked into someone. Before he had a chance to apologize, his victim wheeled around and shoved Cole so hard he almost fell to his rear.

"Watch where you're going, boy!" The man resembled the giant Jax mi Katt in thickness if not in height. Tangled black hair hung in frizzy clumps from his head and chin, and his eyes were like two beetles that seemed to twitch and snap as he loomed over Cole.

"Excuse me." Cole fixed his gaze on the ground and kept going.

Someone stepped into his path, and Cole dared to glance up. The brute had two brutish friends. One with pale hair tied into braids. The other with no hair at all.

"Ain't no excuse for a pimple like you," the first man said.

"What shall we do with him, Osrik?" asked the man with braids.

Cole didn't stick around to find out. He darted around a table filled with taper candles and raced along the southern arc until a fist grabbed the back of his tunic. His feet whisked over the short grass as his body was dragged backward. He clutched his lute and cursed himself for leaving the safety of the keep, where everyone knew him.

The first man, Osrik, threw Cole against the castle wall. His head hit the stone and smarted something fierce. Suddenly, Cole found himself back in the Battle of Armonguard, cornered against a fallen chunk of stone wall by an Eben warrior, convinced he was going to die. There were too many people, too much screaming, too much blood.

"You hear me, boy?"

A slap to the face brought Cole back to the present. His pulse pounded in his ears, his heart flailed inside him, but he kept his face plain and used his fiercest voice to say, "Leave me be. I've no interest in fighting."

Osrik's brows rose, and he smirked at his friends. "He's not interested, I guess."

"He's outnumbered, is why," said the bald man.

"Three against one," said the man with the braids.

Steel rang against wood. "Make that three against *two*."

Kurtz Chazir stalked toward them, brandishing his longsword, Kingsguard red cloak rippling in the breeze. "Put him down, Os," he said.

"Friend of yours?" Osrik asked Cole.

"A good friend," Cole said. Perhaps *only* friend.

Osrik shoved Cole, which knocked him so far off-balance that he stumbled to his knees. The goons laughed until Kurtz jabbed his sword at them. Then they all ran like spiders when a boot drew near.

Kurtz sheathed his sword and extended his hand to Cole. "You all right?"

"I'm fine." Oh, the lies that rolled off Cole's tongue on a daily basis. He hoped Arman wasn't keeping track. He took hold of Kurtz's hand and let the man haul him to his feet.

"What are you doing over here?" Kurtz asked.

"I heard music. Then I thought I saw Atul Shakran."

"Surely not." Kurtz grabbed the scruff of Cole's neck. "Even if he were still alive, he'd be a fool to come this far south seeing that our prince has won the crown, eh? Now, this is *not* the way to the waterfront. Follow me."

Cole strode as fast as his legs would carry him, and still he had to practically jog to keep up with Kurtz. The warrior was so confident, even his walk resembled a dance.

Cole blew out a breath to calm his thrumming heart. "How do you know that man?"

"Osrik Nath once served in the Kingsguard," Kurtz said. "He's a deserter who now makes his living as a slumlord. His father died and left him with several tenement buildings in the city. Why work when you can live off the rutahs of paupers?"

Cole grimaced at the idea of anyone having that man for a landlord.

Kurtz glanced to his left and slowed, turning his head to locate Cole in the crowd. "Hey, keep up, will you?"

Cole increased his speed and lost his grip on the lute. The instrument slipped, and he lunged to catch it before it hit the grassy ground. He braced himself for another rebuke from Kurtz, but the man's focus had settled on a woman selling pears from a basket.

Cole caught up in time to hear Kurtz promise the woman the world and everything in it if she'd meet him later in the orchard. Cole fought back a grin. Kurtz fell in love at least three times a day.

"That'll be a rutah for the pear," she said flatly, "and I'll be on my way."

"You break my heart, you do," Kurtz said as he handed her a coin.

"Tell one of the minstrels," the woman said. "Maybe they'll write a song about it." She flashed a broad smile and slipped through the crowd like a leaf on the wind.

"Cheeky female," Kurtz said, biting into the pear and spraying droplets of juice onto his short beard. "She didn't even ask if you wanted one." He offered the pear to Cole.

"No, thanks," Cole said.

Kurtz shrugged and took another bite. "You don't think it's the bandage, do you?" He fingered the white fabric on his neck that hid the stitches from the arrow wound he'd received in the Battle of Armonguard.

"I don't think so," Cole said.

"Oh, there's Regov. C'mon."

They continued through the crowded market. Cole paused when Kurtz did and nodded when the man introduced one of his fellow soldiers, but Cole found it difficult to focus. Twice more, he returned to the Battle of Armonguard in flashes, reliving the horrors he'd seen that day. For the past week, he'd been walking around in a half fog, deranged and sometimes uncertain he hadn't died and was haunting Armonguard as a ghost.

Which was why he needed music. It had always been a way to escape the pain life thrust upon him.

Sir Caleb Agros.

The man's voice came magnified in between Cole's ears. Sir Caleb, wanting to message him with bloodvoicing magic.

Cole reminded himself not to answer aloud and thought, *Yes, sir?*

Your shields are down, Cole, Sir Caleb said. *You must keep them up at all times.*

Cole grimaced. He had no bloodvoicing magic of his own, so he continually forgot to shield. *Yes, sir. Sorry, sir.*

Where did you leave the standard from the battle? You didn't have it cleaned, did you?

No, sir. Kurtz gave it to Sir Gavin.

Ah, I'll ask Sir Gavin then. Thank you.

And the man was gone.

Why wouldn't Sir Caleb want the standard cleaned? It had been covered in dirt and blood. Cole shoved away the thought. The prince had given him the day off, and Cole intended to enjoy it.

As he caught up to Kurtz along the waterfront, he picked up the dulcet melody of a nearby songstress and let her clear, hypnotic words roll through his head.

"I don't belong here.
Why do I try so hard to fit?
I have so many feelings in a day.
It's hard to know what to do or say.

I should just leave.
It takes too long to make a space.
It's easier to simply disappear,
Rather than be brave and face my fears."

The profound words reached inside and caressed Cole's heart. He could relate. Escape was always easier than confrontation.

"Now, that's a pretty lass, that is." Kurtz's comment pulled Cole from his reverie. Being shorter, he wasn't able to see over the heads of the crowd and stepped to Kurtz's left to see who the man was admiring this time.

The songstress whose words had been so affecting had coils of hair the color of poppies, and radiant, flushed skin almost as freckled as Cole's. She moved as if music were her master. Cole had never heard a voice with such purity of tone. She looked his age, although that didn't mean much. Everyone thought Cole was younger than his nineteen years.

Kurtz tipped his head toward the girl. "Too young for me, eh?"

Cole shrugged. "That never stopped you before."

"I never chased any skirt *that* young."

Which was completely untrue. Cole allowed himself a rare smile. "What about Lady Averella?"

"I never said a wanton word to Lady Averella."

Cole raised an eyebrow.

"Okay, maybe once. Twice. But the minnow knew I was kidding, she did." Kurtz shoved Cole's shoulder. "Enough of your judgment, eh? I say this girl is for you. Let's go meet her so you can write her some poems."

"No, thanks," Cole said. "I came to play."

"And play you shall. And she will sing. If that's not a match, I don't know one, eh?"

Cole turned his gaze back to the girl crooning out a steady

vibrato, and he drummed his fingers on the lute. "I don't think she'll care to—"

"Trust me, there's nothing like a woman to make you forget your troubles. And cause all new ones." Kurtz gripped Cole's arm and dragged him through the crowd toward the stage. "Don't get all tense, now. I'll arrange an introduction, eh?"

A superficial romance was the last thing Cole needed, but Kurtz still had a grip on his arm, and the band had begun a new song that made Cole forget his protest.

The lutist's calloused fingers danced over the strings with graceful proficiency. Each pluck resonated deep in Cole's chest, wrapping around his heart and patching the worn holes. He closed his eyes and leaned in, holding his breath as he savored the melodic tones.

The tabor thumped in at a much faster tempo and took control of the performance. The lutist strummed, ticking his head back and forth, and the songstress skipped to the center front of the stage and began to sing.

> *"When I pluck lute strings, my fingers play, play, play*
> *When I play those chords, my soul sings, sings, sings*
> *When I sing out loud, my voice rings, rings, rings*
> *When I ring and sing and pluck those strings, I bless my*
>   *King."*

Cole tapped a beat along with them on the body of his lute. What fun would it be to sit on stage and play with them. Chords only, at first. It would take time to get back into practice. He used to be decent at fingerpicking, though nowhere near as gifted as the man on stage.

Kurtz leaned his head toward Cole's ear. "They any good?"

Cole nodded.

"How much should we give them?"

Cole glanced at the stage and the scarce collection of coins the audience had thrown down. "I don't have any money with me."

Kurtz shoved his hand into his pocket. "I have plenty. How much?"

Cole shrugged. "More than what's on the stage. What a terrible way to earn a living." Tragic, really. Music gave so much to so many. Why didn't people appreciate it more?

Kurtz offered a fistful of coins to Cole.

Cole nodded at the performers. "Put them on the stage."

"I thought *you* should put them on the stage, you should," Kurtz said. "We want her to like *you*, not me."

Cole shifted on his feet, rolled his shoulders, and glanced at the girl. An awkward meeting with the vocalist held no interest for him. What would he say to her? Nice song choice? You sing good?

"You do it," he said.

Kurtz released a sigh so filled with exasperation you'd think Cole had insulted the man's honor. "All right, but if I get the chance, I'm telling her it was your idea."

Kurtz edged forward and tossed his handful of coins. The songstress's green eyes turned on Kurtz, and she rewarded his offering with a glowing smile. Something in her expression reminded Cole of Nya, the marshal's daughter back in Mitspah. He suddenly felt like a fish on a dock, recently caught and quickly losing air. He rocked from one foot to another and glanced behind him, looking for a way out.

Across the grassy expanse of the plaza, Cole again caught sight of Atul Shakran, this time talking to a short Jaelportian woman in a red cloak.

Was this real? Or was Cole merely seeing things again?

Atul started to walk away, and the hairs on Cole's arms stood on end.

Like Kurtz's jaunty stride, Atul also had a signature walk—the silent, creeping glide of a prowling thief. It had always felt out of place in his role as Mitspah's temporary steward.

Cole glanced toward the pretty songstress, who was in the middle of the second chorus, and Kurtz, standing at the edge of the stage with plans to embarrass Cole.

Another time, perhaps.

Cole slipped through the crowd and followed Atul.

The girl would prefer Kurtz's company anyway.

CHAPTER TWO
MISTEL

SOMETIMES, SONGS GREW OLD—EVEN favorites.

Mistel Wepp clapped along, trying to rouse the audience as Rispen and Burch played through the interlude. Four of the dozen people standing in front of the stage halfheartedly put their hands together. Lands! This audience. Had they no appreciation for music? Her gaze passed over each person. Who had the most coins in their pockets? Who might actually spare some? None of the women, likely. Women saw her as competition. Mistel bet on the old man down front or the broad-shouldered soldier who'd just wandered over. Both, if she were lucky.

One last chorus. Mistel grinned at the crowd, hoping her smile would encourage a few more coins to fall at her feet. She took a deep breath and sang:

"When I beat that drum, my fingers pat, pat, pat
When I pat a rhythm, my feet tap, tap, tap
When I tap my feet, I long to dance, dance, dance,
When I pat and tap and dance and sing, I bless my King."

As the boys finished off the last measure, Mistel threw out her arms and bowed with as much pomp and flourish as she could muster. The old man down front threw a coin that rolled in a circle before coming to a ringing halt.

One rutah. Was that truly all?

The clang of multiple coins pulled her attention to a soldier. Thank Arman! Perhaps tonight she and Edera would get more than bread alone.

If she could get away. Osrik Nath was lurking at the bottom of the back steps with his cronies *and* Lander Gysel, of all people. Mistel couldn't imagine how the two of them had become acquainted. She didn't like the look of Osrik's half-starved leer or Lander's cold hatred. Neither man had offered even one rutah, the stingy hunxes.

Mistel again bowed to the applauding crowd, enjoying the attention, if not slightly annoyed that their praise hadn't motivated more generosity. Far too many of them stood watching and listening and ogling every inch of her. The least they could do was toss her a coin.

Rispen trilled out the drumbeat, waiting for Burch to strike the final chord. Mistel gathered the coins on the edge of the platform. Three rutahs here. Two more there. And five from the soldier. Ten didn't divide evenly. Mistel had taken the overage last time, so today's extra coins belonged to Rispen.

What cheap ingrates lived in Armonguard! Three rutahs wouldn't even buy a loaf of bread in the island market.

Burch strummed the last cord, Rispen struck his tabor a final time, and Mistel spun back to face the audience—all six who remained—and curtsied.

Then she extended her hand to Burch. "Ten rutah," she said. "Rispen gets the extra."

His thick fingers plucked three coins from her palm, and she dropped what was left into Rispen's outstretched hand.

"First day back since the battle closed the castle," Rispen said. "I wouldn't worry."

"We might get more if you'd ask," Burch said.

The words made her weary. The performance had been a complete waste of her musical talent, and Burch somehow considered that her fault? These middle-aged men had no idea what it was like to be a young woman on a stage.

"I'll ask when I'm not being stalked." She jerked her head toward Osrik and his gang, who were still loitering by the back steps with Lander.

She did not want to talk to any of them.

Thankfully, the soldier still stood in front of the stage. Cetheria had protected her today, praise the goddess. If the soldier had five rutahs to spare, he likely had deep enough pockets to buy her a meal too.

Mistel met the man's gaze. He raised his chin and offered a little wave.

Oh yes. He would do nicely.

"See you tomorrow," she told the boys, then put as much effort as she could into performing a sultry walk to the front of the platform.

It was a game, this flirting. She wasn't trying to sell herself. Only needed to get enough so she and Edera could eat, then she'd disappear.

"Why, hello there." Mistel gazed down on the soldier. Broad shoulders and deep-brown eyes. Sandy-blond hair tied back in a tail and a short, reddish-blond beard. Bandage around his throat. Probably wounded in the battle. "Like what you heard?"

"Very much," he said. "And I have a young friend who admired you even more."

Two soldiers? Interesting. "Is that so?"

His gaze panned the crowd. "I was hoping you'd come and say hello, I was. Between you and me, Cole is a bit shy, eh?"

Mistel scanned the crowd for another young man in uniform, but this mysterious Cole was nowhere to be seen. "Help me down, please?"

Strong hands gripped her waist. She grabbed his shoulders as he whisked her off the stage and set her in front of him. This close, she had to tip back her head to see into those dark-brown eyes.

"You a northerner?" she asked. "Couldn't help notice your accent."

"Kurtz Chazir. Grew up in Tsaftown, I did." He smiled then, and dimples tucked into his cheeks.

Oh my. Not at all bad-looking, *and* he knew it. If she wasn't careful, this one might be trouble. "Where the cham bears roam?" she asked.

"Not many cham enter the city. Most keep to the woods. But I've had my share of run-ins with the beasts, eh? I ran one off that was trying to raid a food wagon of a young family headed south. Another time, I helped skin the one our Crown Prince killed."

Mistel perked up. "You know the prince?"

Kurtz pushed out his chest. "Fought beside him in the war. My young friend, Cole, is his squire, he is."

Mistel gasped as she made the connection. "I know who you mean. Round face with lots of freckles?" Encountering anyone with more freckles than Mistel was unusual, so when she'd first glimpsed the squire during the parade the other day, he'd caught her attention.

Kurtz nodded. "That's the man."

"Man, is he? I wouldn't mark him at a day past fifteen. How old is he really?"

"You'd have to ask him, miss. It's not good manners to go spouting a friend's age."

"Isn't that only in the context of women?"

"It's as true for men as it is for women. Maybe truer, eh?"

If that wasn't the biggest longtale she'd ever heard. "How could it be truer? It's men who declare unmarried women spinsters at the age of twenty."

He folded his arms across that thick barrel chest. "Yet you accused the king's chosen squire of childhood based on a few freckles."

My, but he liked to banter. She set her hands on her hips. "I judged his age on his height. I happen to like freckles."

"Come now, we could go on for a day like this. Why not meet the man and ask him yourself, Miss. . . Forgive me. I came upon you midperformance and didn't hear your name."

"Mistel Wepp." She looped her arm through his, determined not to lose her chance at a full meal. "I would be honored to meet your squire friend."

They explored the market, but Kurtz did not see Cole, which seemed to put him on edge.

"Surely you're not worried about the king's squire?" Mistel said. "Such a man must be more than capable of protecting himself."

A soft grimace passed over Kurtz's features, but he said, "Oh, it's not that. Cole is a blade dancer, he is. But I'm due for drills. Lingered too long, I did, listening to your captivating voice."

Lands! This man was a bigger flirt than she was. "You must be famished," she said. "A strong man like you. What say we grab a quick bite to eat?" She patted his arm. "Your treat."

He chuckled and slipped his arm from hers. "I took luncheon an hour ago. No, I'm not hungry. Just late. You'll have to meet my friend another time, eh?"

"It would be my honor."

"Until then, my lady." He took her hand.

But no! She couldn't let him leave yet. As Kurtz raised her hand to his lips, the beaded bracelet Edera had made slid down her wrist.

"You must take this token," she said, removing the bracelet. "It's dear to me, but I would sell it to you if it might bring joy to your friend."

Kurtz eyed the beads and grimaced. "How much?"

"The beads were handmade by the finest artisan." Mistel twirled the bracelet in her fingers and gazed at it as if it were a treasured heirloom and not something Edera had thrown together from two broken necklaces. "I couldn't bear to part with it for less than a copper."

One side of Kurtz's mouth hitched up, like he suspected her of a con, yet he dug into his pocket and withdrew a handful of coins. A bronze was worth twenty rutah, a copper worth one hundred, so she forced herself to remain calm at the sight of a half dozen bronze and coppers and two silvers amongst all the coins. Kurtz plucked out one of the coppers and held it up as he dumped the bulk of his wealth back into his pocket.

"A token from the famous Mistel Wepp will be treasured, I'm sure," he said.

Mistel tucked the copper into her reticule, then Kurtz used two hands to pull the bracelet off her wrist, all the while gazing into her eyes.

My, she had little doubt this man was a rogue, yet he seemed determined to set her aside for his friend. A pity the squire had vanished. If she could work out a way to meet him, perhaps she could earn dinner for the entire week.

"Promise me you'll bring the squire by tomorrow," she said. "I long to meet him."

"Will do, my lady." Kurtz held up her bracelet and winked. "Thanks for the bauble, eh?" Then he walked away.

Well! She'd made more money in five minutes of flirting than in an hour of singing. She didn't like what that said about her talent as a songstress.

Mistel sashayed through the market, feeling like a wealthy heiress with a clinking reticule at her side. It was still a bit early to take home dinner. She might as well enjoy herself.

She wove her way right to her favorite fabric vendor and searched for the blue cobalt. A pang ran through her when she didn't see it up front as usual. Had someone purchased it? Her gaze roamed the bright colors until she finally spotted it on a shelf in the back.

She didn't have enough money to buy even a half yard of anything in this booth, let alone enough to make a gown, but her success with Kurtz emboldened her to duck inside anyway. She touched everything as she made her way back—fine satins, plush velvets, and linens embroidered with silk threads.

She reached the cobalt silk and ran the soft, fine fabric through her fingers. If only she were rich enough to buy the things she wanted. She had traded favors with friends to make sure her clothing was stylish and upper-class, even if she wasn't. How lovely would it be to own more than three dresses? And capes and slippers to match. And earrings and bracelets that jangled on her wrists as she clapped to Rispen's tabor beat.

The vendor appeared. An older man, mid-fifties. "Can I help you, miss?"

Just this once she allowed herself to dream, to pretend her reticule was always full. Mistel wrinkled her nose. "I'm not sure. The other day, the cobalt silk caught my eye, but I have plenty of blue gowns. Now that I'm inside, I don't see anything its equal."

"Not true, miss. Why, this crimson is of the very same weave. I have it in emerald and gold as well."

"I do like the emerald shade. Do you deliver?"

"Of course, miss. Would you like to try one of them?" He gestured toward a small platform in front of a narrow mirror.

What could it hurt? Rich women were incredibly fickle. The man would be disappointed when Mistel bought nothing, but with her in her best dress, and with her jingling reticule, he would never suspect she was a pauper.

"Oh, very well," she said. "Let's try the cobalt anyway."

The next thing she knew, she was standing on the small rectangle of wood while the fabric vendor's wife—Gletta—wrapped one end of the fabric around Mistel's neck, then crossed the excess length tightly around her torso like a bodice.

"That color is beautiful with your complexion and hair." This from one of two female patrons who had stopped to watch Mistel's impromptu fitting. With them was a towheaded boy, weaving between the bolts as if they were a maze.

"Thank you." Mistel gazed at her reflection, admiring the way the silk pleated at her waist. Gletta unwound the remainder of the bolt in whorls at her feet, making it easy to imagine what a beautiful gown the silk might make.

"I would pay anything for your figure," the woman said.

"You must buy some," said the other.

Their words pleased Mistel too much. Were these women really shoppers? Or had the vendor planted them to sprinkle sugar on his customers?

Such thoughts! Mistel had lived among the poor for too long and had grown cynical.

"Don't touch that!" The vendor ran toward the boy, who dropped a filigree brooch that had been pinned to a fabric display.

Mistel caught sight of a familiar reticule in his hands.

"Thief!" Her stomach sank to her toes. She leaped off the platform, but the unforgiving silk tangled around her legs. She fell onto the floor and desperately tried to wriggle free from the fabric.

"My lady, try to stay calm." Gletta's hands found Mistel's and pulled her to her feet.

"That boy took my reticule!" Mistel said. "All my money. . . I must find him."

"Forgive me, my lady," the vendor said, the filigree brooch in his hands, "but he will have vanished by now. I am sorry I did not see him for what he was." He turned his dour gaze on the other two patrons. "I thought he belonged to one of you fine ladies."

"Certainly not," said the first woman. "I would never take a child to the marketplace."

The second woman held up her purse. "He didn't get mine."

"Nor mine," said the first woman, patting her pocket. "I don't doubt he sidled right up to us, trying to act like he belonged. I'm sorry I didn't know what he was about, or I would have sent him on his way."

Mistel unwound the silk from her neck. If she hadn't been so wrapped up in her own vanity, she wouldn't have made herself a mark for a thief.

"My lady, I feel responsible," the vendor said. "To make amends, I would be happy to give you half price on anything we sell."

Even half-priced silk was beyond her budget. "Thank you, sir, but I have lost all my money. I cannot pay you."

"I would give you credit, of course," he said. "I would need only a moment to check your references."

Oh yes. That was just what Mistel needed. The vendor discovering she lived in a tenement house and could barely afford her daily meals, let alone rent.

"Thank you for the offer." She handed the end of the silk to Gletta. "My heart is not in it today. Perhaps another time."

Mistel dragged her feet back through the market. To have been so lucky in one moment and so unlucky in the next. . . What was Cetheria trying to say? Mistel had not been very devout of late. There was no temple of Cetheria in Armonguard. Unsurprising considering the prince's allegiance to Arman, the Father God who had helped him push back Darkness.

Mistel shivered at the memory of hearing Achan's voice in her head, singing.

No darkness have we who in Arman abide. The Light of the world is Câan.

All the years they'd spent together in Sitna, she'd never once heard him sing. Yet he had a decent baritone.

He must have converted to the Armanite faith to secure the crown. Who wouldn't? His magic had allowed him to speak to every mind in Er'Rets. He'd asked the people to join him in worship and prayer, which had brought back the sun—had vanquished Darkness for good.

Mistel didn't want to think what that meant about Cetheria. She supposed it wouldn't hurt to leave an offering for Arman.

What was she saying? An offering of nothing was nothing. She had nothing to give.

She would simply have to remedy that.

While most of the people in Armonguard were friendly enough, most were also poor. That's why Rispen had them play at the island market. Guards had more money than the general populace, and such men were willing to part with their coins when a pretty girl batted her eyes or shared her tale of woe.

Mistel didn't like outright begging, though. She wasn't yet ready to sink so low as that. But Edera needed sustenance, and Mistel *would* beg, if need be, to bring food home to her friend.

She would also wash dishes, though that was another last resort.

She kept her eyes peeled for targets. Guards old enough to be her grandfather were usually willing to contribute to her plight without expecting anything in return. Young men were the worst, of course. She had been mistaken for a prostitute more times than she cared to admit.

She wasn't trying to trade. She wanted a handout, free and clear of any conditions.

Unfortunately, she had been in Armonguard long enough that most locals recognized her as a songstress. She didn't want begging to destroy her hard-earned, good reputation.

She steered her gaze over the crowd and hit a mark. To her right, a man in an Old Kingsguard cloak. Old enough to be her father, and if the concern in his expression was any indication, he just might do. She sighed and leaned against a lamppost, clasping her hand to the neckline of her dress and dabbing away a fake tear as she thought up a story to inspire pity.

Her stolen reticule was reason enough.

The old guard started toward her. Perhaps this wouldn't be so hard after all.

"Mistel!"

She jerked at the bite in that voice. On her left, Osrik Nath pushed through the crowd.

Thunder and rats! That man would be the death of her. Which was exactly why she kept avoiding him. At least this time she saw no sign of Lander Gysel at his side.

She was about to run when a familiar young man stepped out from between a fruit vendor and someone selling spices. He wore plain clothes and held a lute under one arm, but there was no mistaking those freckles. They gave him a friendly demeanor, and his short brown hair seemed so overly average that it was completely endearing. He had an athletic build and stood only a few inches taller than her.

"Cole!" Mistel thrust her hand into the air, waving as if she knew him.

As she approached, his gaze settled on her. He had kind and expressive hazel eyes. A moment of recognition passed across his face, then confusion wrinkled his brow.

She linked her arm with his free one. "I've been looking for you everywhere." Surely the squire to the Crown Prince of Er'Rets would help her. And if she played her cards right, he might even buy her dinner too.

CHAPTER THREE
COLE

HOW MUCH HAD KURTZ PAID HER? The songstress clung to him and smiled, as if pleased to see him. Her touch sent goosebumps up his arm, which he tried to ignore, knowing she didn't mean to be affectionate. Not really.

A few moments ago, Cole had watched Atul board a small boat down at the docks. If the villain was planning to harm the prince, he likely wanted to get inside the castle. So why leave? Perhaps Cole had been mistaken, and the man hadn't been Atul Shakran after all.

"Why were you looking for me?" Cole asked the girl.

Before she could answer, a man yelled, "Mistel, wait!"

That voice drenched Cole in ice. He glanced through the crowd and spotted Osrik Nath pushing toward them.

"Please tell me your name isn't Mistel," Cole said.

She grinned and tugged his arm in the opposite direction. "Come with me and my name will be whatever you want it to be."

Huh. Maybe Kurtz *hadn't* paid her. Clearly, she hoped to use him as a reason to lose Nath, yet she also didn't seem the least bit frightened by the man. She couldn't possibly know about the altercation Cole had gotten into with him earlier, but since Cole had finished following Atul, leaving seemed like a wise plan.

It wasn't like *he* wanted to run into Nath either.

"All right," he said.

Before he could decide which way to go, Mistel led him up the stairs along the castle wall to the western gate. As they climbed, her orange curls bounced hypnotically.

"Where are we going?" Cole asked.

"Taking a shortcut to the Crescent."

Cole glanced over his shoulder, glad to see no sign of Osrik Nath on the stairs below. He might as well tag along with this girl and see where it led. He had the day off, and it would please Kurtz to hear about it later. Stop the man from nagging him so much.

Cole should say something. "Uh, I saw you sing earlier." His face flamed as the words left his mouth. "It was nice."

Commence awkward conversation.

Her gaze shot to his. Specks of blue flecked her green eyes. "You heard me?"

"I was with a friend when we came across your performance in the plaza," Cole said.

She grinned, and the top row of her teeth revealed a slight, entirely endearing overbite. "Sir Kurtz Chazir. He wanted me to meet you."

So, she *had* met Kurtz. Likely fancied him. Most women did. "He's not a knight," Cole said, as if that might make him and Kurtz equals. "Not yet, anyway." He wanted to add that Kurtz was afraid of the dark, but Cole couldn't betray his friend, even to impress a pretty girl.

"He sure looks like one," she said.

He did. Plus, Kurtz arguably had earned the knighthood ten times over, yet he'd also committed twice as many blunders. While Sir Caleb and Sir Gavin were making sure Kurtz was properly punished for his most recent infraction, the prince wouldn't forget him for long. Achan was a man of second, third, and fourth chances.

"Nice lute," she said.

"Thanks." Cole tried to think of something to say. "I enjoyed 'I Don't Belong Here.'"

Her eyebrows rose. "Most people prefer 'I Bless My King.'"

"Oh, that one is catchy, but the lyrics in 'I Don't Belong Here' say something deep. Provoke feeling."

They continued to climb, and when she looked at him again, something had changed in her expression. Had he insulted her? He wished he'd kept his mouth shut.

But then she said, "That's actually my favorite song."

Yet she seemed upset. Why was it so hard for Cole to read people? He swallowed his nerves and tried again. "The line 'It takes too long to make a space' is brilliant."

"Thank you." Her lips curved into another smile, this time with no teeth showing. Head tipped back, she half closed her eyes and bumped her shoulder against his. "I wrote it."

"Did you?"

"You sound surprised." She pulled away. "I suppose you think women can't write songs."

"Oh, no. I don't think that."

"But you assumed someone else had written it."

Cole shrugged, eager to make amends for whatever slander his words had effected. "I'm sorry. I don't know much about music."

What? Why had he said *that*?

At the top of the stairs, Mistel stopped and folded her arms. "You, who carry a lute, don't know much about music?"

Cole's chest grew tight from the lack of air, and more lies escaped. "This? It's not mine."

No, no. Why was he lying to this girl? About something so stupid too?

They were standing on the landing between the gate that led

inside the castle and the drawbridge that led to the Ridge Road and the Crescent.

Mistel grabbed his left hand and ran her thumb over his fingertips. "Liar." She threw his hand back at him. "Your calluses tell a different story." She stomped onto the drawbridge, made it about four steps, then wheeled around, hands on her hips. "Why would you lie about that?"

He didn't know.

No, that was a lie too.

He lied when he was afraid. Of being judged.

His pulse pounded in his head. He wanted to run back to the sanctuary that the castle and his position as the Crown Prince's squire provided him, but her lyrics sprang to mind. Before he could stop himself, he said, "Because 'It's easier to simply disappear, rather than be brave and face my fears.'"

Oh, Arman. Could he have said anything *more* embarrassing? His face flamed, likely matching the color of her hair.

She rolled her eyes and made a sound like she was clearing her throat. "Men." She stomped toward him, grabbed his hand, and tugged him over the drawbridge. "Come on."

Cole followed obediently, pleased his use of her own lyrics had smoothed things over. Mistel had clearly escaped Osrik Nath, so wanting to spend time with Cole after he'd lied made no sense at all. But considering Atul had left on the boat—and since this songstress was enchanting—he would happily follow her wherever she wanted to go.

Mistel led Cole through the winding alleys and narrow lanes of the Crescent. He had been here a few days ago for the parade to celebrate Arman's victory over Darkness. The way the buildings were stacked next to one another like bricks had shocked him.

How could people live so close to one another when there was so much more space elsewhere in Er'Rets?

In the dusk, the tall, narrow buildings conspired to hide the sunlight, which chilled the air and more keenly brought on the stench of rotten filth. The flickering flames of streetlamps swept the ground with yellow light and the long black shadows of their wooden posts.

Cole blinked down a dark alleyway and could have sworn he saw an Eben giant swinging an axe. A second look revealed nothing but shadows.

The web of streets was filled with the steady clip of hooves and wooden wheels on uneven cobblestones, the clamor of merchants closing their stores and packing up stalls into carts, and the bantering of co-workers.

It all felt like trouble, which reminded Cole what had brought them here. "How do you know Osrik Nath?" he asked.

Mistel shot him a glance. "How do *you* know him?"

"He's a Kingsguard deserter." Cole liked how that made him sound enmeshed in all matters of the army when it was really all he knew about the man besides the strength of his arm.

"Is he?" Mistel asked. "He owns the building I live in. He'd like to own me, but I'm not interested."

"Ah." Cole should have known that with a man like Nath it was something like that.

They made their way down a muddy street spotted with horse manure, patches of compost, and swaths of wastewater that had been thrown from windows.

Unfortunate that anyone called this place home.

They approached a building with swinging front doors. Lively music, boisterous laughter, and the sounds of clinking tankards leaked onto the street. A sign hanging from wrought-iron chains on the eave of the roof proclaimed The Crooked Arrow.

People filled the interior like worms in a can. At least two dozen dancing, and that many more folded into cramped tables, eating or drinking. Dozens of candles and a roaring fireplace bathed the faces and rough-hewn wooden tables and walls in glows of gold and bronze. Two men fought near a smoldering hearth. Several shouted to be heard over the din.

The music drew Cole's gaze to a smoky corner where a band of five played a jaunty tune. A lutist, a flutist, a harpist, and two on percussion—one playing a tabor, the other a tambourine. Cole had seen the lutist before but couldn't place him.

Mistel tugged his hand toward the melee. "Dance with me."

He dug in his heels, and their arms stretched a taut line between their clasped hands.

She pulled harder. "Please, Cole."

How strange to hear this girl speak his name. It happened so rarely from anyone not part of the Crown Prince's entourage. "My lute," he said.

She nodded toward an empty table. "Leave it there."

He considered the weathered wood tabletop, still soiled with breadcrumbs and drops of liquid from its previous occupants.

"The lute will be fine." Mistel shimmied toward him until they were toe to toe, her nose almost touching his. Never breaking his gaze, she tugged the lute from his hand and set it on an unoccupied bench, then slid her fingers down the backs of his arms until she caught his free hands in hers.

Cole felt as though he'd stepped into the hearth fire as Mistel pulled him out with the dancers. The crowd forced them to stand so close that Mistel's skirt whipped his legs with every twist and twirl. As they moved together, their gazes remained locked. Cole sensed some unspoken conversation between them, a shared understanding of song and dance. He penned lyrics in his head to match the moment.

She sees me,
She reads me,
In the darkness of a dance.
The music swells,
A melody tells,
How our hearts are in a trance.
She takes my hands and—

BAM!

The noise silenced the tavern and blasted Cole back to the battlefield. A tanniyn rose from the water and smashed its head through the tower wall.

A man inside the tower screamed. The prince was up there.

He gripped the worn wood of the standard pole in one hand, his sword in the other, and ran toward the tower. "For Arman!" Cole yelled, because that was what Achan had told him to say. Chunks of stone and white dust began to rain from above. Cole hunched his shoulders and darted out of the way, but a stone knocked the sword from his hand. When the debris stopped falling, he went back to look for his sword, but an Eben giant stepped out from the dust, spear clutched in one hand, shield in the other. Three lines of black paint slashed across his forehead, signaling his allegiance to the enemy.

"Lee-lee-lee-lee-lee!" the Eben sang.

Without a weapon, Cole turned the flagstaff and pointed the end at the giant.

"Cole!"

A sharp breath brought him back to the tavern, eerily silent as all heads faced a young man standing over a tray of food at his feet.

"Sorry!" the young man said.

The crowd applauded—someone whistled—as the server set about cleaning up the mess.

Cole's gaze snagged on the lutist, who was glaring at him like *he'd* been responsible for the rude interruption.

"Emory? From the top." The drummer beat his tabor—one, two, three, four—and the band started up again.

The noise slowly surpassed its original level. Excessive dancing. Jarring music. Abrasive people. The lutist continued to glare.

"Cole, what's wrong?"

He blinked away from the scene to Mistel, whose green eyes were fixed on his, filled with something like pity.

He wanted his life to change, but this was too much, too fast.

A man reached for Cole's lute at the table.

"Hey! Don't touch that!" Cole lunged in front of the man and grabbed the instrument.

The man lifted both hands. "Sorry, mate. Didn't know it was yours."

Cole swallowed hard.

"Are you hungry?" Mistel stepped close and touched his cheek. "It's long past dinnertime."

Cole shook his head. "I'm sorry." Unable to last another moment, he darted out the swinging doors and sprinted toward the castle.

Chapter Four
Mistel

T ODAY, BAD LUCK FOLLOWED MISTEL like a shadow.

She stood on the porch of the Crooked Arrow and watched as the squire ran around the corner, out of sight.

There went dinner. Again.

What had she done to spook him? Touching his face, perhaps? That soldier, Kurtz, had said Cole was shy. But no. While he'd seemed startled by her touch, she'd lost him before. Frix dropping his tray had blasted Cole into some kind of trance.

She sighed and tipped her head back to the sky, annoyed at how the golden sun mingled with the darkening sky, because the sunset signaled the nearness of night.

She had never worked so hard only to end the day with nothing. She spun on her heel and marched back inside. A thorough study of the patrons of the Crooked Arrow brought nothing but disappointment. She knew each of them well enough to be certain she would not get a rutah from any of them.

Especially not from Emory Harp. Mistel made a special point of avoiding his stare as she walked through the tavern. Cole was far more dashing than the annoying minstrel. Perhaps Emory had noticed.

Mistel had one last option to bring Edera something to eat. She hated it more than anything, but at this point, she was desperate.

As she made her way back to the kitchen, a dark-haired man intercepted her.

Lander Gysel.

Had someone cursed her that she would have such luck today? "What do *you* want?"

"I've made a deal to get you out of your troubles," he said.

"I have no troubles," Mistel shot back. Hard to believe she'd ever thought this man handsome. Despite his dark hair and crooked grin, the rings around his eyes hinted at his depravity.

"To help Edera, then," he had the nerve to say.

Mistel folded her arms. "You've decided to stop trying to blackmail her?"

Lander faked a smile. "I've decided to forgive her debt as long as you sing at Speedwells."

"I am *not* singing at Speedwells." Any girl who did was more harlot than songstress. Mistel tried to walk past him, but he sidestepped to block her way.

"Osrik will pay Edera's debt *and* your salary," he said.

Of all the nerve. "What does Master Nath get for his money?"

Lander shrugged and dared look sheepish. "That's between you and him."

"The answer is no." Mistel shoved past him and slipped into the kitchen, her heart hammering.

Men! Hunxes, all of them.

As always, Nanette wore her white apron with a matching kerchief tied over her curly blonde hair. The sight of the portly woman standing over three boiling pots at the hearth with no sign of the woman's dour husband brought a glimmer of hope. One less bully of a man to deal with tonight.

"Nan?" Mistel wrung her hands and waited for the woman to glance her way.

"Excuse me, Mistel." Frix appeared behind her, holding a tray filled with the mess of all he had dropped. He had his mother's unruly blond hair, though he was slender, like his father.

"Bring it here." His mother motioned to the waist-high table in the middle of the kitchen. "We'll sort it out, wash the tray, then replate everything."

"I'm sorry, Mam," Frix said, setting the tray on the table.

"Happens to everyone," Nanette said, "and don't you worry about it."

The kettle on the hearth sang, and Nanette ran toward it. "What do you need, Mistel? As you can see, we're frightful busy tonight."

"You once told me to check in if I had a bad day," Mistel said. "Well, my day was the worst. I made coin enough for dinner, but a lad in the market stole my reticule."

"Aw, that's a shame," Frix said, his brow furrowed.

"Could you use some help tonight?" Mistel asked. "I've nothing to take Edera, and she's still feeling poorly."

"You can take my tips," Frix said.

"No, you may not," Nanette said. "Boy, I love your generosity, but those tips aren't yours to be giving away. You can work for food, Mistel, as I offered you before. We'd be glad to have the help tonight. You can start by washing the dishes on that tray, drying them, and filling three bowls with stew."

"Thank you, Nan." Mistel rolled up the sleeves of her best gown, tied on an apron, and went to work.

To think Mistel had once thought the life of a songstress would be glamorous and easy. In the end, she almost always had to succumb to manual labor to make ends meet.

Her feet ached as she trudged up the third flight of stairs to the room she shared with Edera on the fourth floor of the tenement building. She carried a linen sack of food in one hand, a warm pot of stew in the other. The pot had been the only way to transport stew home, and Nanette had made Mistel promise to bring it back first thing in the morning.

When Mistel reached their room, she set the food on the floor and removed the key from the chain tucked into her bodice to unlock the door.

She entered to a sickly sweet smell, like someone had boiled sugar wine in some sort of spicy soup. "Edera? I've got a pot of Nan's stew, warm potatoes, and half a loaf of her best bread. I hope you're hungry."

Mistel moved the pot and sack inside the door, then used her key to lock it again. Last thing she needed was Osrik or Lander showing up to cause trouble.

The long, narrow room had two beds on the back, a fireplace on the inner wall, and opposite it, a small table before a narrow window. In the front corner by the door, a standing screen hid a privy bucket. Mistel grimaced. That must be what reeked. She'd have to empty that outside, or their room would stink for a week.

But first, dinner.

She carried the food to the table, then walked to Edera's bed. She gently shook her roommate's shoulder. "Edera, dinner is here. A little food will give you some energy."

When Edera didn't stir, Mistel grabbed her shoulder and rolled her onto her back.

Edera's eyes were open.

And her mouth.

"Oh!" Mistel jumped back so far that her legs knocked against her own bed, and she fell onto the thin straw mattress. She pressed her hands over her heart as tears leaked down her face.

"No, no, no." This couldn't be! Edera had a cold. How could anyone die from a cold?

She caught herself staring at Edera and scrambled back to her feet. She pulled the quilt over her friend's head and paced the length of their room.

Cetheria, why?

Mistel reached the door, turned, and walked to the fireplace, which was still burning, though the embers were low.

Edera couldn't have been gone long.

A strange piece of wood lay in the coals. Mistel knelt at the hearth and grabbed the poker. A little shifting, and she managed to move the wood out of the heat.

A carving. Of a girl.

A girl who looked strangely like Edera.

CHAPTER FIVE
COLE

W HO?" ACHAN ASKED.

Cole followed the prince and his personal Shield, Shung, up the steps to the fifth floor. Despite the prince being but sixteen years of age, both he and Shung were over a head taller than Cole, and in their presence, he always felt small. Besides their height, they also had in common long black hair tied back in a tail. There the similarities ended. Shung, of Berland heritage, had pale skin, brown eyes, and was hairy everywhere—neck, chest, arms, legs, ears, not to mention his bearded face. He was also twice as thick as the prince, all muscle.

The prince, however, was lean with brown skin, blue eyes, and the shoulders of a woodsman. Rumor said he'd cut firewood while living as a stray before he'd discovered his true identity. He now kept up his strength with daily sword-fighting drills.

"Atul Shakran," Cole said. "Lord Yarden's temporary steward. He abducted Lady Averella from Mitspah and compelled a cham bear to attack you. I saw him at the island market today but lost him when he boarded a boat."

"Oh, *him*." The prince pulled a face. "He can't still be alive. I stabbed him. If he'd recovered, he would have been with Esek the rest of the way down here."

"Little Cham is right," Shung said as they stopped outside the prince's chambers. "We would have seen the weasel outside Allowntown and fighting here in Armonguard."

Cole wasn't so sure about that. *I know what I saw.* But he also wasn't about to argue with the prince about anything.

"If you see him again, let me know," Achan said. "Now, if there's nothing else, I'm exhausted."

"Nothing else, Your Highness," Cole said.

Shung and Achan entered Achan's chambers, and Cole returned to his own. He walked to the window and peeked out past the open shutters to the dark night. His room, on the bottom side of the northern arc, overlooked the lake and the eastern pier. Out on the dark water, several small boats with hanging lanterns—night fishermen—bobbed in the water.

Laughter and applause came from the waterfront, and from those making merry, the occasional cheer. The drumbeat carried louder than the faint melody, and people were clapping along.

A heaviness filled Cole, weighted his arms to the point he had no energy to even lift his lute. What did it matter if he could play? He had no one to play with.

Why was it so hard for him to make friends? To talk to strangers? To talk to someone like Mistel?

Why in all Er'Rets had he run from her? A pretty girl wanted to dance, and he ran. What would Kurtz say to that?

Hopefully, the man would never find out.

Cole sighed and sat on the stone sill of his window, keeping one foot on the floor. If not for Kurtz, Cole would be nursing more than his pride. The narrow escape from Osrik Nath, along with the bruise on the back of his head, only made him feel more on edge.

He would never leave the keep out of uniform again.

But he'd seen Atul. He knew he had. So he would go out into

the market tomorrow and continue watching for the man. Wear his uniform and take along a guard or two in case he ran into Nath again.

Arman only knew what Cole would say to Atul if he found him. "You're under arrest for trying to kill—"

Knock, knock, knock.

The hair on Cole's arms stood at attention. He slid off the windowsill and approached the door, wondering who would call at such an hour. Anything important and Sir Caleb would have messaged with his bloodvoice.

"Master Tanniyn?" Trizo Akbar's voice. One of the prince's personal Kingsguards.

Cole opened the door immediately. Trizo was tall with dark-brown skin and wide shoulders. He wore his hair in short warrior braids, an ancient practice that had recently come back into fashion.

"What is it?" Cole asked.

"Beg your pardon, sir," Trizo said, "but there's a young woman come for you. She's hysterical. Says she knows you and that it's an emergency."

Cole instantly thought of Madam Hoff, the prince's childhood friend. She had been emotional of late due to a host of reasons. The loss of Master Rennan, the attempts on the prince's life, the announcement of his wedding date, and her own pregnancy. "Did she give her name?"

"Mistel Wepp, sir."

A tingle raced up Cole's back. Had she followed him here? Why? "Take me to her."

Cole followed Trizo down to the grand staircase that circled both sides of the foyer. Sure enough, Mistel Wepp stood below, wringing her hands as she gazed up at a massive painting of King Trevn the Explorer. Cole started down the red tile steps, and the sound of his boots caused Mistel to spin around.

"Oh, thank you for coming, sir." The girl curtsied. For him. After she had held his hands and they had danced so close in a tavern in the Crescent. Moisture coated her face in streaks from eyes so red that a knot cinched in Cole's gut.

Someone had hurt her.

"Osrik?" he asked.

Her eyes widened. "Oh, no." She shook her head and met him at the foot of the grand staircase. She reached for his hand, stopped herself, then fell to her knees. "Please, Master Tanniyn. I need your help. My friend has been murdered."

When in doubt, ask Sir Caleb.

That's what Achan had said when Sir Caleb had admonished Cole for asking too many questions of the prince, who was "Soon to be king and too busy to be bothered by every little thing."

Which was why Cole now stood just inside Sir Caleb's quarters in the middle of the night, hands tucked behind his back to keep from fidgeting, gaze fixed on the wall so as not to be accused of looking toward the bed where Sir Caleb's wife lay sleeping.

The king's chamberlain paced before Cole in his dressing gown. "How do you know this woman?"

"I met her earlier today, sir. In the marketplace. She came here asking for help."

Sir Caleb moved his hands to his hips. "The constable and the city watch are an unfortunate bunch. She is unlikely to receive timely assistance from them—if they help her at all. His Highness has yet to appoint someone to oversee crime in the city, and—"

"Didn't he choose Sir Gavin?" Cole asked.

"Sir Gavin is over the army. He has no authority over local affairs. And don't interrupt." Sir Caleb stopped and stroked his beard, his gaze settling on Cole. "With so many tied up with the wedding preparations, you might be the right man for the job."

"Me, sir?"

"Yes, you. You're a bit green, but you've shown yourself capable—a great deal more than that inept constable. Take Sergeant Bazmark with you and Master Donotan, the coroner. Ask the sergeant to bring along a half dozen of his most trusted men. He'll need them to question bystanders, to keep people out of the tenement, to follow any leads that arise, or if—Arman forbid—the killer is still nearby."

Cole imagined walking into a tenement where a murderer lay in wait. He shuddered.

"And take whichever guard is with the girl now." Sir Caleb met Cole's gaze, his eyebrows high in his messy hair. "Who is with her now?"

"Trizo Akbar, sir."

"A good man. Take Master Akbar as your own personal guard. Conduct a formal investigation and discover what you can."

Cole's stomach dropped. "But, sir. I don't know how to conduct an investigation."

"You most certainly do. You've helped me accomplish that very task on countless occasions. A good investigator is observant, asks lots of questions, and takes notes. Who? What? Where? When? How? Why? Don't fidget."

Cole tucked his hands behind his back again. He could not think of one time he had helped run an investigation of any kind.

"I see from the vacant expression on your face that you doubt me." Sir Caleb counted off on his fingers. "One, we searched our chambers in Mitspah for poison. Two, we found the prince in the forest where he had killed the cham. Three, we found him in the vineyard when he'd gotten himself injured in the attack on Carmine. Four, we questioned over a dozen prostitutes and maids and uncovered Kurtz's mischief with the processional wagons. And but three days ago we captured an assassin who tried to kill the prince by arrow. Need I go on?"

Cole shook his head, his thoughts drifting between the situations Sir Caleb had mentioned. He wanted to point out that he had done little to help Sir Caleb in any of those circumstances. He had merely followed along, dumbly listening as Sir Caleb worked things out, sometimes transcribing, sometimes nodding or shaking his head when he sensed he should.

Plus, none of those events had involved an actual murder.

"Cole? Are you with me?"

He blinked back to the present and Sir Caleb's wild stare. "Yes, sir."

"Can you do what I've asked?"

While Cole's head screamed, *No, absolutely not!* he heard himself say, "Yes, sir."

"Off you go, then."

Cole blinked. "Now? It's the middle of the night."

Sir Caleb's glare caused Cole to inch back. "One cannot risk letting others tamper with the location of the incident. Go now."

"Yes, sir." Cole walked into the hallway, and before he had fully turned back to face Sir Caleb, the man shut the door.

A deep breath. How did Cole get himself into such things?

CHAPTER SIX
COLE

CONFIDENCE WINS A FIGHT, BEFORE a single word is spoken.

Cole sang the lyrics in his head as he and his men followed Miss Wepp—whom Cole had put on Bart, the piebald pack horse. She led them, lanterns in hand, along the winding cobblestone streets of the Crescent. Cole tried to convince himself of the truth of the song's words as he considered his task of seeking out a murderer in the dead of night.

Miss Wepp stopped Bart in front of a tenement slum house that rose five levels high, its weathered timber frame sagging beneath a shroud of tattered thatch. The air was thick with the stench of refuse and human waste.

Cole's stomach churned. Thankfully, he knew Matar Bazmark and the soldiers the sergeant had chosen for this mission. They had been with the prince in Mitspah, and that gave Cole a measure of courage. But he also knew he would never succeed in this endeavor as his bashful self. While he had little experience playacting, when he finally dismounted Cherix and gave his first order, he did his best to imitate Sir Caleb in posture, stride, and voice.

"Sergeant, leave two of your men here to wait with the horses and to take down the name of anyone who enters the building. The rest of you, with me. Where is your room, Miss Wepp?"

"Room D, sir," Mistel said as she dismounted Bart. "On the fourth floor."

Mistel had been calling Cole "sir" ever since she'd spoken to him in the castle foyer. The term felt too big, like the armor Sir Caleb had first made Cole wear to practice swordplay. Plus, Mistel was no longer gazing at him as if she wanted to dance but as if she wanted him to save her. Those were two very different expectations, and Cole wasn't at all confident he could succeed in the latter—not that he'd done all that well dancing either.

"Sergeant Bazmark, lead the way." Cole followed the man inside and wrinkled his nose as the musty odor of damp wood and stale air mingled with the acrid smell of sweat, feces, and rot. It took him back to his childhood home with the Fawsts.

"Reminds me of the Prodotez," Bazmark said, referring to the pit in the Ice Island prison where the worst offenders were kept. Bazmark had been one of them, pardoned by Achan himself.

Up the creaking stairs they went to the fourth floor, lantern light spinning over the narrow stairwell. Even at this late hour, distant conversation and the clatter of dishes could be heard through the rough-hewn timber walls.

At room D, Cole could see no sign of the door having been forced open. Either the killer had a key or had been invited inside. He remembered Sir Caleb's instructions to take notes and removed from his pocket a scroll of blank parchment and a charcoal pencil. He squinted in the dull light as he noted his first clue.

"I'll not go in again," Mistel said, her voice cracking. "I cannot look on her face."

"Very well," Cole said, not at all eager to see the dead girl himself. No doubt the sight would whisk him back to the Battle of Armonguard. At least if Mistel were in the stairwell, she would not witness his weakness again. "Master Gebfly, please wait here with Miss Wepp."

"Yes, sir." The thin man stepped forward. Brien Gebfly had a reddish-brown braided beard that formed a thin, curling coil off the bottom of his chin.

Cole held his lantern high as he stepped inside, bracing himself for. . . he knew not what. The room smelled like hot maple syrup and onions, strangely enough. The space was as wide as his chamber in Castle Armonguard and slightly longer. He saw no sign of struggle. What few belongings the girls owned were tidily in place on the sideboard or wall hooks. A cutting board lay on a table with a knife and the remnants of an onion, golden peels thin and curling.

Cole set his lantern on the table and scratched these observances onto parchment, grateful Lunden had taught him to write. His handwriting wasn't the best, but if it was good enough for writing songs, it was good enough to solve a murder.

He frowned, not finding that thought very logical.

"Where is the body?" Master Donotan asked. The coroner was a man in his fifties with salt-and-pepper hair slicked back over his head.

"Miss Wepp said she found her friend in bed," Cole said.

"I'll start there." Master Donotan carried his own lantern along with a leather bag toward the back of the room, where two beds each claimed a corner.

Cole stalled by approaching the fireplace. On the iron grate sat a small pot filled with liquid—some kind of sediment had sunk to the bottom. Cole touched the pan and found it cold. Had Mistel imagined the wooden figurine she'd told him about? Not so. A small, partially burnt carving of a woman lay on its side at the edge of the grate.

He withdrew his handkerchief and picked up the carving. It didn't seem detailed enough to resemble anyone in particular.

Strangely, little Xs had been carved over the eyes. He was about to sketch it onto a clean sheet of parchment when Bazmark spoke over Cole's shoulder.

"Well, break me open. That looks just like the dead girl."

Cole glanced up at the sergeant. The man was taller even than the prince, had straight black hair tied back in a tail, and a short beard.

"How so?" Cole asked.

"That braid and the belt." He indicated a fat plait etched down one shoulder and a zigzag carving around the statue's waist.

Cole didn't see how a braid and a few scratches of a belt could construct a likeness to anyone. "You sure?"

Bazmark stepped back into the center of the room and gestured toward the beds. "See for yourself."

The coroner sat on the edge of the bed on the left. Cole supposed he must see the body at some point. Might as well get it out of the way.

He passed Bazmark and approached the beds, tightening his grip on his parchment and pencil, knowing he might slip away to the battle at any moment. The syrupy smell was strongest back here, which reminded him of Nonda Fawst's fear about noxious odors of night air being contagions.

He stopped in a place where Master Donotan was still blocking his view of the body. "Is it safe to breathe in here?" he asked.

"Most certainly," the coroner said. "Contrary to what many believe, contagion cannot be caused by miasma."

So many words Cole didn't know. He swallowed and inched forward.

Then he saw her.

Edera Duwal didn't seem dead to Cole. Eyes closed, she looked as if she might be sleeping. She had brown skin and black hair that had been twisted into one fat braid that lay over her left shoulder.

Remnants of crusty paste streaked her forehead. She wore a wrap over a nightdress and a macramé belt tied snugly around her waist.

Cole held up the statue and immediately understood why Bazmark had seen a likeness.

"Uh. . . have you determined what killed her?" Cole asked.

"I have not. It's most mysterious. She has no lesions, but you can see the remnant of a poultice on her forehead, and she's still wearing one on her chest."

Master Donotan wore thin muslin gloves. With the side of his pinky finger, he drew aside the neckline of the girl's robe and gown to reveal layers of wet muslin covering pasty white mud.

"Miss Wepp said she'd been ill," Cole said.

"Indeed. You'll find more evidence of her ministrations there." Master Donotan gestured to a small table between the headboards of the two beds. On top of it lay a collection of small jars and several paper packages, one open, the creases of its pouch filled with the remnants of an herbal mixture. Cole picked up a coiled scroll from the center of the mess.

For the migraine take a handful of barley, two pinches of betony, vervain, and mint. Boil them well together, then spread them on muster cloth and lay it to the sick head to make it whole.

For congestion of the lungs, thinly slice an onion and fry it in oil with two cloves mashed garlic and a pinch of ginger. When warm enough to touch, layer over the lungs and cover with strips of muster cloth.

For hot stomach and digestive concerns, take an equal measure of anise and cumin, steeped in white wine and

*strained by a muster cloth. Drink the liquid and it shall
    settle the stomach and void the bowels.*
*Take one tablespoon of theriac two times each day with
    food.*
Saren Perroy
Apothecary
6 Haven Row, Southwalk

That explained the onions. "What's theriac?" Cole asked. "And why onions?"

"Theriac is a tincture said to remedy all ills and poisons," Master Donotan said. "Onions have expectorant properties that help open airways."

"So, she could have died from not being able to breathe?" Cole asked.

"It's a possibility. Another is that she was poisoned, but that will be difficult to deduce without a postmortem examination."

More words Cole didn't know. "Do you make anything of this?" He held up the statue.

Master Donotan glanced up and squinted. The moment he saw the statue, his eyes widened, and he plucked it from Cole's hands. "Where did you find this?"

"In the fireplace," Cole said.

The coroner held the statue up to Miss Duwal and sighed heavily. "This changes things. See how the eyes have been marked out? It appears this was an effigy killing."

Curse Cole's limited vocabulary. He did his best to write that down on his scroll as he clarified. "What do you mean by that? Aren't effigies made to honor the dead?"

"Life-sized ones, yes." Master Donotan held up the statue. "This, however, is black magic. A mage creates an effigy in the likeness of the victim. A totem, if you will. I've seen them made from wax or clay or wood. Whatever the mage does to the effigy happens magically to the victim. I find it strange the effigy is here. Normally, it would be with the killer, not the victim. But since it was found in the fire, Miss Duwal likely died of smoke inhalation."

A magical murder? Cole instantly recalled the eerie magic of the black knights and how Lord Nathak had magicked Silvo Hamartano into dust. "Could it have been a black knight?"

"No, black knights don't bother with this type of sorcery. Effigy magic is prevalent in Cherem and Magos. Possibly Jaelport as well."

"Is there any way to prove who did it?" Cole asked.

"Not usually, though someone could have hired a mage. If you can find the mage, you might cut a deal with them to turn over their patron."

Let the mage go free in order to arrest the person who'd ordered the killing? "Shouldn't the mage be convicted as well? Who's to say that whoever hired them would have killed her without the mage's magic?"

"That is for the prince to decide," Master Donotan said, "or his council or bloodvoice mediators or whatever system he sets up to deal with crimes like this."

That there might be more such crimes churned Cole's stomach. "How can I help you?"

"I'd like to move the body to the castle, where I can conduct my examination."

"It will be done." Cole sent two men to fetch a wagon to have the body transported back to Master Donotan's laboratory, then Cole and Bazmark started the tedious task of questioning the residents of the tenement house to see if anyone had witnessed anything suspicious.

No one had. Not one clue.

But Cole was not without suspects. And at the top of his list was Mistel Wepp.

Chapter Seven
Mistel

BAD NEWS DIDN'T IMPROVE WITH AGE like cheese or wine. It proofed like yeast.

Mistel sat in the stairwell outside her tenement home, Master Gebfly, the guard, standing by like she had been the one to kill Edera. It must be nearing dawn. She felt like she'd been waiting here for hours. Heart heavy with grief, her eyes stung from weeping and lack of sleep. She had declined Cole's invitation to join him as he questioned her neighbors. As if she would want all of them looking on her with pity and suspicion.

Master Gebfly had called her a suspect. Mistel had been shocked at first. How could Cole believe she would kill her friend? Though he didn't really know her. He likely found it suspicious that she had run from Osrik. And she *had* tried to extort dinner from the squire.

Thankfully, the tall sergeant with the black beard had gone with Cole. He was practically a giant, and she didn't like the way he stared as if he were raking her very soul.

"Please! Let me pass." Frix's voice carried up from the stairwell below. What was *he* doing up at such an hour?

Oh dear. The poor boy would be devastated to hear about Edera.

Master Gebfly peeked over the railing. "Who is that?"

"Someone to see Master Tanniyn," said a voice from below.

The clatter of bootsteps, creaking steps, and lantern light grew as Frix and whoever was bringing him up approached. They arrived, single file, two strong Kingsguards with lanky Frix sandwiched between. He still wore his apron over his clothes, but most of his curly blond hair had come loose from its thong and hung wild around his face. His eyes, small on either side of a rather pointed nose, rolled frantically as they sought her out.

"Mistel!" Frix pushed between the guards and ran to the foot of the stairs on which Mistel sat. "Tell me it's not true. Tell me Edera is well."

Mistel gripped his arm. "I'm sorry, Frix."

"Ahh!" Frix sank to his knees on the landing outside Mistel's door and keened. The smallness of the stairwell magnified his moaning to an overwhelming degree.

Mistel knelt beside her friend and wrapped one arm around his shoulders, fighting back her own tears. "I'm so sorry," she said.

"Who are you?" Cole's voice, strangely demanding.

Mistel twisted around and leaped to her feet. Cole stood on the landing above them, his giant of a sergeant behind him.

When Frix didn't respond, Cole asked again, "Your name, sir?" This time he sounded almost regal, which felt odd coming from that boyish, freckled face.

Frix panted a few breaths before turning his tear-streaked face to Cole. "Frix Swain, sir."

"You work at the Crooked Arrow," Cole said, and Mistel knew he must recognize Frix as the servant who had dropped the tray. "How did you know the victim?"

"Edera worked at our tavern," Frix said, his voice soft, resigned. "Until a few weeks ago."

"Why did she leave?" Cole asked.

"My father fired her." This came out with a bite, and Mistel ached for her heartbroken friend.

"What's your father's name?" Cole asked. "Do you know why he fired Miss Duwal?"

Fritz sighed deeply. "My father is Bero Swain, sir. He fired her to keep us apart. I wanted to court her, but she said no."

Cole wrote something on a curl of parchment, balancing it awkwardly on the banister. "Did that make you angry?"

"No, sir. Just sad."

The sergeant came down to the landing, leering at Mistel with each step. He took position by the door to her room. Mistel pulled Frix to his feet and used him to stand between her and the half giant, who suddenly smirked at her like he'd read her thoughts.

Mistel turned her gaze on Cole. "You don't honestly think Frix would harm Edera, do you?"

Cole didn't so much as glance at her. "Master Swain, where were you last night between the hours of half nine and midnight?"

Apparently, he could.

"Where I always am," Frix said defensively. "Working at the Crooked Arrow. My mother can verify it, as can Mistel."

"We were both there working until well after midnight," Mistel said.

"How did you hear the news?" Cole asked Frix.

Mistel wondered that herself.

"Lander Gysel came into the tavern and accused me not ten minutes ago," Frix said.

Lander? "Who told *him*?" Mistel asked.

Frix shrugged and kept his shoulders high.

Cole wrote faster. "Lander Gysel is. . . ?"

"Edera's former beau," Mistel said.

"Where does he live?" Cole asked.

"I know not," Mistel said.

"His father has a shop on Weaver's Row," Frix said. "He's a fabric merchant."

Cole scribbled something else on his parchment. Mistel rose onto her tiptoes, trying to see. She felt the gaze of the half giant on her and made the mistake of glancing at him.

Sure enough, he was staring and grinned.

She huffed. Odious man.

"Can I see her?" Frix asked.

"Certainly not," Cole said. "This is a murder investigation, and you are on my list of suspects. Go home, but do not leave Armonguard. Is that clear?"

Frix's eyes flashed wide, proof he'd understood the seriousness of Cole's instructions. "Yes, sir."

One of the guards followed Frix down, leaving Master Gebfly, the sergeant, and the younger guard with the warrior braids on the landing outside her door.

Cole sat down on the steps. "Have a seat, Miss Wepp." He nodded to the step beside him.

Mistel stiffened at his formal tone, so different from the nervous boy she had danced with. The sergeant and the remaining guards eyed her, and she was tired of being scrutinized. "I didn't hurt her, if that's what you think."

"It is my job to prove who did, and I must question everyone." Cole patted the step beside him. "Please sit."

She supposed that was fair. Mistel lowered herself to the bottom step. Her nearness to Cole's warmth in the chilled stairwell made her pulse leap. This handsome young man had come running when she'd asked for help. But like Master Gebfly had said, Mistel *was* a suspect, at least until Cole could prove otherwise. She leaned against the wall, not wanting to give Cole the wrong idea. There were times to flirt, but this was not one of them.

"Where were you last night after I left the Crooked Arrow?" Cole asked.

Mistel didn't miss the way the sergeant raised one eyebrow at Cole. Brutes like him thought they were better than everyone else. She rather liked letting him get the wrong impression about her and Cole. "I was there until I came here. I worked in the kitchen with Frix and his mother until closing."

"Madam Swain can verify that for both of you?" Cole asked.

"Yes, her name is Nanette."

He wrote that down. "Do you work there regularly?"

She huffed and rolled her eyes. "No, only in dire circumstances."

"You found yourself in such circumstances last night?"

"My reticule was stolen, along with all my money. Edera has been sick, and it was my last chance at providing her something hot and nourishing to eat."

"You were dancing with me so I'd buy you dinner," Cole said, his brow crinkled. "That's why you took me to the Crooked Arrow."

The accusation annoyed her. "So?"

He pressed his lips into a thin line and wrote on his parchment.

She stretched to try and see what he was writing. "Why is that relevant?"

"How long have you known Miss Duwal?" Cole asked.

Mistel sighed and sank back on the step. "About five weeks. We met on the trip down from Sitna. She was from Carmine."

"Do you know anyone who might have wished her harm?" Cole asked.

Mistel rubbed her hands over her face. "I don't know. I've been asking myself the same thing over and over, and I simply don't know."

"Lander. . . " Cole shuffled through his coils of parchment. "Gysel?"

"Perhaps. He was trying to blackmail us both."

His eyes narrowed. "For what?"

"Spite. We ignored his threats, of course, but he kept at it."

"Why would Master Gysel threaten you?" Cole asked.

"He wanted to court me," Mistel said. "I allowed it for a few days but quickly discovered his addictions."

Cole's gaze found hers. "What kind of addictions?"

Her stomach clenched, and she glanced away. "Gambling, liquor, women… I told him I didn't want to see him anymore, and the fool tried with Edera. She rejected him outright. When he discovered that Edera was slandering Emory, Lander thought—"

"Wait, Emory Harp, the minstrel?" Cole asked.

Mistel fought back a groan, annoyed that Cole had heard of Emory. "That's the one. He was playing at the Crooked Arrow last night."

"He's good," the sergeant said.

"He glared at me," Cole said to the both of them.

Mistel rolled her eyes. "Because of me. Emory hates me. And he hates Edera too."

"Why?"

"We traveled with him and his sister from Sitna."

"And…?"

Mistel couldn't believe she was about to tell this to anyone. She lowered her voice, hoping the sergeant and the other guards couldn't hear. "I've known him and his sister a long time. Joya and I were best friends growing up in Sitna. Emory and I both wrote songs and liked to sing. When we left to follow Achan south, Emory made me believe he loved me. That we were going to be… together. But he lied."

Cole frowned as he wrote on his parchment. "What does this have to do with Edera?"

"Emory spent a lot of time in Carmine over the years. Little did I know, Edera felt the same way about Emory as I did. Worse, he let her believe they had a future together just like he did me. We found out about each other when we camped on the coast of the Lebab Inlet. Turns out Emory had a girl in Mahanaim too."

Cole's expression was unreadable, but a darkness sparked in his eyes. "This gives him reason to harm Edera how?"

"Because we made a pact to tell everyone we could what a hunx Emory Harp is. Not only does he steal hearts but he also steals songs. He stole a song from me and claimed he wrote it. He's a thief and a liar, and we wanted to make sure everyone knew it."

"You've been slandering him," Cole said.

Ugh. Such an ugly word. "Is the truth really slander?"

"Wouldn't he want to kill you both?" Cole asked. "Why target Edera alone?"

"When we arrived in Armonguard, I gave up my mission to destroy Emory. I'm not big on revenge. Life is too short. I started singing with Rispen and Burch, and I didn't want other musicians to think me jealous of Emory's success, even though he stole my song. So I moved on. But Edera was madder than ever. She and Emory got into a big fight the last day she worked at the Crooked Arrow. That's really why she was fired. Frix only thinks it was about him. But his father needed Emory to bring in a crowd. Wanted to keep him happy."

"This ties back to Lander Gysel how?" Cole asked.

"Lander thought he could work our situation with Emory to his advantage. Said he was going to tell our employers that we'd slandered Emory. Lander is always desperate for money. I think he hopes Emory will pay to get rid of us, which Emory would never do. Last night, Lander confronted me. Said if I sang at Speedwells, he'd forgive Edera's debts. Worse, he said Osrik Nath would pay me for my time."

Understanding lit Cole's eyes. "Which would put you in Master Nath's debt."

Mistel grimaced. "Exactly."

"What is Osrik Nath's relationship with Miss Duwal?"

"She didn't know him. As I told you last night, Osrik is fixated on me. He's never mentioned Edera."

Cole wrote something down. "What about Frix Swain?"

"He would never harm Edera."

"His parents?"

"Of course not!"

Cole looked up then, and their gazes locked. In the dark light, his hazel eyes appeared brown. Bottomless. No, *fathomless* was a better word. Deep and searching and somehow so much older than his boyish, freckled face.

"How old are you?" Mistel asked.

The question shattered the moment, and he glanced away, up at the sergeant standing beside the door.

"The *master* turned nineteen just last week," the sergeant said.

Cole's whole face darkened, which made his freckles more pronounced.

Lands! Cole Tanniyn was quite charming.

"We'll be moving her body very soon," he said, standing. "Will you be all right to stay here once she is gone? Or do you have another place you could go?"

Mistel's chest seized at the very idea of sleeping in her bed, knowing someone had killed Edera in that very room. "I can't sleep here. I'll figure out something." Though she had no idea what she would do.

Cole's brow pinched adorably. "I need to know where to find you in case I have further questions. Would you be opposed to staying in the castle for a few days? I'd rather know you're safe, especially on the off chance whoever killed Miss Duwal is also intent on harming you."

Tears stung Mistel's eyes as she breathed for what felt like the first time all night. She could hardly believe her luck. To not have to face the uncertainty over where to sleep or how to earn her next meal was a blessing beyond anything she had ever dared hope for. "I would like that, sir. Thank you very much."

Cole nodded. "I'm finished here, Sergeant," he told the big man.

"Trizo and I will escort Miss Wepp to the castle and see that she is settled. Then I'll report my progress to Sir Caleb. You and Master Gebfly remain here to meet the wagoner team. See that Miss Duwal's body is brought safely to Master Donotan's laboratory."

"Miss Wepp can wait here and ride back with us," the sergeant said. "That will free you up to speak with Sir Caleb sooner."

Ugh. Why would the half giant make such an offer? His gaze fixed on hers, and she edged closer to Cole, suppressing a shiver.

"Thank you, Sergeant, but Miss Wepp has waited long enough." Cole turned to Mistel. "I'm sure you're exhausted."

"I am, yes," she said, grateful to stay with Cole and away from that beast of a man.

Cole nodded and gave further instructions to his sergeant. "Tomorrow morning, you and your men split up and bring Bero, Nanette, Frix Swain, Emory Harp, Lander Gysel, and Osrik Nath to the castle."

"Are they under arrest?" the sergeant asked.

"No, I simply wish to speak with them," Cole said.

"We'll see it done," the sergeant said.

Cole gestured toward the stairs. "After you, Miss Wepp."

Mistel didn't have to be told twice. She hurried down the stairs, feeling self-conscious at the prospect of Cole's fathomless eyes on her back.

Was he studying her? Did he think she was pretty? Did he think her a woman of loose morals after telling him that three men had wanted to court her?

Or worse, did he believe she was a killer? He'd said he didn't think so, but men were untrustworthy creatures. She had no reason to believe he'd been telling the truth.

"What song did Minstrel Harp steal from you?" Cole asked.

Ah, so he *was* thinking about her in some way. "His most popular new one," Mistel said. "'The Pawn Our King.'" She paused on the landing between the third and second floor and glanced up at Cole, who had stopped with one hand on the railing. The young soldier with the warrior braids, Trizo, stopped behind him.

"You wrote *that* song?" Cole asked.

"Didn't I just say so?"

Cole continued down slowly, which forced Mistel to keep moving since the steps were so narrow. "It's a great song," he said. "Do you mind if I tell the prince you wrote it?"

Mistel spun around on the steps, a thrill coursing through her at the very idea. "Not at all! Thank you, sir."

He gave her a long, inscrutable look, and Mistel sensed a change in him. "You may call me Cole," he said, "if it pleases you."

Mistel gave him her widest smile. He had no idea how much that pleased her. "Thank you, Cole. I would like that very much."

CHAPTER EIGHT
COLE

B Y THE TIME COLE HAD HANDED OFF Mistel to Lucia—a maid in Castle Armonguard—it was half past four in the morning. Where so much time had gone, he couldn't say. He decided to update Sir Caleb in the morning, rather than bothering him again tonight. He dismissed Trizo and went to bed.

Dreams of effigies marching in the Battle of Armonguard, making men fall dead with a glance, haunted his sleep. Atul Shakran was there too, controlling the effigies himself.

Sir Caleb Agros.

Cole opened his eyes.

Sir Caleb Agros.

"Yes, sir?" he said aloud, his voice raspy from sleep.

Your suspects are being held in a room near the armory. I suggest you don't keep them waiting.

"Suspects?"

Apparently, this is now a murder investigation?

The dead girl. The crossed-out eyes on the wooden carving. Mistel's tear-streaked face. It all came rushing back. *Yes, sir,* he thought, knowing Sir Caleb didn't like him to speak aloud in a bloodvoiced conversation. *I'll be down right away, sir.*

How did it go last night? Sir Caleb asked.

What to tell Sir Caleb? That Miss Duwal had already been sick? That he'd questioned all the residents and no one had seen anything? That Master Donotan had called it an effigy killing?

I don't know much yet, he thought, *but I have a lot of notes.*

A knock on the door made Cole jump.

Best get to it, then, Sir Caleb voiced.

Yes, sir.

Cole got up and found Trizo outside. "They're waiting in the long-room, just off the armory," Trizo said. "It has an attached storage room. I put a desk and some chairs inside. Thought you could use it for privacy when conducting your interviews."

"Brilliant idea, Trizo. Thank you. I'll be down soon."

Cole shut the door, yawned, and rubbed sleep from his eyes. Everything in him ached. He touched the back of his head and found a tender lump from Nath's attack earlier today.

Yesterday.

What day was this?

Cole slapped his cheeks. He had slept in his clothes, so he quickly changed and pulled on his new black Kingsguard cape. The red one Sir Caleb had given him to wear in the Battle of Armonguard had been ruined. Although soon enough, all Kingsguard capes—black or red—would have new crests sewn upon them as part of Achan's plan to unite the soldiers of two regimes under one banner.

Cole had no water for washing, but he ran a comb through his hair, grabbed a fresh clutch of blank scrolls and his charcoal pencil, and headed downstairs.

As expected, the suspects were waiting in the armory long-room with Matar Bazmark, Trizo Akbar, and Brien Gebfly. The Swain family huddled together in one corner. Emory Harp stood alone in the adjacent corner, while Osrik Nath leaned against the wall opposite the entrance. A slender young man who could only be Lander Gysel paced the room like a caged wolf.

The moment Nath saw Cole, he shoved off the wall and advanced. "Tattled to the prince, did you?"

Trizo and Brien stepped in front of Cole.

Bazmark drew his sword. "Back away, sir."

Nath, realizing he was outnumbered, stopped. "You have no right to hold me here," he said. "I barely touched him."

"Touched who?" Bazmark asked.

"The squire!" Nath yelled.

Cole had no desire for everyone to learn about his altercation yesterday with Osrik Nath. "Master Gebfly, I'll speak with Madam Swain first." He summoned his acting skills and emulated Sir Caleb as he strode toward the storage room. The chilled, dank room was uncomfortably cold. He spun around. "Master Akbar, have someone fetch a brazier for this room."

"Yes, sir."

Trizo left, and Brien led Madam Swain inside. Behind them, Master Swain and Frix stood on the threshold of the room.

"Close the door, Brien." Cole motioned to the chairs across the table from where he stood. "Please, have a seat, Madam Swain."

The plump blonde woman fingered a charm around her neck. "I don't know anything about that dead girl."

"Be that as it may, I still have questions," Cole said. "Please, sit?"

She lowered herself to one of the chairs, and Cole sat facing her and the door.

He would start with verifying Mistel's whereabouts, then move on to questions about Edera Duwal. "During what hours was Mistel Wepp with you at the Crooked Arrow last night?"

"She helped me in the kitchen from about sunset until an hour or so after we closed. It was probably just after midnight when she left."

Cole allowed himself a faint smile, relieved to hear that Mistel had told the truth about working at the tavern.

"She promised to bring back my stewpot first thing this morning." Madam Swain folded her arms and shivered. "But I haven't seen her yet. Or my pot."

"She is staying here in the castle," Cole said. "Your pot is likely still in her room in the tenement, but I am sorry to say it cannot be returned until the investigation is over."

That made him think of Mistel, safe in the castle but with none of her belongings. He must ask Lucia to find a spare dress or two for Mistel until she could return to her home.

The woman frowned. "That's unacceptable. Have you ever tried to make soup without a pot? I have a kitchen to run."

Cole had not meant to make light of her loss, but he could not give away something that might be evidence. "Speak to Master Brien on your way out, and we'll see that you are given a new stewpot." Time to switch topics. "When was the last time you saw Edera Duwal?"

"A week ago, maybe? The day Bero fired her."

"Why did he fire her?"

"She was causing mischief with our son. Frix adored her, but we both knew she wasn't interested. It was affecting his work."

"It had nothing to do with Emory Harp?"

Madam Swain shifted in her chair. "Well, I suppose it did a little, yes," she said carefully. "Minstrel Harp wronged the girl in some way, and she meant to make him pay for it. Bero didn't want any trouble, so the girl had to go."

"She was bad for business, that girl," Bero Swain said. He had clearly given his son, Frix, the same slender build, though Master Swain had no hair at all on his shiny bald head. "As soon as Emory stepped foot in the place, she'd start in on him. A little jab here. A dig there."

When Cole had finished questioning Madam Swain, Trizo had brought in a brazier and started a fire. Now the tiny storage room was heating up nicely.

"Did you ever see Minstrel Harp argue with Miss Duwal?" Cole asked.

"No. He ignored her as best he could, but the girl didn't make it easy. What happened between them wasn't my problem. I have a business to run, and Emory draws a crowd."

"There are other minstrels in Armonguard," Cole said.

"Since when is it a crime to hire the minstrel I want to hire?" Master Swain barked.

Cole fought back a critical comment about true artists versus con men who stole other people's songs. "Where were you last night when Mistel Wepp came into the Crooked Arrow?"

"At my mother's house. She lives in Southtip. She's been ill, and I was taking care of her. It's high time she moved in with us, if you ask me, but the woman is stubborn."

"Do you believe Minstrel Harp wished harm upon Miss Duwal?" Cole asked.

"Not Emory." Master Swain leaned across the table and lowered his voice. "The man's a great actor when putting on a performance, but he's a chicken-heart when it comes to violence. Hates confrontation. He wouldn't have harmed that girl."

"Might he have paid someone to do it for him?" Cole asked.

Master Swain chuckled and sat back in his chair. "I doubt that very much. Emory is the biggest pinchfist I've ever met. He makes plenty of coin, trust me on that, but he'd rather be publicly reamed than give up a single rutah." He leaned across the table again. "You want to know who *I* think killed her? Bring in Lander Gysel next. He's a broken, desperate man."

"Why do you say that?"

"I hear he has a lot of debts. Gambling, for one. He tried to blackmail me. And I know he was blackmailing the dead girl."

And trying to get Mistel to sing at Speedwells. The man seemed to threaten a lot of people. "Tell me how he tried to blackmail you."

"Said if I didn't pay, he'd tell everyone I was employing a libertine. I told him to go right ahead and spread the word. Audiences love a scoundrel. Rumor like that would only bring in more patrons to see Emory perform."

Cole doubted Master Swain would care that Emory had stolen Mistel's song as long as customers came in to hear it. "How was Master Gysel blackmailing Miss Duwal?"

"That, I don't know," Master Swain said, "but I overheard him talking to her a few days before I fired her. Whatever he said, he'd upset her to the point of tears."

Before Brien could shut the door, Master Gysel snapped, "You've no right to summon me here." The slender man appeared to be in his mid-twenties. He had a shadow of a dark beard, and eyes so pale they looked like ice.

"Yet here you are." Cole gestured to the empty chair. "Take a seat."

Master Gysel put both hands on the table and leaned over Cole. "I don't know anything about a murder."

"You knew she'd died before anyone else," Cole said. "How did you find out?"

"I saw her body." He jabbed his thumb against his chest. "Because *I* found her."

Cole perked up and grabbed a fresh piece of parchment. "Where? What time was this?"

Master Gysel pressed his fingertips against his eyes. "Uhh,

around eleven? Quarter past, perhaps? She'd been feeling ill, so I went by to check on her."

Cole wrote that down. "At such a late hour?"

"Edera always stayed up late to wait for Mistel." Master Gysel circled the space between the table and the door. "She was sick. Why do you assume she was murdered?"

"We found evidence," Cole said. "After you found her dead, what did you do next?"

Again, he turned direction. "I got out of there. It stank to the Lowerworld and back, and I didn't want to catch it, whatever it was. I went to the constable's office and reported it. You can ask them. They said they'd get to it when they could. So I went to the tavern—the Crooked Arrow. I hoped Mistel would still be there. Would have some idea of what to do. But she'd already left. That dumb kid, Firk, got all wound up over seeing me, and we had words. So I told him Edera was dead and he needed to move on. He lost it and took off running to see her."

That matched up with Frix's arrival at the tenement last night. "What do you do for a living, Master Gysel?"

"I work with my father. We sell fabric."

"What were you doing before you stopped by to visit Miss Duwal?"

"Playing cards at Speedwells."

Cole withdrew a spare piece of parchment and laid it on the table. "Write down the names of at least three people who saw you there last night. I also want the name of whoever you spoke with at the constabulary."

"Can't," Lander said. "I can read but never learned to write."

"Dictate to me, then."

Lander sat down at the table again. "Man named Ronnel worked at the constable's office. At Speedwells, you can talk to Tomyl Matz and Nikko Orban. Oh, and Laille and Darice. Don't know the women's last names."

Cole took down the information. Even with this list, the fact that Lander Gysel had been the first to find the body made him the prime suspect.

"You attempted to persuade Mistel Wepp to sing at Speedwells," Cole said. "What do you gain by this?"

Master Gysel paled slightly. "I'm assuming Miss Wepp is the one who told you that, and if I'm right, that means you know as well as I that she's lovely to look upon. She also sings like a lark. The owner told me he'd forgive my debts if I could get her to perform at the club for the next few months. Three, at least, he said."

"The owner's name on this list?" Cole lifted the parchment in question.

"Yeah, Nikko Orban."

Cole made a note. "Where does Osrik Nath fit in?"

He shrugged. "Os and Nikko do deals like that all the time. You'd have to ask him."

Cole certainly would. "Why were you blackmailing Miss Duwal?"

"I wasn't."

"I have witnesses who claim otherwise," Cole said.

Master Gysel sighed and slumped back in the chair. "I needed the money, and I thought she could afford it."

"You've seen where she lived. How could someone of her meager means afford anything?"

Master Gysel shrugged one shoulder.

"What did you have on her?" Cole asked.

"She was being courted by a foreigner. I figured she didn't want her employer to know."

Cole frowned. "What kind of foreigner?"

Another shrug. "Olive-skinned bloke. Looked Jaelportian. Everyone knows how the Crown Prince feels about that place. I figured it might be bad for her if word got out."

"What was the man's name?"

The question sent Gysel back to his feet, and he paced before the desk. "She wouldn't tell me, and I couldn't figure it out. I saw them together in the marketplace, holding hands. I think he might live in her building, or at least nearby, because I also saw them outside the tenement."

When Cole asked Frix Swain about the Jaelportian man, it brought tears to the young man's eyes. "No, I never saw anyone like that. Who said that? Lander? He's a liar. He'll tell any lie if he thinks he can make money off it. Edera loved me. I *know* she did. But it was hard for her to work at the tavern with the minstrel always singing songs about her."

"What did he sing?" Cole asked.

"Oh, what they all sing. Songs about love and such. Edera said he wrote those songs for her. That she'd inspired them. But Emory said the same things to Mistel. Ask her about it. She'll tell you."

"I'll do that," Cole said.

Instead, Cole called in Emory Harp.

"Listen," the minstrel said, slapping the tabletop. "Women are fickle flirts who are all out to trap me in matrimony. But I've made it very clear that I'm not looking to settle down. A wife would destroy my career."

Cole had been pretty sure he disliked Emory Harp after talking to Mistel last night. Now, he was certain. "How so?"

"Women make up three-quarters of my adoring public. I get hitched, I lose."

"Did Edera Duwal desire to marry you?" Cole asked.

"They all do, yes. When Edera realized I wasn't going to ask, she became a demon."

"In what way?"

"Heckling, mostly. She and Mistel would come to my performances and boo. Yell lies over the music. Say I was a lecher who had done them ill."

"Did you?"

"No!"

"You've never taken advantage of any young woman? If I asked the Crown Prince about your behavior in Sitna, what might he say, do you think?"

Emory flushed. "I know how it looks to people, but the truth is, women love me. And I love women. But I'm a sworn bachelor. Not for sale. Yet women are delusional. So many truly believe they'll be the one to finally tame my wild heart. I'm actually working on a song about that very thing. Want to hear it?"

"Thank you, no," Cole said. "Where were you last night after your performance at the Crooked Arrow?"

"Home. With my sister, Joya. She'll vouch for me."

Cole dismissed Minstrel Harp and read over his notes. He had thoroughly questioned everyone except Osrik Nath. He straightened the papers on his desk and steeled himself.

Nothing to do but get it over with.

Chapter Nine

Cole

Like Lander Gysel, Master Nath refused to sit, though the man didn't pace. He simply stood across the table from Cole, arms crossed over his broad chest like some kind of Shield. Clearly his Kingsguard training had stuck, though he could use a few lessons in grooming, as his tangled black hair resembled tree moss.

Cole took a deep breath to bolster his courage. "When did you last see Edera Duwal?"

Nath's brows sank. "Never heard of her."

"She's one of your tenants," Cole said.

"The majority of my tenants are peasants," Nath said. "I've got a man who collects the rent."

"But you do know Mistel Wepp."

A slow grin crossed Nath's face. "Aye, and I hope to know her better very soon."

Heat pulsed in Cole's chest, and he clenched his jaw to keep from saying something foolish. "Edera Duwal was Miss Wepp's roommate."

"Oh, sure. I know who you mean. The dark-haired girl. She's a nice morsel too."

"She's dead," Cole said.

Nath's brow twitched. "So that's why all you soldier types are swarming the place like ants without a hill."

"A young woman was murdered," Cole said.

Nath leaned over the table and grinned. "Well, if my memory serves me correctly, I only touched one person yesterday. And I left *you* alive."

Brien moved to step in, but Cole stood and leaned over the table as well. The act fairly terrified him, but he was determined to behave as Sir Caleb would, with confidence and intimidation—not that it was working with Osrik Nath.

"Where were you last night between the hours of nine and midnight?" Cole asked.

Nath backed up a step. "Out and about. I suppose you want the names of my companions?" He glanced at the scrolls on the table. "You going to write them down?" He flicked a scroll, and it rolled off the edge and onto the floor.

Cole set his charcoal on the table in front of the man. "No, sir. You are."

Nath released an animalistic part sigh, part growl. He kicked his chair aside, stalked over to the scroll, and caught it up. He then fell onto his chair and scraped it toward the table so loudly Cole winced. Nath made a show of writing the names of three people so big the words completely covered the parchment.

Brien lingered beside Cole's desk rather than taking up position by the door as he had during the previous interviews.

Nath finished writing and shoved the parchment across the table, upsetting Cole's tidy stacks.

"There you go, little pimple. I don't know the woman's surname."

Cole sat and collected the scroll. Read the names Nath had

written. The first two were Nath's friends from the wharf green yesterday morning: Wolferam Turl and Mar Rudlin. The third name was female: Akina.

"Mistel Wepp will be looking for a roommate, then?" Nath asked.

The leer on Nath's face filled Cole with the urge to draw the sword he was not wearing. "No," he said. "She's currently residing in the castle."

"With you, you mean?"

"Certainly not," Cole said. "She has her own quarters."

"She's moved out of my building, then?"

"She has not," Cole said. "But while we are conducting our investigation, and while there is a murderer on the loose, she's safer here. Which brings me to my next question. What is the relationship between you and Nikko Orban?"

"Nikko and me are friends," Nath said. "Fellow businessmen. He owns a gambling den."

Cole imagined Sir Caleb correcting Nath's speech. *Nikko and I.* "Why did you agree to pay Mistel Wepp's salary if she agreed to sing at Speedwells?"

Nath smirked and scratched his beard. "I view her as an investment."

"What kind of investment?"

"The kind that brings more patrons into Nikko's club and puts Miss Wepp in my bed."

Fire lit through Cole's chest. "Master Nath, do not be crass."

Nath chuckled and folded his arms. "I'm being honest. Isn't that what you investigators prefer?"

"I would prefer you keep your distance from Mistel Wepp," Cole said, then forced himself to add, "until this investigation is over."

"I'm sure you would. Look, if she's really moving out, I need to know so I can rent the room to someone else." Nath stood, again making his chair scrape loudly over the stone floor. "Be careful

out there, pimple. Whoever killed the girl might get you next."
He faked a forward lunge, stomping his boot hard on the floor.

Cole ducked as chunks of stone fell from the sky. Across the expanse, the Eben strode toward him.

"Lee-lee-lee-lee-lee!"

"Sir?"

A shake of Cole's arm changed the sky to a stone ceiling. He was crouched behind the table, hands over his head. On the other side of the table, Osrik Nath cackled.

"My, what a fierce investigator! One noise puts you on the floor. The squire to our noble prince. Pathetic. A bunch of babies going to rule Armonguard now, it looks like." Nath stalked to the door. "Well?" he said to Brien, who was shorter and half as thick.

"Master Tanniyn hasn't dismissed you yet," Brien said.

Nath glanced back and chortled. "Master, are you?"

Cole's face burned. He pushed to his feet and straightened his cape. "He may go."

Brien opened the door. Nath spat on the floor by the guardsman's feet and walked out. Brien started after him.

Cole called out, "Let him alone, Master Gebfly. I do not believe he is our killer. Trizo, dismiss the others. But tell them not to leave the city."

"Yes, sir," Trizo said.

Brien stepped inside the room and shut the door. "You all right, sir?"

Cole couldn't meet the man's gaze. "Where did you fight in the Battle of Armonguard, Master Gebfly?"

"With the main army," Brien said. "Sir Gavin led us down from Noiz. You carried the standard for the prince's division, didn't you?"

Cole nodded, unable to deny that he had indeed carried it.

"That's mighty admirable," Brien said. "Soldiers need to see their colors flying. See what we're fighting for."

That's exactly what Achan and Sir Caleb had said, yet Cole couldn't help thinking if he'd been a better swordsman, he would have been asked to stay with the prince.

"Don't you let that ruffian get to you," Brien said. "If he isn't the killer, then who is?"

Ah, Brien thought Cole was upset by Nath's rude behavior. "I don't know. Master Nath has no reason to kill her. Lander Gysel had the opportunity and found her before anyone else."

"Yet he has no reason either," Brien said.

"Precisely. A dead woman cannot pay her blackmailer. We must check all the references. If they are true, I cannot think of a reason to accuse anyone I spoke with here today. My only other lead is to ferret out the identity of Edera Duwal's mysterious Jaelportian suitor."

The door opened, and Trizo entered. "I've sent them all away. What shall I do next, sir?"

That these seasoned soldiers continued to call Cole "sir" made him want to laugh. "Get some rest, both of you. When you're able, go out and speak with the people Masters Gysel, Nath, and Harp listed as references. Meet in the great hall at midday and tell me what you've learned. Then we'll visit the apothecary together."

"Yes, sir," Brien said.

"You've a good start," Trizo said as he smothered the fire in the brazier.

Cole offered the guardsman a weak smile. "Thank you." He'd done the best he could, yet he still had no idea who had killed Edera Duwal.

The large rectangular expanse of the great hall with its ribbed, vaulted ceiling sat at the top of the western arc of the castle with two double-door entrances on each side wall. A raised dais that spanned the narrow southern end of the hall commanded attention. Above it, stained-glass windows depicting the Kinsman mythos cast colorful rays of light upon the stone floor below. Throughout the hall, banners of crimson and black hung proudly, displaying the new sigil of the Crown Prince in four quadrants—a castle, a tree, a crown, and a cham bear.

Cole spotted some members of Tsaftown's Fighting Fifteen at a table in the back. The majority of the visiting armies of Carmine, Zerah Rock, and Berland that had fought in the Battle of Armonguard had started their long journeys home. The Tsaftown army, however, remained camped north of Armonguard as they helped with repairs to the city and castle and awaited Lord Livna, Captain Demry, and the Fighting Fifteen, who were staying in the castle for meetings and to await Achan's wedding and coronation.

Cole chose a table on the floor, close to the dais in case the prince finished his meetings early and entered the hall. As he ate, he thought over all he'd learned that morning. Lander Gysel had the means to kill Miss Duwal, but in light of him blackmailing so many others, his motivation was flimsy.

A bowl of stew clunked onto the table beside Cole. Kurtz climbed over the bench and sat.

"You ditched me," Kurtz said.

"I beg your pardon?"

"Never beg." Kurtz took a bite of soup, smacked his lips, and reached for a shaker of salt. "You disappeared yesterday."

"Oh. I had to follow Atul." Had that only been yesterday?

"You missed meeting the girl," Kurtz said. "She was very fetching, and she gave you this." He pulled from his pocket a beaded bracelet, which he dropped on the table beside Cole's bowl. "I promised her I'd bring you by this afternoon to meet her."

Cole picked up the bracelet, curious why Mistel hadn't said anything about it. "I already met her. Yesterday. Her roommate was killed, and I'm investigating the murder."

Kurtz gaped, spoon heaped with stew halfway to his mouth and dripping. Cole rather liked being able to shock this man for once.

"Killed?" Kurtz ate the bite off his spoon, which must have still tasted bland, because he added more salt. "Think she did it?"

"No! Of course not."

"You sure?"

"You and I saw her singing in the plaza. After that, she was with me. And later—"

"*With* you, was she?" Kurtz raised an eyebrow.

Cole swallowed. "Not the whole time. After I left the tavern, she worked until closing. I've verified that with the owners."

"Why is a dead girl your concern?" Kurtz asked. "Don't you have other things to do? The prince is getting married."

"Yes, well, Sir Caleb told me I must investigate, so I'm doing my best. Besides, I don't think he needs my help planning the wedding. Perhaps this is a convenient way for him to keep me busy."

Kurtz grunted. "Sir Caleb likes investigations and hates parties. I'm surprised he hasn't taken over and let you plan the wedding." He elbowed Cole, a wicked grin twisting one side of his mustache. "You took that pretty young lass to a tavern?"

Cole inhaled a long breath. "Actually, she took me."

"Heh hay! Well, that tracks better, it does. No offense. But still, a step in the right direction, lad. Well done, eh? Now you just need to write her a sonnet, and that'll be that."

"Please don't make more of this than there is," Cole said. "I'm duty bound to find her friend's killer." Besides, beautiful girls like Mistel tended to choose men like Kurtz or Achan or even Trizo over someone like Cole. Best to not get his hopes up about her.

"What's the dead girl's name?"

"Edera Duwal. She worked as a maid at the Crooked Arrow until she was fired for dallying with both the minstrel and the owner's son."

"Now things are getting interesting, they are. You have any other suspects besides the minstrel and the boy?"

"I interviewed six people this morning and Mistel yesterday. You'll like this. She lives in one of the tenements owned by Osrik Nath."

Kurtz growled softly. "There's your killer."

"That was my first inclination," Cole said, "but there's no evidence. And Nath produced names to back up his story. Besides, Miss Duwal was killed by effigy magic, which doesn't seem like something Nath would bother with when he has two lethal weapons as hands."

"What in flames is effigy magic?" Kurtz asked.

Cole explained the wooden carving.

Kurtz whistled low. "Sounds like the lass was involved with some dark characters."

"Or someone paid to have her cursed."

Kurtz jabbed a crust of bread at Cole. "That, more like. You're good at this."

"Master Tanniyn, can I speak with you, sir?" Brien approached their table.

"Have a staff now, do you?" Kurtz asked.

"If this is about the investigation, you may speak in front of Kurtz," Cole said.

"I went over to Speedwells and talked with Nikko Orban," Brien said. "He confirmed Lander Gysel was there last night around midnight."

"I'm not terribly surprised," Cole said.

"He also admitted to the deal that he'd forgive Lander's debts if Miss Wepp would sing at the club. Said she's a songbird."

"She is that," Kurtz said.

"What about Osrik Nath?" Cole asked.

"Trizo spoke with his friends, who said they were with him,"

Brien said, "but he can't find the woman without a surname. And Miss Joya Harp said her brother was home at that hour."

Cole sighed, mulling over the fact that he must cross off every suspect from his list. Nothing to do but press onward. He stood and said to Kurtz, "We're off to visit an apothecary. Care to join us?"

"You know I can't," Kurtz said. "Besides, Sir Gavin has called a meeting. Wants us captains to help him come up with ideas for recruiting more soldiers. Lost too many in the battle."

At that depressing thought, Cole caught sight of Esek Nathak entering the great hall. He gasped at the sight of the villain he knew was dead and pointed him out. "Who is that man?"

Kurtz and Brien turned in unison as the false prince made his way toward them.

"Who, Akbar?" Kurtz asked.

"Akbar?" Cole looked again. Sure enough, Trizo Akbar approached. Cole turned slowly in a circle, examining the tables for that familiar face, but Esek Nathak was gone.

CHAPTER TEN
MISTEL

HAVING WEALTH AND PROSPERITY WAS the only way to truly experience life.

While Mistel had barely slept last night, she'd greatly enjoyed the feeling of that glorious feather bed. After having experienced the luxury of Castle Armonguard, how could she ever return to the squalor of the tenement?

Yet she couldn't start her life anew until Edera's killer was found. Mistel liked Cole Tanniyn, but she knew better than to trust anyone, especially a young man. In this life, she trusted only herself.

Mistel rose early and walked to the mansion in Hamisha Hills where her friend Joya Harp worked as a caretaker for the Earl of Idez's three children.

Joya had already heard about Edera's death from Emory, her brother, and Trizo Akbar, who had come to question her about Emory's side of the story. The girls cried afresh over the loss of their friend, then Joya fed Mistel breakfast while Mistel told Joya everything she knew about the investigation. She hoped that Joya, who seemed to know everyone in the city, might see some sort of clue that had been missed.

And she did.

"Not just anyone can carve wood to specific likenesses," Joya said. "I can think of two. One is out of the city at present for his niece's birthday. The other I met at a party where Emory was playing. His name is Dewin Sattah? Sittol? Something with an S. He's young. And sooo talented. Has a shop in the Crescent on the corner of Broad Street or Haven Row. One of them. Where it crosses Walcot Lane."

Which was how Mistel ended up in the Crescent near midday. The roads were muddy after a morning rain and packed with pedestrians, men and beasts pulling carts, and children running wild. A beggar roamed the street just ahead, talking to himself about prunes. He had already asked her for money. Twice. And twice she had refused him. Even if she wanted to share, she had nothing to give thanks to that pesky island market thief.

Mistel edged close to the steps of a tenement building on Walcot Lane as a wagon filled with vegetables drove by, squishing through the mud coating the road.

As she watched the wagon, she caught sight of a man behind her. She jumped, certain at first it was that abominable Sergeant Bazmole. But no. While they had similar coloring and both walked like soldiers, this man was shorter, thinner.

He likely meant no harm.

At the corners of Broad Street and Walcot Lane, she found no sign of a carver's shop, so she continued on. Reaching Haven Row, she paused to examine the four corners. Next to her stood a cobbler's shop that sold men's work boots. Across the street to her right sat a tobacco store that also sold pipes. Catty-cornered was an apothecary. The beggar had turned the corner there, headed, no doubt, toward the castle and deeper pockets than the Crescent could supply. This inspired Mistel to glance back at the soldier-like man, but he was gone.

Good.

She turned her gaze across the street on her left to a haberdashery. Normally, such a place would have drawn Mistel right inside. Alas, the hats on display were also geared toward male clientele and were more utilitarian than stylish.

Someone stood at the window. She startled when she realized it was the man who'd been following her, and if she wasn't mistaken, he seemed to be watching her reflection in the panes of glass.

The urge to run overcame her, but perhaps some breezy conversation could uncover his intentions. It wasn't like he would harm her in the light of day. Right?

Focus, Mistel. She had better things to do at present. She studied the buildings on the intersection again but saw no sign of any carver's shop.

Dash it! How peculiar. Joya was not usually wrong about such things.

"Spare a coin, sir? Anything will help."

The beggar's voice drew Mistel's gaze to four Kingsguard soldiers on horseback, approaching from the south. The one riding a brown horse with a blond mane and tail slowed long enough to toss a coin to the beggar.

"Thank you, sir!" the old man cried.

Movement across the street drew Mistel's gaze. The man who'd been watching her was now striding quickly away from the Kingsguards. How curious.

Back on the street, three guards reined their horses at the corner and waited for the fourth to catch up. When he did, rather than ride on, all four dismounted and tied their horse's reins to the hitching post on the corner.

That's when Mistel recognized Cole as the one who'd tossed a coin to the beggar.

Her heart leapt at the sight of him. She fisted her skirt, glanced both ways, and ran across the street as quickly as she could without stepping in the myriad of mud puddles that pockmarked the intersection.

"Master Tanniyn, wait!" she called.

Cole glanced around until his gaze met hers. A hint of a smile flashed before disappearing entirely. Was the man afraid to be caught smiling? Well, she would fix that little quirk, or her name wasn't Mistel Wepp.

When she reached him and was certain she stood fully on dry ground, she smoothed her skirt and said, "Hello there. Are you following me?"

"I wish I could admit I was," he said, "but I am merely tracking the clues of my investigation."

She fought to keep from rolling her eyes. "I surmised that much, but I'm afraid the carver's shop is not here."

Cole's brow wrinkled. Lands, what a sweet face. "Then it's a good thing I've come to speak with the apothecary." He gestured to a sign above the door that said "Apothecary."

"Whatever for?" she asked. "You're not feeling poorly, I hope?"

Again, that ghost of a smile. "I am well, but Miss Duwal was a patron of Master Perroy. I found instructions in his hand along with several treatments on her bedside table. You didn't know she'd come here?"

Mistel gazed up at the sign, curious when Edera had found the time to visit this part of the Crescent. "I didn't."

"You said something about a carver shop?" Cole asked.

"Oh, yes. Well, I—"

A bell rattled, and the door to the apothecary opened into the space where Mistel stood. She lunged back to avoid being struck, lost her balance, and would likely have needed to step into a deep puddle if not for Cole, who grabbed her arm to steady her. His nearness made her skin tingle, but then he released her, and the sensation abruptly vanished.

A ruddy-faced balding man stood on the stoop. He wore an

apron tied over a fine tunic and a pair of trousers. "Master Tanniyn, is it? From the castle?"

Cole gave the man a quick nod. "Yes, sir. You are Saren Perroy?"

"I am. Do come inside. It looks like it might rain yet again. I daresay these streets will not react well."

Cole opened his mouth to reply, then turned his gaze to Mistel. "Would you like to join us, Miss Wepp? Your perspective would be a welcome addition."

She had no idea what Cole was going to ask the apothecary, but she certainly wanted to learn as much as she could about Edera's death. And she didn't mind spending time with Cole, either. "Yes, thank you."

"Sergeant Bazmark and Trizo, with me," Cole said. "Brien, keep watch over the horses."

Only then did Mistel take in Cole's companions. She recognized all three men from last night. The kindly, older Master Gebfly, who had sat with her for so long in the hallway. The handsome, younger Trizo with the short warrior braids, who had escorted Frix up from the street and questioned Joya. And the creepy half giant who, sure enough, was staring into her soul again, the boorish hunx.

Cole gestured for Mistel to go first, so she followed the apothecary inside. A gust of warmth from a lit fireplace met her, accompanied by the smell of spices, dried flowers, and mint.

Behind their group, the wooden door creaked closed, its bell rattling softly. Mistel stayed at Cole's side as he followed the apothecary, their footsteps loud on the polished floor.

Shelves built of dark wood lined the walls, giving the space an expensive feel compared to the rest of the neighborhood. Some shelves held bottles, jars, and vials. Others were lined with tiny drawers filled with dried spices and herbs. A long table in the center of the room was littered with bowls, tongs and tools, mortars and pestles, scrolls, and an inkwell and quill. A stand of lit candlesticks sat in one back corner of the table. A set of scales had been arranged in the other.

Above the table hung sprigs of lavender, thyme, and mint. Steep ladder-like stairs in the back of the room ran up to a second level of shelves filled with books.

"How can I be of service to you, Master Tanniyn?" asked the apothecary.

"First, know that I have not come to accuse you, but to ask your expert opinion," Cole said.

"I'm glad of that," the man said.

Cole reached beneath his cloak and removed a scroll, which he handed to the apothecary. "A young woman has died, and I found this on her bedside table."

"How tragic." Master Perroy's eyes shifted as he read the scroll. "Ah, yes, I remember her. She complained of a host of ailments. Headache, congestion, irritable digestion. Couldn't sleep. Had vivid dreams. That often happens with digestive issues and fatigue. I made prescriptions based solely on her ailments. Do you know how she died?"

"The royal coroner has determined the cause of death to be asphyxiation due to a black magic effigy spell," Cole said.

Master Perroy slumped forward, catching himself with a hand on the table. Jars clinked as he pushed them aside for support.

Cole strode around the table and gripped the man's arm. His head turned as he perused the room. "Trizo." He nodded toward the fireplace. "Fetch that stool, please?"

Trizo ran to obey. Mistel found herself standing alone beside the half giant and quickly joined Cole on the other side of the table. Though, now she could see the sergeant watching her, which she didn't like either.

He smiled at her and winked.

Vile man!

Cole helped Master Perroy sit on the stool beside his worktable.

"Thank you, sir," the apothecary said. "It's been years since I've encountered such magic, and it has never been by choice. Never!" The man's face darkened, and his eyes flashed, haunted by something in his past.

"What can you tell me about it?" Cole asked.

"Mantic witches. . . " He glanced at Mistel. "Not only females, mind you. They call on evil spirits to carry out curses upon the innocent and unsuspecting. People become terrorized, manic. I'm terribly sorry such a diagnosis didn't occur to me. It's been so long." He withdrew a handkerchief from his apron pocket and dabbed his forehead.

"Did Miss Duwal experience any manic symptoms, Miss Wepp?" Cole asked.

Mistel thought about it. "She complained of several bad dreams. Nothing specific. She was overly spiteful toward a certain minstrel we spoke about before. I thought she was taking her bitterness too far. She saw much greater misdeeds in the man than I ever did, and I daresay he wronged me far more than he did her."

"Did she toss and turn in the night?" Master Perroy asked.

"For the past week, at least," Mistel said. "I believed it a side effect of her cold. I honestly expected to come down with the same thing. Thought myself lucky that I hadn't."

"You lived with the girl?" the apothecary asked.

"I did," Mistel said. "Our beds were but two paces apart."

"Then you certainly should have caught her ailment by now," Master Perroy said. "The fact that you did not corroborates the coroner's cause of death."

Mistel shivered, horrified that a mantic had methodically killed her friend.

"Do you know anyone capable of such magic?" Cole asked. "I need a list of names."

Master Perroy barked a laugh. "No, sir, I do not. No self-respect-ing apothecary would be able to provide one. We do not consort with their type. Though you might ask around the ring."

"I'm sorry, where?" Cole asked.

The half-giant sergeant's deep voice turned Mistel's stomach. "The Magosian part of the Crescent."

"Magosians live in Armonguard?" Cole asked.

"All nationalities live in this, the oldest Kinsman city in Er'Rets," Master Perroy said.

Cole sighed deeply, glanced up at the dried sprigs. He seemed agitated, and Mistel wondered what was so bad about Magosians.

"Thank you, Master Perroy, for your time," Cole said. "May I call again, should I have more questions?"

"Certainly, sir."

They left the apothecary in a heavy silence.

"Where to next, sir?" Trizo asked.

Cole rubbed his face, and Mistel noted the creases under his eyes. His attention fell on her, and for the space of several breaths, he simply stared. Then, "Miss Wepp, before Master Perroy interrupted us, you mentioned a carver's shop. What did you mean by that?"

"Oh, yes," she said. "My friend thought there was a woodcarver's shop near here, but I couldn't find it."

"There's one just there," the half giant said, pointing around the side of the apothecary shop.

Mistel stiffened at the way the sergeant's wanton gaze seemed to strip her bare.

"Show me," Cole said.

The order, thankfully, sent the sergeant away. He led them a few steps to a single door sandwiched between the apothecary and an upholsterer's shop. An oak sign above the entrance was chiseled with a single word: Woodcarvings.

CHAPTER ELEVEN
COLE

COLE GAZED UP AT THE WOODWORK-ing sign, confused why Mistel had been seeking a carver's shop. Could this be where the effigy had been made?

"It was right here all along," Mistel muttered.

"Not everything is what it seems at first glance," Bazmark said to her.

She scowled at Baz and edged closer to Cole. He couldn't help admiring the way her ginger hair curled against her rosy skin peppered with orange freckles. She wore her hair up today, though much of it had escaped the wooden pins. She smelled nice, too, though it could be that they all smelled like the lavender from the apothecary shop.

He shook such thoughts away and asked Mistel, "Were you down here searching for the person who carved the effigy?"

"Mm-hmm," she said, grinning. "Joya thinks—"

"You could have been killed!" Cole said.

Mistel had the decency to look ashamed, but her expression quickly shifted and she lifted her chin. "I'm not afraid."

Before Cole could lecture the fool girl further, she stepped forward and knocked on the door. He followed at her side, biting back another rebuke. Yet at the same time, he didn't want her to be angry with him. "I spoke with the Swain family," he told her. "You've been cleared as a suspect, as have they."

"That's a relief," she said. "Edera was my friend. I hope you have some ideas as to who might have killed her."

"A few. I should add Master Perroy to my list, though he has no motivation." This time, Cole knocked on the door.

"He sure seemed terrified about the use of black magic," she said.

"Rightly so," Cole said. "I've seen enough black magic to know it's extremely dangerous." He had no desire to enter the Magosian ring either and see such sorcery firsthand. Perhaps he could send Trizo who, if Cole remembered correctly, was fluent in the old language.

Cole tried the knob, and the door opened. "Perhaps we're meant to let ourselves in?"

"Allow me, sir." Steel scraped against wood as Bazmark drew his sword and pushed inside the shop.

Mistel practically jumped on Cole in her attempt to get out of Bazmark's way. Cole clutched her waist. He'd done it to keep her from going inside, but he couldn't help notice how nice it felt to hold her so close.

"Brien? Trizo?" Cole nodded after Baz.

Only when all three soldiers had entered and declared it safe did Cole follow with Mistel. The door was too narrow to enter side by side, so he regretfully had to release her.

"I'm sure there's nothing here worth all this fuss," she said.

"It's best to take caution." Cole dragged his gaze away from the tendrils of hair dangling down the back of her neck and took in the shop. "Especially with a murderer on the loose."

The space ran long and narrow with a workbench along one side and a wall mount above that held chisels, sandstones, files, saws, and sharpeners. Shelves on the opposite wall contained hundreds of carvings. The majority were figurines and statues, though some shelves held relief panels, signs, furniture embellishments, masks, utensils, or toys.

On the far end of the room, a fireplace stood cold. Sawdust and wood shavings covered the floor. The chill and smell of fresh-cut wood tickled Cole's nose.

Bazmark picked up a carving of a cham bear from a shelf. "There's no money in woodcarving," he said, tossing the bear back. "Cabinetmaking or furniture is the way to go."

Brien shuffled through a pile of parchment on the workbench. "Looks like our carver's name is Dewin Sessit."

"That's right," Mistel said. "Like I tried to say before, Joya said Dewin knows Emory. She thinks Dewin might have carved the effigy or that he might know who did."

That Dewin knew the minstrel made Emory more suspect. He could have paid a mantic to cast the effigy spell that'd killed Edera. For that matter, any of Cole's suspects could have done so, which meant he couldn't dismiss any of them, really. Not even Mistel.

That didn't sit well with him.

Cole joined Brien at the workbench, where he scratched a note about Emory's connection to Dewin onto a fresh scroll.

Brien patted a stack of parchment. "Invoices for special commissions," he said.

"See if you can find an order for Edera Duwal or any of our suspects." Cole watched over Brien's shoulder as the guard turned over the orders one at a time.

You're not shielded. Achan's voice boomed in Cole's head as the prince messaged with his bloodvoice. *Where are you?*

Cole blinked, uncertain if Sir Caleb had told the prince anything about the murder. "I'm outside the castle at the moment."

Brien turned to Cole. "What's that, sir?"

Cole shook his head and tapped his temple. "Sorry. The prince..."

"Ah." Brien went back to the invoices.

Where, Cole?

Cole swallowed and remembered to think his answer rather than speak aloud. *In the Crescent, sir.*

What in flames are you doing out there?

Sir Caleb tasked me with an investigation, sir.

Of course he did. Well, I had a mind to cross swords, but since you're not here...

Shung is a better sparring partner than me, sir.

Enough with the sirs. I wasn't wanting to spar for myself but for you.

Oh. I see. Achan was still determined to see Cole improve as a swordsman. It was a lofty goal, but Cole didn't want it nearly as much as the prince did.

Not to worry, Cole. Perhaps this afternoon... No? Ah. Apparently, I have a fitting this afternoon for my wedding ensemble. As if I don't already have enough fancy clothes.

Mistel gasped and grabbed Cole's arm. "Is that a... person? In that chair?"

Cole followed her gaze to a chair sitting before the cold hearth, its back facing the room. "Baz?"

The big man's boots clomped over the floor as he approached the chair. "Hey there, friend. Wake up." He leaned down and snapped his fingers.

Mistel spun toward Cole and tucked her face against his shoulder. Her hair tickled his chin, and while he wanted to savor the moment, all he could think about was what Bazmark was seeing across the room.

"Is he dead?" Cole asked.

The sergeant glanced up and said, "Looks like."

Who's dead? Achan asked with his bloodvoice.

Cole unhooked himself from Mistel's grip and approached, but as he stepped around the chair, he found himself outside the tower in Castle Armonguard, staring down onto the face of a dead soldier.

Cole? What's wrong? Achan asked.

Cole backed up a step and bumped into someone. Spun around to a pale, muscled chest draped with animal skins. The Eben glared down on him.

"Your Highness," Cole said. "We are under attack. Ebens!"

Where are you? How many Ebens are there?

Something struck the side of Cole's head. He found himself on his knees on the floor beside a chair that held the body of a young man with olive-green skin, black hair, and dark eyes that stared at nothing.

Ah, Cole had hoped the body had been part of the vision.

Alas, Dewin Sessit was dead.

Cole, I can see through your eyes, and I see no Ebens, Achan said.

Oh. What could he say to the prince? *I was mistaken, sir. I'm sorry.* Then he concentrated and raised the shields around his mind.

Cole instantly felt a twinge in his head and heard the prince's bloodvoiced knock, formally introducing himself for a magical conversation. *Achan Cham.*

As Sir Caleb had taught Cole long ago, bloodvoicers needed permission to speak to a shielded mind. If Cole did not lower his shields, the prince could only knock. He glanced around, wondering if he had won, or if Achan would persist.

Another twinge. Nope. The prince knocked again. *Prince Gidon Hadar.*

Cole frowned, still not wanting to answer. "Trizo, fetch the coroner."

"Yes, sir." Trizo exited the shop.

Pain spiked in Cole's temples as Achan persisted. *The future king of Er'Rets.*

Mistel crouched at Cole's side. "Why did you hit him?" she asked Baz.

"The boy's battle broken," Baz said. "He needed to snap out of it."

Battle what? Another stab of pain in Cole's head. "Ah!"

Knock, knock, my friend.

Mistel tucked Cole's hair over one ear. "Are you all right?"

Bazmark chuckled and stepped closer. "Fool boy. You're ignoring the prince?"

Cole whipped his gaze to Baz. "He's talking to *you*?"

"What does 'battle broken' mean?" Mistel asked.

"He can't stop thinking about what he saw in the war," Baz said. "It spooked him."

Cole ground his teeth and snapped out a reply. "I'm not afraid."

Baz leaned down, propping his hands on his knees. "Yet you fell over just now."

"Because you struck him!" Mistel yelled.

"Enough," Cole said. "Let's continue the search while we wait for Master Donotan." Yet he didn't move. He simply stared at Dewin Sessit's chest and watched the slow but steady rise and fall. "He's still breathing."

Trizo returned with three more guards and Master Donotan, who took one glance at the woodcarver's body and agreed with Cole.

"This man has been stormed," the coroner said, "but if his soul is not found, he'll die soon enough."

Bazmark sank onto the floor beside the fireplace and leaned against the wall. "I'll go in and see if he's nearby."

Cole opened his mouth to argue but could find no reason to do so. Since his primary experience with bloodvoicing magic was to keep his mind shielded against potential spies and answer when his superiors used their magic to talk to him from a distance, he often forgot that some bloodvoicers had other abilities as well.

To be stormed was to have one's soul pushed by a bloodvoicer from one's body into the Veil, which was the world between the physical realm and the eternal realms of Shamayim and the Lowerworld. It was a horrible thing to do to a person and often resulted in death when the stormed soul could not find its way back to its body. Beings in the Veil could see into the physical realm, yet those in the physical realm could not see what was in the Veil.

Not every bloodvoicer had the ability to enter the Veil, whether to storm or to go in and try and find a stormed soul. Cole supposed that Bazmark searching the Veil was the best way to try and find Dewin Sessit's soul and bring him back.

Bloodvoicing magic unnerved Cole almost as much as witchcraft. That someone might be in his head—or even in the Veil—watching and listening without him knowing gave him the shivers. Though he was rather certain he was shielded at the moment. Or the prince had given up.

He suddenly remembered that the prince had been in his mind when Cole had flashed back to the Battle of Armonguard. What had Baz said? That Cole was weary from the battle? The very idea brought on a rush of shame.

"What's he doing?" Mistel took hold of Cole's arm, but her gaze was on Baz, who looked to be napping.

The question brought Cole back to the present. "He's gone into the Veil."

She frowned, her mouth a grim line. "Can *you* bloodvoice?"

"No," Cole said. "Though they talk to me often enough."

"Who does?"

"The prince, mostly." Hopefully, Achan wouldn't be too angry that Cole had ignored his knocks. "And Sir Caleb. Occasionally

Kurtz or Sir Gavin or Sir Eagan. Baz and Brien are capable but have never spoken directly to me."

Mistel's eyes widened. "So many? What's it like?"

"Disturbing. But sometimes helpful too. Let's keep working."

Cole searched through the figure carvings. Most were people or animals, but there was an entire shelf of idols of the various Er'Retian gods. On another shelf, a bust of the Crown Prince stared back at Cole, so lifelike he leaped back and dropped his scrolls and charcoal. For the briefest moment, he thought Achan had hidden amongst the carvings to get a verbal answer to his knocks.

Once Cole had caught his breath, he studied the other carvings on that shelf. All were either the prince or Lady Averella. His gaze fell upon some smaller full-body carvings of Achan that resembled the effigy he'd found in Mistel's fireplace. He reached out a shaking hand and picked up one. Everything was the same except the likeness and the fact that the eyes were not X'd out.

"Brien." He held out the carving.

The guard whistled a low note. "I don't like the looks of that."

Mistel appeared between them. "What's wrong with it?"

"Besides the fact that it's in the same style as the carving of your roommate?" Cole asked.

"That's not surprising," she said. "Many vendors sell carvings or paintings or sculptures of our Crown Prince and his bride-to-be. There's a lot of money in it."

True. Cole had seen them himself. "But this man could be our carver. The fact that he's been stormed makes it even more likely." His gaze fell on a muslin drape nailed up in the far corner of the room. "What's back there?" Still holding the carving, he walked to the corner and drew the fabric aside. This revealed a tiny room filled with a cot and small table. "Looks like he lived here."

At Cole's shoulder, Mistel gasped, then pushed past him into the room. She headed straight for the table, picked up a bracelet, and held it aloft.

"This is Edera's," she said.

Cole entered the tiny space and examined the bracelet. Its twin hung in his room in Castle Armonguard.

"How do you know?" Brien asked from the doorway.

"Because she made two of them," Mistel said. "And gave the other to me. And I gave it to. . . " Those green eyes met Cole's.

"To me," Cole said.

"Sir?" Trizo called from the main room. "Baz is back."

Cole rushed out to where Bazmark sat beside the fireplace. "Well?"

"No sign of anyone nearby in the Veil," Baz said, pushing to his feet. "What did I miss?"

"We found Edera Duwal's bracelet and about a hundred of these." Cole handed Baz the effigy-like carving of the prince.

"Looks like we found our carver," Baz said.

Cole frowned at the unconscious man. "What's left of him, anyway."

Cole stood with Mistel outside the woodshop, watching his men load Dewin Sessit's body onto the coroner's cart. He needed a break to clear his head and think, so he asked Brien to go back to the castle and see that Dewin Sessit was taken to a room and cared for, then he asked Bazmark and Trizo to investigate the Magosian ring without him.

"Head back to the castle first and change out of your regalia," he told them. "Then saddle up some pack horses. You need to appear common before venturing into Magosian territory."

"Good plan, sir," Brien said. "Those witches won't be too keen on conversing with Kingsguard soldiers."

They certainly wouldn't. "See if you can find anything about effigy rituals or killings," he told Trizo. "And be careful."

Giving orders to the men in front of Mistel made him feel both important and like an impostor. He tried not to show either emotion on his face, including the twinge of shame from having weaseled his way out of a trip to the Magosian ring.

"Miss Wepp," he said, "I apologize for keeping you so long. Would you like a ride back to the castle?"

Bazmark patted the saddle on his horse. "You can ride with me, if you like."

Mistel's eyes widened as she looked Baz over. "No, thank you," she said. "I walked out here. I can certainly walk back."

"You could ride with the coroner in the wagon," Brien said, gesturing to the cart where Dewin Sessit's body lay shrouded.

Mistel wrinkled her nose and turned her back on the other men. She petted Cherix's flaxen mane and said softly to Cole, "Can a horse really carry two people at once?"

"For short distances, yes," Cole said. "Especially a big horse like Cherix."

She inspected the animal. "That saddle seems small for two."

"With this saddle, one person has to ride behind," Cole said. "Though if you'd rather ride alone, you could take Cherix."

That brought those lovely green eyes back to his. "Then you'd have to walk."

Cole shrugged. "I don't mind."

She lit up with a grin so wide and bright that it drew attention to her endearing overbite and compelled Cole to grin back, completely stupefied by her beauty. This somehow made her smile wider.

Heat shot through Cole from head to toe. Blazes, he liked having her around. How she could remain so calm through the entire investigation impressed him, and with her amazing singing voice and that hair, if he continued to spend time with her, his heart would soon be in trouble.

It might already be too late.

Bazmark's hearty chuckle broke the moment. "You'd best ride with the boy, Miss Wepp. You two clearly like the look of each other, and together you weigh less than one of me. That won't bother the horse none."

Cole frowned, now hot for an entirely different reason.

But Mistel's answer of, "All right," diffused any offense Cole felt toward Bazmark's slight. She wanted to ride with Cole, not Baz. Did that mean she fancied Cole? At least a little?

"Ride on, then," he told the men. "When you're done in the Magosian ring, meet me back at the castle."

"Will do," Trizo said.

"Aye, sir," Brien said.

"Best hold on to him, Miss Wepp," Baz said. "In his battle-broken state, we wouldn't want him to fall off."

Cole squeezed his fists, smiled too wide, and laughed too loud as Bazmark rode away.

He was quickly growing to dislike that man.

CHAPTER TWELVE

COLE

SHORT PEOPLE HAD A GOOD PERSPEC-tive on the world since they were always looking up. That's what Lunden, the stable master from Mitspah, had told Cole when Lord Yarden had mocked him for his short height. Cole reminded himself of the adage as he hoisted Mistel onto the saddle, then used the hitching post to boost himself up behind the cantle to sit on Cherix's bare back.

He managed the task with some grace, thankful Mistel was facing forward and talking to Cherix instead of watching him scramble up behind her.

And that Bazmark was not here to make rude remarks.

As Cole reached around Mistel's slender waist to take hold of the reins, he instantly questioned the wisdom of riding double. The cantle put space between their hips, but as she was sitting sidesaddle on a regular saddle, her shoulder and back rested fully against his chest, and her hair tickled his face. She smelled of lemon and mint, which strangely made him think of the chicken he'd eaten a few nights back. This made his stomach growl.

Arman, please don't let her have heard that.

Cole nudged Cherix forward, and the horse took off at a walk down the street. It was only about ten city blocks to the castle—he could see it from here—yet he could not imagine riding so far in such an awkwardly alluring scenario. Until Mistel turned, and her hair brushed over his face, and her eyes were so close she blurred before him like a bouquet of poppies and white roses.

"Have you always lived in Armonguard?" she asked.

"No, I'm from Mitspah."

"Look out!" a man yelled.

Cole jumped. Cherix had veered into the path of an oncoming cart, its driver waving madly. Cole steered Cherix out of the way. "Sorry!" he called as they passed by.

He leaned to the side, trying to keep an eye on the road lest he run someone else down.

"How did you come to meet Ach—I mean, the prince?" Mistel asked.

Cole wasn't about to tell Mistel the whole truth of that story. "He and his army visited Mitspah for several weeks this past summer. I worked in the stables there and had the opportunity to care for his horses. He, uh, liked my work and spoke to Lord Yarden about taking me with him. Lord Yarden agreed. The rest is, as the minstrels sing."

"An epic." She grinned. "Do you miss home?"

"Mitspah is a beautiful place," Cole said, "but it's never been home for me. I've always felt home was a place I had to find myself. I was eager to leave."

"That's how I felt about Sitna, though I never thought it was beautiful. It thrilled me deeply to leave. My first adventure. I've barely had time enough to discover Armonguard yet, but it holds so many possibilities. I can see myself finding a home here. What about you?"

He breathed her in, a rhyme about lemons and poppies swirling in his head. "More and more every day."

"When did you get promoted to the prince's squire?"

"After the Battle of Reshon Gate."

"You fought in that battle?"

Cole had done nothing more than care for horses, watch over Matthias, and check dead bodies for weapons. "I did my part," he said, letting her draw her own conclusions.

"And now you're battle broken? Because of what happened at the castle?"

The lie flowed easily off his lips. "No," he said. "Bazmark likes to jest."

"But you said Ebens were attacking."

Had he?

Thankfully, they had reached the castle, and Cole changed the subject by telling Mistel about the different gates. When Cherix carried them into the stables, Cole dismounted first, then helped Mistel down, liking the feel of her waist in his hands. He released her and set to work on Cherix.

"You don't have to wait," he said, loosening the girth strap on the saddle.

"Aren't there workers to do that?" she asked.

"None that will take better care of Cherix than I will."

Mistel walked around front and petted Cherix's nose. "Is he yours?"

Cole pulled off the saddle and put it away. "He is. The prince gifted him to me."

"He's beautiful," Mistel said, then to Cherix, "Yes, you are. What kind of horse is he?"

"A flaxen chestnut." Cole grabbed a currycomb. "Would you like to brush him?"

"I've never groomed a horse before," she said.

"It's not difficult." Cole rubbed out a wet spot. "We're not trying to make him pretty. We're removing the sweat and dirt. Get air to his skin so he can dry out."

"Why?"

"Because if we don't, he can develop sores and infections. Plus, it's a nice way to reward him for carrying us around. It massages his muscles and helps the blood flow."

She came to stand beside Cole. "Will you show me how?"

"Sure." He handed her the comb. She grabbed it wrong, so he took it back and adjusted it in her hand. Such tiny, slender fingers. He set her hand and the comb against Cherix's coat and, with his hand over hers, guided the comb along Cherix's side.

"Go against the grain," he said, trying not to be obvious about smelling her hair. "Scrub him really good. You won't hurt him."

He let her lead their hands on the next stroke, doing much better this time. Combing might ease Cherix's muscles, but it made Cole's tense. He grabbed another comb and worked on the other side, where it was cold and smelled only of manure.

Cherix released a breathy sigh.

"He likes it," Mistel said.

Over Cherix's back, Cole watched her face light up, which made him grin. "You've made a new friend."

Then Mistel began to sing.

"Cherix, the horse with mane of gold,
He roams through the Crescent, brave and bold.
Carrying passengers is his quest,
Now Cherix receives his well-earned rest."

Cole stared at Mistel, spellbound, until Cherix nickered and broke the silence.

This girl never ceased to surprise him. "Are you trying to steal my horse?" he asked.

She giggled and continued to work the comb.

"How are you always so upbeat?" Cole asked. "So happy?"

Strangely, the question destroyed Mistel's smile. Had he upset her? She scrubbed a spot on Cherix's side, and Cole wished he hadn't asked. Then she finally said, "If I'm not, the darkness will catch me."

A knot formed in the pit of Cole's stomach. "What darkness?"

Mistel closed her eyes and smiled, lips closed. She stayed like that a moment, as if posing, then shook her head. "Another time. What do I do when I'm done with the comb?"

All right, then. Cole got the hint, and when they'd finished brushing Cherix, they walked out of the stables. While Cole steered toward the keep, Mistel angled toward the front gate.

"If you're not too busy," she said, "I'd like to introduce you to my band. I haven't spoken with them since yesterday, and I need to let them know what happened."

Cole couldn't help but feel jealous of these men who got to make music with Mistel every day. That she wanted to introduce Cole to them seemed promising. If they got to know each other better, then someday she might be comfortable enough to share what darkness was chasing her, and he might be able to help.

"All right." Cole offered her his arm, and she took it.

They exited the western gate on foot and took the stairs around the scalloped outer wall until they reached the wharf green. As they made their way through the marketplace toward the waterfront, Cole felt like a different person than he'd been the day prior. All because of Mistel and the way she looked at him. He didn't want to overthink it—jinx it or get his hopes up—but he liked spending time with her.

She came to a sudden halt, squeezing the life from his arm. "That's the boy who robbed me." She nodded toward a waif no bigger than Matthias—eight or nine years of age—who was watching a puppeteer make a wooden jester dance.

"Let's see what he has to say for himself." Cole slipped up behind the boy and grabbed him around the middle.

The boy yelped and thrashed as Cole carried him away from the audience. "Let me go!"

Members of the audience turned toward the boy but seemed to relax when they saw Cole's Kingsguard uniform.

Cole turned so Mistel could see the boy.

"Where is my reticule?" she asked. "You stole it from me yesterday, and I want it back."

"I don't have it," the boy said.

"Listen here," Cole said in his ear. "I'm squire to the Crown Prince, and if you don't return what you've stolen, I'll put you in the dungeon."

The boy turned his head to try and get a look at Cole. "Will I get two meals a day?"

The question softened Cole's heart, but he said, "Not thieves. Guards cut off their hands and feed them to the tanniyns."

The boy resumed his fit. "Let go!"

"If you return the lady's purse, I will," Cole said.

"I told you I don't have it. I gave it to the man."

"What man?" Cole asked.

"The man who made me do it. He gave me a whole mince pie when I was done."

Cole dropped to his knees and turned the boy in his arms so he could see his face. "What man? Describe him."

"Tall with black hair and whiskers. He came into my head and made me take it."

A chill ran over Cole. "You heard his voice in your thoughts, did you?"

The boy nodded, his eyes huge. "The pie was still warm."

Cole withdrew some coins from his pocket and gave them to the boy. "I'm sorry he did that. It was wrong. Don't steal anymore, you hear? If you're hungry, come into the stables and ask for Cole. Tell them I sent you. That clear?"

The boy stared at the coins cradled in both hands. "Yes, sir. I will, sir."

"Good," Cole said. "Now go get another of those pies."

The boy scampered away like a squirrel, and Cole pushed back to his feet.

"That was sweet," Mistel said. "But what about my money?"

"It's long gone." Cole didn't want to frighten her, so he didn't tell her a bloodvoicer had compelled the boy to steal from her. Might Sir Caleb have a way to catch such a thief?

"I'll replace your money," he said, again offering his arm. "Let's find your band."

He and Mistel walked through the plaza toward the sound of music. They found Mistel's band sitting under a leafy oak tree. Both men were middle-aged. Burch played the lute. His black hair had receded, though he kept it cropped close to his scalp. He seemed to have some Otherling blood, as his skin held a grey tint. Rispen, the drummer, looked fully Kinsman with dark skin and eyes. He'd braided his greying beard into a frizzy tail.

"How did you all come to meet each other?" Cole asked.

"Rispen is Joya and Emory's cousin," Mistel said.

"We were thrilled to meet Mistel," Rispen said. "We lost our last singer to matrimony, and her husband didn't want her performing anymore."

"Is that what's happening here?" Burch narrowed his gaze at Cole. "You taking Mistel from us, boy?"

Heat flooded Cole's face. "I'm not—"

"No," Mistel said quickly, which sent a slight twinge through Cole's stomach. "This is the squire to the Crown Prince."

She told them what had become of Edera, and they instantly sobered. Cole felt like an intruder as the men embraced Mistel and offered condolences.

"Cole is a musician," Mistel said. "He plays the lute."

Burch lit up. "Is that so?" He offered his instrument. "Play us a little something?"

"Oh, I couldn't." Cole shook his head, yet clasped the neck of the lute for fear Burch might let go and the instrument would fall.

"Please play for us," Mistel said. "I've been longing to hear you."

Cole rather liked the sound of that. "If I play something you all know, will you join in?"

They agreed and admitted to knowing "Light of the World," so Cole picked out the melody and began to strum. His body grew warm under the scrutiny of Mistel and her band. He had never led a group in song like this. He was so nervous that he missed his entry point into the song and had to play through another measure. The second time, he did not miss his cue.

"Er'Rets was lost in the darkness within.
The Light of the world is Câan!
Like sunshine at noonday His glory shone in.
The Light of the world is Câan!"

It had been too long since Cole had played with other musicians. He'd sung along at many a campfire on the journey to Armonguard and made his own jingle stick. He'd stolen one moment with another man's lute and had once been permitted to play a tabor drum, but most musicians didn't loan their instruments to strangers. That Burch had passed over his lute so freely honored Cole to no end.

He played the full song, then Mistel asked him to play "Mountain Song." Cole began right away. Mistel had sung "Light of the World" with a rich soprano voice, but for "Mountain Song" she lowered her range and sang an alto harmony to match Cole's lead. Burch sang in a deep baritone, and Rispen led the pace on his tabor.

The music so overwhelmed Cole that he closed his eyes to enjoy the way their voices and the instruments wove together.

After his final strum on "Mountain Song," Cole handed back the lute before Mistel or anyone else could make further requests. He didn't wish to hog another man's instrument or abuse the privilege of playing with these new friends.

"Thank you," he said to Burch. "It's a fine instrument."

"A lute is only as fine as its player," Burch said. "You're quite skilled. When did you learn?"

"I've been playing for six years," Cole said. "Haven't been able to play for several months, though, so I'm a bit rusty."

Burch raised his brows. "If that's rust, young man, I'd like to see you polished."

"You're wonderful, Cole," Mistel said. "Your voice gave me chills."

"Oh." He flushed. "Thank you. Uh. . . I should go. I need to check on Dewin Sessit."

"Friends with Dewin, are you?" Rispen asked.

Cole perked up. "You know him?"

"Young woodworker," Rispen said. "Carves the occasional flute. Can play, too, though we haven't seen him in a while." He gestured to Mistel. "He and his sister live in your building."

Cole met Mistel's shocked expression.

"I didn't know," she said. "I've never seen him before. I swear."

"What's his sister's name?" Cole asked.

"Akina," Rispen said. "Dewin do something wrong?"

Now, this was news. Could this Akina be the same one Osrik Nath had been with the night of the murder? "We don't know yet," Cole said, "but he may be tied to the attack on Miss Duwal."

"Oh, Dewin wouldn't hurt anyone," Rispen said.

"Definitely not," Burch added. "He's a good lad. Though I keep telling that boy to get his own place. His sister is a bad influence."

"How so?" Cole asked.

"It's the company she keeps," Burch said. "She's friends with some shady people."

Nath certainly fit that description. Cole wanted to follow up on this lead right away. "I should go," he said to Mistel.

"Are you going to look for his room in my old building?" Mistel asked.

"As soon as possible," Cole said.

"What about lunch?" she asked. "Have you eaten?"

"I ate before I went into the Crescent," Cole said. "But if you're hungry, you're welcome to eat in the great hall."

Her eyes lit up. "I'm famished."

They bade farewell to Rispen and Burch and made their way back across the wharf green. A chilled breeze inspired Cole to step a little closer to Mistel so that their arms touched. He wished they might linger out here, perhaps go on a boat ride the way the prince and Lady Averella liked to do, but the clue connecting Akina and Dewin was too important to brush off.

"What's it like to live in a castle and eat in the great hall?" Mistel asked as they started up the stone steps that curved along the outer sentry wall of the castle.

"Surreal," Cole said. "Honestly, I haven't lived here long. Before that, we were on the road for a few months, living in tents."

"And before that?" she asked.

Cole didn't want her to know he'd been a stray, sleeping in the stables on a bed of hay each night—or worse, about his life with the Fawsts before Nonda had sold him.

"Busy caring for horses in Mitspah," he said.

They passed inside the western gate, walked through the bailey, and entered the western arc of the keep. On the threshold of the great hall, Lucia intercepted them.

"Miss Wepp, I've been searching for you all day," said the maid. "Might you have a moment to look at some fabrics and maybe allow me to take some measurements?"

"Whatever for?" Mistel asked.

"Master Tanniyn commissioned some new dresses for you. But

I don't know what fabrics or colors you would prefer, and I dare not guess."

Mistel pinned Cole with her gaze. "New dresses?"

Cole hoped she wasn't upset. "I forced you to leave everything behind. It didn't seem right for you not to have any spare clothes. Lucia, can Miss Wepp meet with you afterward? She was about to eat."

"Oh no," Mistel said, patting Cole's arm. "Thank you, Master Tanniyn, for your generosity. Lunch can wait. I would like to see the fabrics now."

Lucia lit up. "Right this way, miss."

The ladies walked away with Lucia prattling on about green, blue, and red fabrics she had pulled aside to show Mistel.

Cole watched them go, admiring how the length of Mistel's hair swung from side to side as she walked. Then he remembered what he'd learned about Akina Sessit.

He had a feeling that Osrik Nath was somehow involved in all this. A woman named Akina had been on his list of people he'd been with the night of the murder. Now Cole had discovered that Dewin, the stormed carver, had a sister named Akina. That could be no coincidence.

Cole asked a page to inform him the moment his men returned from the Magosian ring. They needed to visit Nath, who would hopefully confirm his Akina's last name as Sessit, then tell them exactly where to find her.

The sooner Cole solved Edera Duwal's murder, the sooner he could go back to his task of befriending some musicians to play with, and at the top of his list was a ginger-haired songstress who could write songs off the top of her head, just like him.

With a voice enchanting, beyond his ken,

That captivates both beasts and men.

CHAPTER THIRTEEN
MISTEL

AFTER MISTEL HAD CHOSEN TWO FABrics—one a deep maroon, the other cobalt blue!—and allowed Lucia to take her measurements, she entered the great hall. Never had she stood in such a large room. The ceiling was higher than three regular ceilings, with great curving beams. Stained-glass windows on the narrow ends of the hall illustrated history, only some of which Mistel recognized. The dais was empty, but she eyed the matching thrones hungrily, wishing Achan and his betrothed were sitting there now so she could marvel in the wonder of their amazing story.

Simply glorious.

Cole was nowhere to be found. Not that Mistel needed his presence to enjoy the moment. Dining in the castle presented a golden opportunity to connect with influential individuals. Yet, as she surveyed the occupied tables, her options seemed limited. She could share a meal with a group of middle-aged soldiers or ancient-looking servants. Given the choices, she'd rather eat alone.

She chose an empty table, and a maid brought her a bowl of stew, two rolls, and a tiny basket of figs. Mistel thanked her and dug in. The stew was warm and rich with a peppery flavor that triggered a moan from her lips that turned several heads at a nearby table.

Such pleasure brought on a sudden pang of sorrow. Just listen to her! Edera was dead, and here sat Mistel, relishing all the wonderful opportunities that had come from it. Was she a horrible person for enjoying her new room in the castle, the dresses Lucia had ordered, the food, and singing songs with the cute squire?

Though Mistel had only known Edera for a month, she had loved her dearly. Sorrow would not bring her back, but what could she do?

She gasped as a sudden idea gripped her. She could write a song about Edera. That would not only honor her memory, it would also give Mistel a way to immortalize her friend.

She released a happy sigh. Cole was good with his lute. Mistel should ask his advice before she put music to "Gone Too Soon."

She grinned and bit into a fig. Well, look at that. She already had a title.

> *Dearest friend, deserves to bloom,*
> *Because she is, gone too soon.*

Mistel ate more stew and continued to compose lyrics about Edera.

> *Like a rose, wilts away,*
> *Forever young, you will remain.*
> *Like a song, stuck in my brain.*

Mistel wrinkled her nose, not liking the word *brain* in her song.

> *Like a song that will not wane.*

That was better.

What else about Edera? Mistel hadn't known the girl long.

This made her think of Cole. His freckled face. Soft brown hair. Lips turned in a tender frown of determination, as if he were composing complicated lyrics at all times. And those impossibly thick eyelashes framing a constant, almost pleading gaze, blending sorrow and contemplation at all times. Always watching.

She liked how he watched her.

Men always did, so it didn't surprise her. But Cole wasn't undressing her with his stares like that horrible Sergeant Bazilrat. No, Cole simply observed her, as if fascinated. As if he wanted to say more but was taking his time to find just the right words.

He *had* to be a songwriter. She wanted to hear his work and find out if it was equal to her own. She hoped it was as good as his singing voice. She wanted it to be.

As she munched on her figs, another idea budded. What if she could convince Cole to sing with their band? They were good enough without him, of course. But a woman singing alone tended to attract men, while a troupe with both a male and female lead appealed to both genders. Such bands could sing a more diverse selection of songs too.

"May I join yeh?" a man asked.

Mistel jumped, so lost in her daydreams that she hadn't heard anyone approach. She glanced up and her heartbeat took off at a run. Middle-aged and rail thin, this was the man who'd been following her in the Crescent. This close, she noticed a thin scar that ran through his top lip.

She forced herself to smile, not wanting to show fear. Unfortunately, he took her smile as an invitation and boldly set his hand on her shoulder.

"Haven't I seen yeh with the young squire?" he asked, his voice as greasy as his looks.

Repulsed, she shrugged out of his grasp. "You have. May I help you?"

He had the audacity to sit across from her, his dark eyes boring through her, the same way the sergeant's did. "'Tis empty 'n here, and yeh seemed kind."

Oh. Well, Mistel might have judged him too harshly, but she sensed something dark about this man that she'd rather not test. She stood and gathered her remaining figs into her hand. "Thank you, sir, but I was just leaving."

She strode away from the table, grateful he didn't call after her.

See? This was exactly the kind of thing that wearied her. Things Sergeant Baskold and Osrik and Lander did daily. The kind of thing someone like Cole would never do.

The idea of singing regularly with Cole thrilled her. He was not only talented and dashing, but he knew important people. Achan and Lady Averella, likely Prince Oren and a host of lords and ladies. He could get their band in front of important audiences.

Cole could help her achieve her dream.

Sure, he was a tad on the serious side and a bit skittish. But he was kind and generous and thoughtful. She'd enjoyed singing with him today. How much more fun would it be to sing with him on a regular basis? Maybe kiss those frowning lips until she coaxed them into a smile.

She popped a fig into her mouth and chewed. Oh, yes. She liked this plan very much.

Now she simply had to convince him.

Cole had likely sung in front of Achan before. If he hadn't, he likely could. Where did a prince listen to performers? In the great hall? Or did he have a more private venue?

As she climbed the stairs to her room, she wondered where Achan's room might be in relation to hers. It was still early, and she wasn't tired, so she decided to wander a bit and see if she could find it.

Only the first two levels of Castle Armonguard were finished inside with wood and richly adorned. The higher she climbed—

and the more she wandered various corridors—the colder the finishings became, transforming to cold grey stone and simple board-and-batten doors with black iron ring handles.

By the time she'd finished the last of her figs, she was so lost she had no idea where she was. She felt fairly certain that the prince's rooms were on the fifth floor, but nothing looked all that different up here. In her wanderings, she met only two people—both servants who'd paid her no mind. The corridors in this section did seem wider, though, so perhaps she was close.

Suddenly, two soldiers, both wearing red tabards emblazoned with the Hadar sigil, rounded a corner. Behind them, a third man followed, who was slightly older with chin-length blond hair swept back over his head.

"May I help you?" one of the soldiers asked.

"Um… I was searching for…" But she couldn't remember. "My room? I… got lost." Hadn't she?

"Take the stairs to the bottom floor and try again," the other soldier said.

Mistel frowned. "The stairs?"

The second soldier pointed over her shoulder. "Back that way. You can't miss them."

Well, he was quite rude. What if she couldn't find her way back? "All right." She sighed heavily. "Though I'm worried I'll be wandering this castle until my hair turns grey."

The third man approached. He wore a fancy surcoat of brown wool and embossed leather that was embellished with brass studs and gold embroidery. A matching leather belt cinched his narrow waist but held no sword, though the man's gait and the width of his arms suggested he knew how to wield one. Surely he was someone of importance.

"What is your name, miss?" he asked.

"Mistel Wepp."

"Ah, yes." His eyes lit. He'd heard of her. "You should be in the western arc. I'd be most happy to escort you there. We cannot have that hair of yours turning grey."

Well, at least she wouldn't get lost on her way back. "You know me, sir, but I'm afraid I don't know you."

He bowed his head. "Sir Caleb Agros, miss. I am the king's chamberlain."

"Oh." Mistel suddenly felt like she'd been caught doing something wrong. "Pleased to meet you, sir."

"If you'll come this way, Miss Wepp."

She followed the chamberlain toward the stairs, confused as to how she'd come to be lost in the first place. Her room was not difficult to find.

As they passed by an arrow-loop window, she could see that the sun had not yet set. It was far too early to be banished to her room.

"Sir Caleb," she said. "Is there a place to mingle in the castle at night?"

He turned and gave her a look, lined creases wrinkling across his forehead. "*Mingle?* With whom?"

"Well, I'm a songstress, you see, and I like to meet other musicians."

"Ah, I do see." He glanced away and sighed, in that moment reminding her a great deal of her father, always displeased with her. "I would not want to find you in the barracks with the soldiers."

Heat rushed to her face, and she twisted her hands together. Was that an accusation? "Certainly not, sir!"

"Forgive me, I meant no offense. But that's the only place I know where music is played publicly in the castle, unless there is a ball or celebration of sorts, which tonight there is not." He shook his finger. "Actually, I daresay you might find some maids and their families out in the bailey. There is a place that some of the servants congregate for dinner and sometimes play music and sing. It's between the laundry and the weaver's dyeing vats. You'll find it in the western arc. I can take you partway."

Well, that would do for now. Mistel certainly wouldn't meet any nobles in such a place, but she could ask the servants enough questions to find out what important people she should be trying to meet.

"I appreciate that, sir," she said.

As Mistel walked down the stairs in silence with Sir Caleb, she pondered his words, wondering if she had made an enemy in this man. True, she probably should not have been wandering around the castle, but did that give him reason to assume the worst of her? The fact that he'd heard of her likely meant Cole had spoken of her—or of the investigation.

Oh, she hoped she hadn't done anything that might bring trouble upon Cole. He had been kinder to her than anyone she'd ever known. She considered raising the topic, telling Sir Caleb how much she appreciated Cole's help, but she feared that would only make matters worse.

At the foot of the stairs, Sir Caleb followed the curved corridor until a set of double doors came into view. "Outside those doors, you'll be in the western arc of the outer bailey. Look for the laundry and you'll have found it."

Mistel curtsied, wanting to give the chamberlain as much respect as possible. "Thank you, Sir Caleb. You are very kind."

"Yes, well. We shall see."

CHAPTER FOURTEEN
COLE

WHILE COLE WAITED IN THE GREAT hall for Mistel, the page arrived with word that Trizo and Bazmark had returned. He walked to the stables, a bit disappointed to have missed eating with Mistel. He hoped she'd enjoyed her dress fitting and that he might see her later.

Cole met the men at the stables, where he told them what he'd learned about Dewin having a sister named Akina.

"We must ride to Osrik Nath's house and question him about Miss Sessit," Cole said. As he saddled Cherix to ride, he asked Trizo for a report of what they had learned in the Magosian ring.

"A priestess gave us a tour of the temple," Trizo said. "Priestesses do effigy purifications in the courtyard."

"Do I want to know what that means?" Cole asked.

"Apparently, an effigy must be cleansed and purified before it can be used," Trizo said.

Trying to imagine such a thing made Cole frown. "Used for killing?"

"She refused to speak about using effigies for killing," Trizo said.

"Got angry and said effigies are used to heal and appease angry spirits or to avenge wrongs. Not to kill."

"Well, someone used one to kill," Cole said. "If Dewin Sessit did the carving, perhaps his sister acted as priestess for cleansing?"

Trizo shrugged. "Could be."

Cole had never understood the fairness of a world where villains prospered. He pondered this thought as he, Trizo, and Bazmark rode a quarter of an hour up Ridge Road to the edge of the city and Osrik Nath's home. The sprawling residence had been built of stone with a facade of gleaming white marble. They dismounted, tied their horses to a lattice fence covered in climbing roses, and approached an entrance framed by pillars of polished granite.

Bazmark knocked on the door, and Cole leaned against one of the pillars as they waited. It seemed ridiculously unfair that someone like Nath would live in a house like this while his tenants lived in his slums.

The door opened, and by some blessing of the gods, Nath poked out his head. Cole felt slightly better knowing the man kept no servants.

"What do you want now?" Nath asked.

Cole pushed off the wall and slipped between Baz and Trizo to face Nath. "I need to know the room number for Dewin and Akina Sessit. They reside in one of your tenement houses."

Nath glared down on Cole. "I'll have to ask the manager. I don't know every person who lives in every building."

"You mentioned being with Akina at the time of the murder," Cole said.

Nath frowned, though one corner of his mouth betrayed him with its smirk. "You know, I never knew she lived in my own building. Small city, Armonguard!"

Cole had no time for games, but it pleased him that Nath did not deny that his Akina's last name was Sessit. "I have an edict signed by the Crown Prince that says you'd better find the room number and tell me, or you'll sit in the dungeon until you do."

Bazmark raised an eyebrow at Cole's lie. There was no edict, but Nath would never know that.

"Fine, you little pimple. I have a roster somewhere. Wait here." He shut the door in Cole's face.

"Nicely done, *pimple*," Baz said.

Cole set his jaw. His pulse was throbbing from that interaction, and Bazmark's goading didn't help. In fact, he couldn't allow Bazmark to continue to mock him. He didn't know what had turned the sergeant against him, but it needed to end. So he forced himself to play the part of Sir Caleb again. "Would you like to sit in the dungeon too, Sergeant?" he asked.

Baz narrowed his gaze. "You can't send me to the dungeon."

"On the contrary," Cole said. "If you insist on disrespecting me, I will happily send you to the dungeon. Perhaps even speak with Sir Caleb about a demotion."

Baz looked as if he'd sucked on a lemon. Before he could respond, the door opened and Nath emerged holding a ream of parchment. "Sessit, 1K." He dropped the list to his side. "Anything else?"

Excellent. "Not at this time, Master Nath. Good day." Cole spun on his heel and walked toward Cherix.

It took about a half hour to ride back to the tenement house where Edera Duwal had been murdered. Cole hated the mere sight of the stooped and weathered building, which somehow appeared worse in the light of day, with its shredded thatch roof the color of soot. The surrounding narrow cobblestone alleys echoed with the distant cries of street vendors and the clatter of wooden carts.

Cole tied Cherix to the hitching post and bade Trizo guard the horses. Then he tried to ignore the pungent scent of rot as he and Bazmark went inside.

As they made their way down a narrow hallway, the distant sounds of laughter and argument drifted through the thin walls. Cole counted the numbers carved into the doors as they passed by each. A and B across from one another. Same with C and D.

"How was the ride back to the castle with your little chicken?" Bazmark asked, his voice soft as they passed by rooms E and F.

Cole jerked his gaze up to the man walking beside him. "Chicken?"

"Isn't that what Miss Wepp smells like to you? Maybe you should tell her." He chuckled.

A chill ran over Cole's arms as he pieced together Bazmark's meaning. He slowed outside room G and quickly shielded his mind. "You spied on my thoughts?"

Bazmark continued past rooms I and J. "Bloodvoicing is good for a great many things, it is," he said. "Looking into your thoughts. Looking into hers."

Icy fingers clawed at Cole's soul—peeled back the scab that had long ago covered the years of helpless humiliation at the hands of his stepbrothers. How dare Bazmark invade his private thoughts? "I command you stop at once!"

Bazmark laughed and turned around, walking backward. "All right, then. But you're not very good at remembering to shield. Would you believe me if I said I stopped?"

Cole frowned as he took in the smirk on Baz's face. "No, I don't believe I would."

The sense of betrayal festered, igniting a rage Cole rarely felt. This wasn't just an insult—it was a violation, a trespass into the sacred space of his mind and heart. And Mistel. The idea of her private thoughts being exposed to this man's twisted amusement was unbearable.

"What are you going to do about it, then?" Bazmark asked.

"Put me in the dungeon? Do that and I'll never stop sifting your thoughts. Or hers."

The sneer in Bazmark's voice was the breaking point. Heat surged through Cole like wildfire, and he charged the man, his vision narrowing with the force of his fury. But Bazmark danced aside so quickly that Cole rammed into the wall. Pain shot through his shoulder, but it was nothing compared to the ache in his chest.

He was about to attack again when Bazmark said, "Oh, look. It's room 1K," and knocked on the door.

Though Cole felt like his heart were trying to bust out of his chest and take on Bazmark single-handedly, he forced his hands to his sides as the sound of footsteps moved within the room.

Bazmark sighed happily. "Smells like chicken."

Cole gritted his teeth. He didn't want to fall for Bazmark's baiting games. That he had done so once already embarrassed him. He must behave like Sir Caleb: calm and wise and always in control.

The door opened, and a woman peeked out. "Yes?"

"Good afternoon," Cole said. "Are you Akina Sessit?"

She looked him up and down, then did the same to Bazmark. Cole slid his boot into the door's opening just as she closed it.

Footsteps ran through the room. Cole pushed inside in time to see the woman slide out the window. He sprinted after her.

"Catch her outside!" he yelled to Bazmark as he swung out the window and into an alley.

The woman turned a corner at the end of the building, and he ran to catch up. When he rounded the bend into another alleyway, she had already reached the far end. Cole sprinted with everything he had in him, but when he turned the next corner, he slammed right into Bazmark.

"Where is she?" Cole pushed to get around the huge man.

Bazmark shrugged. "You let her get away."

"*I* let her. . . ?" Cole caught sight of Trizo walking toward them.

"Did something happen?" Trizo asked.

"You just got promoted," Cole said. "Bazmark, stay with the horses. Trizo, with me."

Cole strode back inside the tenement to room 1K, fuming with every step. "We must search this place for anything suspicious." Hands on his hips, he let his gaze travel a room that was a copy of Mistel and Edera's.

"You mean like this?" Trizo asked.

Cole joined Trizo at the table, and when he saw the parchment and carvings, he almost lost the use of his legs.

A sketch of the great hall in Castle Armonguard labeled "Royal Wedding" and wooden effigies of Achan and Lady Averella, eyes crossed out.

CHAPTER FIFTEEN
COLE

STAY YOUR RAGE AGAINST THE MESSEN-*ger, for his duty is but to relay.*

The lyrics ran through Cole's head as he stood before Prince Oren's desk in Castle Armonguard, having just repeated a word-for-word report of the one he'd given Sir Caleb not ten minutes ago. The prince had been meeting with Duchess Amal when Sir Caleb and Cole had barged in.

"Blasted mantics!" Prince Oren grabbed his cane and limped toward the hearth. After he'd been injured at the Battle of Reshon Gate, the missing lower half of his right leg had been replaced with a wooden peg.

The prince's office had been partitioned off with tapestries around the fireplace to keep it warm. Prince Oren stopped there, grabbed the poker, and stabbed the burning logs, sending up a flurry of embers. Achan and his uncle had similar coloring, though the elder prince had a long, narrow nose.

"Achan is fine, Your Highness," Duchess Amal said, "as is Averella. I saw them both an hour ago. You need not worry. They are not the least bit ill." The diminutive noblewoman wore an emerald-and-cream gown trimmed in black lace, and a black beaded caul net adorned her auburn hair.

"Perhaps the mage has yet to begin the ritual." Prince Oren gestured to the effigies of Achan and Lady Averella that Cole had set on the desk along with the sketch of the great hall. "Did you notice anything different between the effigy of Miss Duwal and these two?"

"Only that the one in the fireplace had been partially burned," Cole said.

"Let's not bother the prince with the whole of this," Sir Caleb said. "I'll tell him there is another assassination concern, but until we know more, I don't want to frighten him unnecessarily."

"Agreed," Duchess Amal said. "They both deserve a nice wedding."

"But how will we stop this?" Prince Oren asked. "In the week since winning Armonguard, my nephew has survived a bowman's attack, a stoning, and now this."

"I do hope the welt goes down before the wedding," Sir Caleb said.

"His hair could be styled to hide it," Duchess Amal added.

"Witches plot to kill our future king, and all you care about is his appearance?" Prince Oren snapped.

"Not all. . ." Sir Caleb said. "We are working on the problem, and his security is as tight as it can be without locking him in a cell."

"But a mantic can kill from afar," Prince Oren said. "They don't have to be near their target to do it."

A moment of silence descended.

"Master Tanniyn," the duchess said. "Do you think the murder of this woman is somehow connected to this planned effigy attack?"

"I believe Miss Duwal was romantically involved with the mage's brother," Cole said. "I think she saw or heard something about Akina Sessit's plans and was killed for it."

"The brother helped kill his ladylove by carving an effigy?" Prince Oren asked.

"He might have carved Miss Duwal's likeness for himself, and his sister used it to kill her," Cole said.

"That theory seems plausible," Sir Caleb said. "Explain to me—"

The door burst open, and Achan strode inside. "So many of you together? I do hope the topic is boring."

Everyone jumped to their feet and bowed. The prince had a way of effortlessly commanding attention by his mere presence. With his tall stature and Kinsman features, he carried himself with ease, always seeming to be smiling, even when he was cross.

Which was why Cole braced himself. He hadn't spoken to the prince since he'd ignored his bloodvoicing knocks at the woodcarver's shop. He hoped the prince wasn't angry about that.

Achan growled and waved them all to sit. "You know that's not necessary."

"You know that it is, Your Highness," Sir Caleb sang. "How can we be of service?"

"I'm looking for Cole. Bazmark voiced me in a tizzy about being demoted."

"Demoted?" Sir Caleb's wild-eyed stare fell on Cole.

Just hearing Bazmark's name set Cole on edge. "He spied on my thoughts. On Miss Wepp's thoughts too. He thinks I'm too young to be in charge." They likely all did.

"Have you been shielding yourself?" Sir Caleb asked. "Because if you're not, then you deserve to be spied upon."

"Oh, Sir Caleb," Duchess Amal said. "No one deserves that."

"He knows perfectly well how to shield his thoughts." Achan quirked a brow at Cole. "Age has no bearing on leadership, Cole. Is this about the investigation Sir Caleb tasked you with?"

"Yes, sir," Cole said, looking up at the prince with only his eyes. "I'm investigating a murder."

"What?" Achan sat on the edge of Prince Oren's desk and

pinned Sir Caleb with a stare. "Investigating a murder seems beyond the responsibilities of a squire, Sir Caleb."

"A young woman asked him for aid," Sir Caleb said. "A knight is duty bound to serve where he can. I thought it would be good training."

"Who is this woman?" Achan asked.

"Mistel Wepp," Cole said. "She claims to know you."

Recognition brought a smile to Achan's face. "From Sitna?"

"Yes, sir. She came south with a group of people following our procession—following you. She's a songstress. Said she wrote 'The Pawn Our King' and that Emory Harp claimed it as his own."

"Really?" Achan folded his arms, grinning even wider. "That strikes me as odd. Emory has always liked Mistel. Do you believe she wrote the song?"

"She's a gifted performer," Cole said. "I've not observed her songwriting skills, but I can see no reason why she would invent such a tale."

"Bring her to me," Achan said. "I want to speak with her."

"Your Highness," Prince Oren said, "this is not the time to be inviting new people into the castle."

"Uh. . . she's already staying in the castle," Cole said.

"Whatever for?" Prince Oren asked.

"Her roommate was murdered," Cole said. "I feared she might be targeted as well. Figured she'd be safer here until the investigation concluded."

"That was a thoughtful decision," Duchess Amal said.

"Thoughtful, yes," Sir Caleb said. "But I wish you would have consulted me beforehand. Just today, I caught the girl wandering around the fifth level of the southern arc. I can only assume she was searching for the prince's quarters with plans to—"

"No, Sir Caleb. Stop right there." Achan set his hand on Sir Caleb's shoulder. "Mistel means me no harm, I promise you. I have known her for as long as I can remember."

"What can you tell us of her?" Prince Oren asked.

"Her father was strict," Achan said. "After he died, she went a bit wild. She likes to be in the center of things. She's always smiling—has a huge smile. Not as big as Cole's, though he hardly uses his."

Cole looked from face to face as everyone glanced his way.

"Could she have killed her roommate to get to you?" Prince Oren said.

Achan scoffed at his uncle. "That would be madness. She hardly needs to plot to get to me. I would be happy to speak with her anytime."

"With your betrothed present, of course," Duchess Amal said.

"Of course." Achan shot Cole a smirk. "On the condition that Cole acts as my chaperone. It's only fair, considering I'm constantly outnumbered by women."

"Don't complain, Your Highness," Duchess Amal said, a subtle grin playing at the corners of her mouth. "It won't last nearly as long as my daughter's season of being outnumbered by you men."

Achan opened his mouth to reply to the duchess's comment, but before he could speak, Sir Caleb jumped in.

"Why not suggest Miss Wepp compose some lyrics so you can gauge her musical ability?" Sir Caleb asked.

For some reason, that annoyed Cole. "Miss Wepp is not a suspect. Nor am I investigating her accusation of stolen lyrics."

Achan chuckled. "You're juggling a great many responsibilities at present, Cole. That much is clear. Now, let's talk more about Bazmark questioning your leadership."

"Your Highness, might we take this discussion to my office?" Sir Caleb suggested. "Cole and I interrupted the meeting here."

"Certainly," Achan said. "We shall leave you to it."

Prince Oren and the duchess stood and bowed.

Achan frowned at them and left, Cole and Sir Caleb on his heels. Shung had been waiting in the corridor, and he walked with the prince.

Once they were in Sir Caleb's office, with Shung guarding outside, Achan said, "Bazmark has a history of misusing his blood-voices. This should be dealt with."

"I agree, Your Highness," Sir Caleb said. "Regardless, Cole does not have the authority to demote him."

"You really don't," Achan said to Cole, then turned to Sir Caleb. "But to take back his words will only undermine his authority over the investigation. Therefore, Bazmark will remain demoted until the investigation is over. I'll take him as a temporary guard, which will give me a chance to speak with him about this."

Cole shook his head. "Please don't say anything to him. It will only get worse."

"It is my duty to speak to him," Achan said. "I pardoned him on the condition that he would behave no more in such a way. You, on the other hand, must learn to stand up to teasing without losing your temper."

"You make it sound simple," Cole said.

"You know it's not," Achan said. "You've seen me go through worse. Here I thought I was helping someone younger than me when I took you out of Mitspah. Imagine my surprise when I discovered you're almost three years my senior."

Sir Caleb frowned at Achan. "You didn't know Cole's age?"

"I did not. No one tells me anything."

Now Sir Caleb was sighing.

"But you need advice," Achan said. "First, stop lying to yourself."

Cole swallowed. "About what?"

"'No one respects me. I'm too young.' Remember, Sir Caleb wouldn't have entrusted you with this responsibility if he doubted your competence. Remind yourself of that truth. Frequently, if you have to. You belong in this role. Be confident, not bossy. Avoid making threats. Instead, when appropriate, seek their expertise and involve them in the decision-making process."

Sir Caleb set his hands on his hips. "Listen to our prince with all his sage advice."

"I was forced to undergo intensive training," Achan said. "But I'm not done. Get to know them. Ask about their family. Where they grew up. And probably most important of all, don't know what to do? Seek counsel from those with more wisdom than you. Surround yourself with trustworthy people and let them help you."

"You've done an excellent job so far, Cole," Sir Caleb said. "Even bringing the girl into the castle... thinking of her well-being. I'm proud of you. What is your next move?"

The question came so fast Cole barely had time to feel the weight of Sir Caleb's compliment. "I must locate Akina Sessit. Three other tenants said a man other than her brother has been staying with her. I'd like to identify him." Cole felt in his bones it would be Osrik Nath. It had to be.

"Good," Sir Caleb said. "Keep me informed."

"Now, about the other thing," Achan said, fixing those blue Hadar eyes on Cole.

"There's more?" Sir Caleb asked.

Cole braced himself for trouble. He had ignored the prince's knocks, after all.

"He's still seeing the battle," Achan said. "Ebens, in particular."

Cole hadn't expected concern. "It's nothing," he said.

Sir Caleb's bushy brows sank over his eyes. "How often?" he asked. "Every day?"

Cole glanced at the door. "I tell you, I'm fine."

"Your resilience is commendable, Cole," Sir Caleb said, "but being battle bruised is not a sign of weakness. It's quite common."

"Toros Ianjo warned me about it on the journey down here," Achan said.

Bruised sounded better than being broken. That Cole wasn't the only one to experience such a thing filled him with hope. "Did it happen to you?"

Achan shook his head. "Not from the battle but the cham bear attack. I couldn't stop thinking about that for weeks. Every once in a while, I still have a dream about it and wake up convinced it's in my room about to eat me."

Sir Caleb gave the prince a funny grin. "You never said anything about that."

Achan shrugged. "I talked to Toros about it."

"I'm glad to hear it," Sir Caleb said. "Toros could help you too, Cole. Or Eagan. He's been helping me work through my *ride* with the sea serpent." He shuddered. "I've been through a lot of things in my time, and I've learned to deal with them quickly. Otherwise, they can fester."

The memories *had* been getting worse. "Too many things make me remember," Cole said. "Noises. People. I thought I saw Esek Nathak in the great hall, but it was Trizo."

"And you thought you saw Atul Shakran." Achan glanced at Sir Caleb.

Yes. . . Cole supposed Atul could have been in his imagination too.

"You were in grave danger and experienced a moral wound," Sir Caleb said. "That it bothered you is normal. But keeping such things to yourself can be terribly isolating, which is why talking about it helps."

"Telling the story helps," Achan said.

Cole wasn't so sure. He hadn't wanted anyone to know about the flashes because he feared being seen as frail. Small. Runt of the litter.

"Allow us to share the load," Sir Caleb said. "Or Kurtz, if you prefer."

Kurtz didn't like talking about hard things, but he *had* admitted to fearing the dark after he'd spent so many years in the Ice Island prison. That Cole's closest friend had made himself vulnerable inspired him to speak.

"When the tanniyn hit the tower. . . " Cole glanced at Achan. Was he really going to do this? Apparently so. "I heard screaming. I knew you were up there, and I worried you'd been hurt. Stone began to fall. Some hit me. Not enough to do damage, really, but one hit my hand and caused me to drop my sword. I ran out of the way, and when I came back to look for my sword, the stones had buried it. I was trying to dig it out when the Ebens came. Everyone was gone, and I didn't have a weapon. Only the flag."

Cole's hands were shaking. He pressed them against his leg. But now that he'd stopped talking, the words lodged inside his chest.

Stuck.

Why had he said anything? Achan and Sir Caleb were staring, which somehow made Cole feel like something inside him had caught on fire.

Achan flung his arm over Cole's shoulders. "I had no idea you were down there alone. I want to hear the rest of the story, but you look spent."

"Do you want to share more?" Sir Caleb asked.

Cole shook his head. "Another time."

Or never.

"I'll hold you to it," Achan said. "At the very least, I'll make sure you talk to someone. And don't ever shield against me again. Is *that* clear?"

Cole nodded, relieved to be done with this conversation and eager to leave. "Yes, sir."

"Arrange for Mistel to meet me in the Veralla Room after dinner tonight," Achan said.

"Your Highness," Sir Caleb said, "we do not know this young woman well enough to—"

"I grew up with her. She's not going to poison me or draw a knife."

Sir Caleb folded his arms. "There are worse things she can do to your reputation."

Achan clenched his jaw. "Vrell will be there, Sir Caleb. Stop fathering me."

Sir Caleb lifted his hands and walked away.

"Tonight, then?" Achan asked Cole.

"Yes, Your Highness," Cole said, hoping he could find Mistel.

"For the hundredth time, Cole, call me Achan when we're not in public. That's a command. Do you hear me?" But the prince was grinning.

Cole really didn't feel right calling the prince *Achan* aloud, but he also couldn't disobey him. "All right"—he swallowed and glanced at Sir Caleb—"Achan."

Chapter Sixteen
Mistel

FAR FROM THE GAZE OF WATCHFUL EYES, *a sanctuary found, where solace lies.*

Mistel hummed as she sought out a tune to pair with the lyrics. She crossed the bailey, heading toward the doors to the castle keep. She had spent the last few hours singing with some new friends she'd met near the laundry, exactly where Sir Caleb had said she might find them.

"Mistel."

At the sound of Cole's voice, she turned. There he sat on a fat stump of pine before a full woodshed. He stood and approached her. "Ach—ah, the prince has requested your presence in the Veralla Room after dinner."

Mistel lit up. This was the perfect opportunity to sing for Achan. If she did well, surely more invitations would follow.

Then her interaction with the guards and Sir Caleb came to mind—how she'd been caught snooping on the fifth floor. "Why should he honor me so? I'm not in trouble, am I?"

Cole grinned, a tiny little twist of his lips that sent sparks into Mistel's belly. "Whatever for? I thought you'd welcome the chance to see him. He said he knows you from Sitna and wanted to speak with you."

Well, that was a relief. "Certainly, I do. I was merely confirming." Mistel slid her hands around Cole's arm, and he led her toward the entrance of the keep. "He's going to be king. Despite knowing him in my childhood, we weren't close friends. I resided outside the castle, and he lived within. I frequently saw him in the Corner, though. Even danced with him once."

Cole glanced at her with something like panic in his eyes. "You danced with the prince?"

Oh, how she loved that little flare of worry. Jealousy, perhaps? Either way, it proved Cole fancied her, and she wanted to set him at ease. "Once. I begged a friend to put him up to it in an attempt to make Emory jealous." She sighed at the memory of Emory tracking them as he sang "Harvest Moon." "It worked. Emory didn't like seeing me with anyone else. Such a hypocrite."

They stepped inside the castle, and the chill of the stone walls seized her arms. She leaned closer to Cole's warmth as they made their way toward the great hall.

"The prince is dining privately," he said. "If you intend to eat something, best do so now."

"I ate my fill at lunch," Mistel said. "I don't usually eat so much in a day. My stomach is not used to it."

"I'm not hungry either," he said.

Interesting. This might be the perfect time to get Cole alone. "I have a small confession. I cannot stop thinking about singing with you today. Might we do that again sometime?"

"Sing what?"

"Whatever you'd like. Our voices harmonize well together, don't you think?

"Yes." He shrugged, his neck flushing pink. So cute.

She caught his hand in her own and tugged him away from the

great hall. "I wrote a song today and want to see how it sounds put to music."

He allowed her to pull him forward. "What kind of song?"

"A song about Edera. A beautiful girl who died too soon. I'd like to try it in a minor key and hoped you might help me."

"I'd need to fetch my lute. We could meet in the herb garden out back of the kitchens?"

But she wanted to see where he lived. Likely close to Achan's room, though why that should matter, she could not fathom.

"I'll walk with you," she said. "An hour is so little time. I can tell you about my song on the way."

"I suppose that would be all right." Cole led her to the southern arc of the castle.

She recognized the grand staircase from when she'd come here the night Edera had died. She reveled in the splendor of the space as she made her way up the shiny red tile steps. Did all the important people live in this part of the castle?

Up, up, up to the fifth floor they climbed, and Mistel told Cole about writing her song. "I want to capture her memory. It's strange to feel her slipping away already."

"A song is the perfect way to immortalize her," he said.

On the fifth floor, Cole led her down a familiar stone corridor. She felt certain they were close to where she'd explored earlier today.

He stopped before an ordinary board-and-batten door, said, "Wait here," then walked inside.

Mistel followed him in, surprised that his bedchamber looked nearly identical to her own. She'd like to think the prince's personal squire had nicer quarters than a peasant guest, but no. A narrow bed rested against one stone wall, no headboard, though the covers were neatly made. Across from the bed, a small collection of armor hung on the wall next to a sideboard that held a lone water basin. And on the narrow end of the room, opposite the doorway, a small, shuttered window, carved into the stone, allowed daylight to filter in past a leafy tree, casting shifting shadows across the rough-hewn floor.

At least he seemed to have a better view.

Cole picked up his lute from a hook on the wall and turned back, nearly colliding against Mistel in the middle of the room.

"Sorry!" He lunged back a step. "I didn't know you'd come in."

She walked deeper into his room, her gaze devouring every inch of the small space. "You're very tidy. Do you have a maid?"

"Uh, no." This earned her another of those almost smiles, which made her all the more determined to get the boy belly laughing in some way.

She had no idea how to do that, but. . . challenge accepted!

She approached the armor and weapons hanging on the wall and glanced over a shirt of chain mail, a dented helm, a pair of gauntlet gloves, and a belt and sword. She fingered the pommel of the sword and shivered, wondering if Cole had killed anyone.

She spotted her bracelet—the one she'd sold to Master Kurtz—hanging from a tiny nail on the sideboard. She stepped over, picked it up, and twirled it through her fingers. "You kept my token."

"Why wouldn't I?" He opened the door and held it wide. "Shall we go?"

She returned the bracelet to the nail. "I suppose."

"After you."

Well, wasn't he a gentleman? She swept out the doorway.

Down they went, a different way than before that took them through the kitchens. Mistel didn't think she could ever find the herb garden again on her own, but she rather liked the idea of getting lost with Cole in beautiful places.

The garden had been built on an old patio between the kitchens and the former great hall. Vegetation grew over the worn wood, creating an ethereal jungle of greens with an array of colorful blossoms from flowering spices.

"It's so beautiful," Mistel said.

Lute in his arms, Cole sat down on a stump beside a cluster of white oregano blossoms and strummed an introduction to "The Pawn Our King," then transitioned it into a minor key. "Let's hear you sing that new song," he said.

Mistel moved a three-legged stool beside Cole's stump. Sitting on it made her a few inches shorter than him. "It's not done, and I don't have a melody yet."

"Tell me the lyrics again," Cole said.

"All right." Mistel fixed her gaze on Cole and said,

> *"Dearest friend, deserves to bloom*
> *Now she is, gone too soon.*
> *Forever young, you will remain*
> *Like a song that will not wane."*

"I like that she's a song," Cole said. "You don't forget songs. They stick with you."

"Exactly." That he understood shot so much energy through her that she bounded to her feet. "The pace should be fast, since the subject is so sad."

Cole hummed a note of disagreement. "Sorrowful songs like this deserve a slower tempo. You want people to feel her, to know her, and if they're too busy dancing, they won't be able to do that." He closed his eyes and plucked out a few notes on the lute.

Notes Mistel liked the sound of. Her breath caught at the melancholy feel of the run. "You can hear it already, can't you?" she asked.

Cole opened his eyes and held out the lute. "I hear something, but I don't want to take this from you. Go ahead and play around with it. See what you find."

She shook her head. "I've never played a lute."

"You'd never groomed a horse either. Until you tried."

"True." She sat down again. "But I'd like to hear what you hear."

He turned to her then, his stare intense. "All right." He repositioned the instrument, picked his fingers along the strings, and strummed a minor chord. When he sang her verse, it came out breathy and rough. Dash it, she loved his voice.

He stopped playing and shrugged. "Something like that, maybe?"

"That was beautiful. Cole, do you write your own songs?"

"I have, but..."

"I want to hear one. Please? Then we'll go back to mine."

"All right." The poor boy looked so uncomfortable, Mistel would think ants were crawling all over his back.

"Uhm..." He strummed a few chords, then sang.

"I saw her,
At the fountain in front of the castle.
She wore red,
Had a flower in her hair.
All alone,
Standing beside the waterfall,
I asked her name,
She said Nnn—"

He stopped midverse, lowered the neck of the instrument, and swallowed. "It's not finished."

But this was an interesting twist. Cole Tanniyn was a hapless flirt unless it was through music, and then, ladies, beware. "Have you ever been in love, Cole? You sing like you have."

He rolled his shoulder, the one closest to her, and she knew her proximity was making him nervous. He finally admitted, "Once. She wasn't who I thought she was."

"What do you mean?"

"She wanted me to be someone else." He plucked a string on his lute, and the sound reverberated. "What about you?"

"Oh, I've been in love loads of times. When I was younger, daily, with every boy I knew."

He chuckled and blinked his long eyelashes her way. "Why does that not surprise me?"

She bumped her arm against his. "None of that was love, though. I only truly loved Emory for what felt like forever. When he started to travel, making himself famous, I used to imagine where he was and what he might be doing. I dreamed he'd take me with him someday. When he first started paying attention to me, I fell hard and fast."

"Was it only the lure of adventure?" Cole asked. "Did you like anything about *him*?"

"I was infatuated with his music and his looks. I didn't even try to get to know him. I couldn't tell you his favorite food or anything like that. He just moved me. That probably sounds foolish."

But Cole shook his head. "He made you feel something."

"He did. He made me feel alive. My father never let me go anywhere—made me cook and clean—and I thought, 'Emory Harp will take me places.' And he did. He brought me here. I wish I could have seen the truth, though. That he was making a half dozen girls fall in love with him all over Er'Rets. It annoys me that I didn't know."

"How did you deal with that rejection?"

She shrugged and tossed her hair over her shoulder. "It was his loss. Life is too short to waste on men like him."

"That pain is powerful, though. You could have written a song about it."

"A depressing song."

"You could make it funny. An eviscerating parody."

"Edera was so set on that path it made her ugly." Mistel tipped her head, hoping to dislodge that thought before it had time to stick. She pulled up a memory of Edera and herself playing on the beach together on the trip south. So much laughter that day.

Mistel's hair brushed Cole's cheek, and they glanced at each other, their faces so close. "Thank you for bringing me here after Edera died," Mistel whispered. "You protected me—made me feel safe."

"I was merely doing my duty."

"The prince trusts you." Mistel set her hand on Cole's knee. "He's lucky to have such a reliable squire."

Cole cleared his throat. "The song," he said. "Perhaps if you sing the lyrics while I play the melody, we can get a feel for how they sound together."

She hummed, gazing at his dark eyelashes, freckled cheeks, the curve of his mouth. "I'm already feeling lots of things, not only because of your music."

She leaned toward him, aching to feel his lips on hers—delighted to see him glance at her mouth. But then he turned his head and strummed a chord, which resounded between them.

Mistel's heart surged like rapids were flowing through her veins. "You were about to kiss me, weren't you?" At the subtle flush in his cheeks, she smiled and tucked an unruly lock of hair behind her ear. "What changed your mind?"

He ran his finger along the neck of the lute. "You have a confidence that suggests you're experienced in matters of the heart. I fear I might not measure up to your past suitors."

She frowned, sifting his words for meaning. What had given him the idea that she'd had lots of suitors? Perhaps her story about falling in love every day? She chuckled and said, "I haven't kissed that many people."

A small furrow wrinkled his brow, and he caught her gaze in his fathomless eyes. "I can't take you to the places you want to go. I live here. I work for the prince. It's truly not as exciting as it sounds. He has meetings all day. Tediously boring meetings."

My, but he was intense. Were they talking about marriage or a kiss? Mistel couldn't think that far ahead. "You've already taken me so many places," she said, feeling the need to reassure him. "Inside this castle, for one. Eating in the great hall. Riding a horse. New gowns. But it's so much more than that." She ran her finger along the back of his hand where he palmed the lute's body. "All my life, I've had to take care of everyone, myself especially. But no one's ever taken care of me until you. I don't trust people easily, but I trust you, Cole."

He shot a sideways look at her, his pupils huge, and leaned toward her, just a fraction.

She tilted her face toward his and closed her eyes, hoping he wouldn't change his mind. She felt the warmth of his breath a moment before his mouth met hers. Her stomach flipped at the softness of his lips. He kissed gently. So different from Emory's wet, strangely fierce kisses.

Cole's hand ran up her arm to her shoulder. His fingers tangled in her curls. He smelled like music, of yew wood and strings rubbed in walnut oil. Kissing him felt like longing, that feeling you get when you're hungry and your mouth waters and your stomach aches to be filled.

Someone cleared their throat, and Cole shot to his feet.

A guard she didn't recognize stood at the garden's entrance. Mistel ducked her head, hoping that getting caught like this would not cause Cole to push her further away.

"My pardon, sir," the man said. "The prince is asking for you and Miss Wepp. He says to bring your lute."

"Thank you," Cole said. "We'll be right there."

An awkward silence fell between them. Never did bootsteps on cobblestone sound so loud as the guard retreated. How on earth hadn't they heard him approach?

"Where did the time go?" Cole asked.

Mistel giggled, but it sounded forced, awkward. "Best not to keep the prince waiting."

Cole grabbed the neck of his lute and stepped toward the door. "Definitely."

CHAPTER SEVENTEEN
COLE

WHEN COLE REACHED THE VERALLA Room with Mistel, Achan and Lady Averella were seated on a pair of thrones and in deep conversation with Sir Eagan, Sir Caleb, and Sir Gavin.

Mistel frowned at Achan. "Did something happen to his face?"

Cole tried to see what she meant. "Oh, you mean the scars on his cheeks. That was Esek the day Sir Gavin presented Achan to the Council of Seven. I wasn't there. I only heard about it. Even after Sir Gavin proved Achan was the real Prince Gidon, the Council still voted for Esek to be king, so Achan and the knights ran. There was a fight. Sir Kenton captured Achan, and Esek cut his face."

"How awful." Mistel's gaze shifted to Lady Averella. "She's so beautiful."

Sir Caleb approached, and Cole remembered his manners. "Sir Caleb, this is Mistel Wepp. Miss Wepp, meet Sir Caleb Agros, chamberlain to the Crown Prince."

"Very nice to see you again, Miss Wepp," Sir Caleb said. "I hope you don't mind waiting. It shouldn't be too much longer."

That's right. Sir Caleb had found Mistel roaming the halls. Cole should have asked her about it, but he'd completely forgotten.

He shouldn't have kissed her.

He was already dealing with the aftereffects of the war—battle bruising, apparently. Now the investigation. Both things had him in over his head. Add this wild, impulsive girl. A girl who had a history with the prince. Undoubtedly, Achan had been counted among every boy Mistel knew in Sitna that she had loved at one point or another. Cole didn't like how that made him feel small. Second.

The real problem? Kissing Mistel had made Cole vulnerable.

Yet her words had swept him away. How she wanted to hear what was in his head. No one had ever said anything so attractive to him. Being seen like that… being understood… It stirred his soul. Still, Cole was different from most men. Deep down, he didn't care what people thought of him, about swordplay or feats of strength, though he wouldn't mind being a few inches taller. Certainly, Mistel would see that soon enough and find him lacking.

Getting involved with her was far too risky.

"Cole."

He jolted out of his reverie. Sir Caleb was waving him over. Sir Eagan and Sir Gavin had gone, and Mistel now stood at Sir Caleb's side, still gazing warmly at the prince.

Cole's stomach sank. Every young woman who looked upon the prince fell madly in love with him. Achan had every bit of what women found attractive: height, strength, quick wit, eloquence, nobility. A freckle-free face with a decent amount of beard, even for one so young.

Cole couldn't even grow a mustache.

"Cole!" Sir Caleb again, this time scowling.

"Sorry." Cole hurried after them.

Achan was on his feet, greeting Mistel. She glowed in his presence, of course. All women did. The prince introduced her to Lady Averella, and Mistel curtsied like a proper subject should.

Then they were chatting about Sitna, the loss of her father, and Mistel's decision to move south. Cole stood by, trying not to let his emotions spiral further.

"Cole tells me Minstrel Harp has taken credit for a song you wrote," Achan said.

"He has!" Mistel said. "Thankfully, it was the only one I shared with him."

"Would you sing it to us?" Achan asked. "Cole can accompany you. Right, Cole?"

Huh? Cole glanced from Achan to Lady Averella to Mistel to Sir Caleb, trying to puzzle out what he had missed.

You are daydreaming, Sir Caleb bloodvoiced. *And you've left your shields down. The prince has asked if you'll play Miss Wepp's song so she can sing it.*

Cole flushed and raised his shields. "Yes, sir." He turned his attention to Mistel and strummed a G chord. "Will that do?"

"Lower," Mistel said. "I'd like you to sing it with me."

"But it's your song."

"It sounds better with two voices. I wrote it for two voices." Mistel stared at Cole, a subtle furrow in those peachy brows, lips parted in a silent plea.

As if he could ever say no to such a face. Besides, she'd said in the plaza that his singing was wonderful. "I'll follow your lead." He kept the same key to give her the melody and picked out a peppy intro.

Before he knew it, they were singing again. Time stilled, and all other noise faded away. Her high, smooth voice melded effortlessly with his raspy harmony. A copper bell and a longsword becoming molten as they were forged together in song. Reddish-brown and silvery-grey tendrils converging in a liquid tapestry of sound. Yielding to one another.

Magic.

Cole glanced at Achan and Lady Averella once or twice but mostly kept his gaze on Mistel, watching her embrace this opportunity for truth and redemption. *She* had written this famous song. Achan's story had inspired *her*, not Emory Harp, and Cole reveled in the justice of this moment. He could see it was true for her as well. She sang with the captivating expression of a storyteller. As she moved, strands of her blazing hair escaped the twist on the back of her head and danced around her face like curling flames.

All too soon, the song ended, and Achan and Lady Averella rose to their feet, clapping.

"Simply brilliant," Lady Averella said. "I am so pleased to learn the truth of who wrote that song."

Mistel's smile made her eyes shine. "Have you been to Sitna, my lady?" she asked.

"I have," Lady Averella said as she and Achan took their seats again.

"Then you know it's a dreadfully small place. My whole life, I wanted to get away from there. When I heard the truth of Achan's identity—I beg your pardon, Your Highness."

The prince waved a hand. "No need to apologize. I'm still getting used to it myself."

"Thank you, Your Highness," Mistel said. "As I was saying, when I heard your story, I couldn't stop thinking about what adventures you must be having. Some people were saying it wasn't true, but they were jealous, I think. That's when the lyrics came to me. I wanted to celebrate your discovery of truth. Your liberation."

Achan chuckled. "You certainly did that. And very well, I might add."

"Your story captured me too, my lady," Mistel said to Lady Averella. "It made me long to escape Sitna."

"Which you did," Lady Averella said.

"I did." Mistel beamed at Cole, and her smile about melted him into a puddle.

He'd been a fool to worry about Mistel and Achan. Singing with her had snapped him out of his irrational melancholy. Cole was the person she trusted, not Achan.

"And Cole!" Achan said. "You mentioned your love of music and that you could play, but not your level of proficiency. You are a marvel."

Cole's face grew hot. "Thank you, sir."

"We should commission a song," Lady Averella said.

"Yes!" Achan said. "Not about me, though. Someone else should be the center of attention this time. Like you." He grinned at his bride-to-be.

"Oh, no," Lady Averella said.

"Oh, yes," Achan said. "This is a most excellent idea."

"Achan, really." Lady Averella twisted her hands. "I know! Write us a song about Sir Gavin, Sir Caleb, and Sir Inko. How they wouldn't give up on their search for the true prince. Never believed in the impostor Lord Nathak presented."

"I don't know if *that's* necessary," Sir Caleb said.

"But of course it is!" Lady Averella said. "Could you write it in time for our wedding?" she asked Mistel. "Cole can help you."

A chill ran over Cole. A wedding a mantic wanted to destroy. He glanced at Sir Caleb, who shook his head at the future king and queen and chuckled.

"Fabulous idea, my lady." Achan turned his attention to Mistel and Cole. "We will pay you, of course. A song about the three Kingsguard knights. Or. . . " He reached for Lady Averella's hand, which she gave him, and he rested them together on the side-by-side arms of their thrones. "A song about Lady Averella's story. I'd like both songs, but try to finish the latter in time to perform it at our wedding."

"Achan!" Lady Averella snatched her hand away.

"Can you do it?" Achan asked, then bloodvoiced Cole, who had again forgotten to maintain the shields around his mind. *I want the song about Vrell for the wedding, Cole. Finish it first, if you can.*

Cole and Mistel regarded each other. Cole loved the idea of writing a song—two songs—with Mistel, but he merely lifted his eyebrows, not wanting to make the choice for her.

Those pink lips curled—just one side, like she was trying not to show how she really felt about the opportunity. *Say it*, Cole thought. *Say you'll do it.*

"If it would please Your Highness," Mistel said. "And if Cole has time, what with the investigation."

"He'll make time," Achan said.

"I'll make time," Cole said, wanting to speak for himself. Wanting to kiss her again. Hoping he would now that they had reason to spend more time together.

"Excellent," Achan said. "Mistel, it was very nice to see you. I pray it will not be long before Cole and his team catch the one responsible for your friend's death and Arman brings it all to a swift and just resolution."

"As will I," Lady Averella added.

"Thank you," Mistel said.

"I hope you will excuse us for not visiting with you longer," Achan said. "Sparrow and I are exhausted. It has been a long day."

Lady Averella glanced at Achan, one eyebrow raised.

"*Lady Averella* and I," Achan corrected with a wink.

"Thank you for speaking with me." Mistel curtsied. "And for your prayers. I'm so grateful the truth about your life has been uncovered."

"As am I." Achan stood and offered Lady Averella his arm.

She rose and took hold. "Good evening."

Achan shot Cole a look as they were leaving. Suddenly his voice was in Cole's head again. *In time for the wedding, Cole. A song about Vrell Sparrow. All right?*

Yes, sir, Cole thought back, then shielded his thoughts at once.

"Would you walk me back to my room?" Mistel asked Cole. "This castle is so big I sometimes get turned around, as Sir Caleb well knows." She chuckled.

Cole met her gaze, and his stomach twisted pleasantly. "I'd be happy to."

"I'm afraid that's not possible," Sir Caleb said. "I have need of Master Tanniyn at present, but Master Akbar can show you the way."

Trizo, who had been standing along the wall with a half dozen other Kingsguards, stepped forward. "Yes, sir. Right this way, miss."

Mistel glanced between Sir Caleb, Trizo, and Cole. "Oh. Thank you."

"Mistel," Cole said. "I'm, um, meeting my team in the great hall tomorrow morning at first bells. We're going back to search the room Dewin Sessit shared with his sister. See if we missed anything. If you're free, I'd like you to join us."

Mistel lit up. "Certainly."

"Then afterwards, perhaps we can get started on the songs?" Cole said. "We have very little time to get at least one of them ready."

"That would be wonderful," Mistel said.

"Tomorrow, then."

"Tomorrow."

Cole watched her leave the room with Trizo. Only when she was completely out of sight did he turn his focus to Sir Caleb, who stood staring at him.

"On a first-name basis with this young woman, are you?" he asked.

Cole's face burned. "She has become a friend, yes."

"And you commissioned not one but two dresses for her? The bill was brought to me this afternoon."

"She had to leave all her things in the tenement," Cole said, "which I closed for the investigation."

"You're paying for these dresses out of your own wages, then?" Sir Caleb asked.

Cole hadn't thought about it. "If I must."

"I see." Sir Caleb folded his arms, and Cole knew him well enough by now to see a lecture coming. "When I caught her wandering around the fifth level of the castle, I assumed she was looking for the prince's quarters, but perhaps she was searching for yours. Has she been to your room?"

Heat simmered up Cole's spine. "Not before today, sir."

"Not before today. . . Be very careful, Cole. This woman has a past with our prince. She could seek to exploit that. Try to get caught with him in a compromising position so she can make claims of impropriety and—"

"Mistel would never do that."

"You know that because you are such close friends. Of two days."

Point taken. Cole recalled Mistel's mention of the darkness chasing her. He truly knew her very little, but that was no reason to condemn her. He took a deep breath. "I will take care, sir."

Sir Caleb squeezed Cole's shoulder and pulled him into a one-armed hug. "That's all I ask, my boy."

Cole bolstered his courage and used his trick of acting like Sir Caleb on the man himself. "I would ask something of you as well, Sir Caleb."

"Go ahead."

"I understand that Kurtz is not permitted to aid me in my investigation without the permission of the prince. Is that so?"

"Ahh. . . I. . . I'm not certain that is the whole of it," Sir Caleb said.

Cole knew better. Achan forgave easily. It was Sir Caleb who made everything a lesson to be learned and was still punishing Kurtz for his mistakes on the Lebab Inlet. "At this point," Cole said, "I need a man at my side who I can trust implicitly, as the prince suggested. I'm prepared to go to His Majesty and ask his permission for Kurtz to help me, but I thought such a small matter might be decided without the need to bother him. Would you agree?"

Sir Caleb's mustache twitched, and his eyes lit with humor. "When you put it like that, Cole. . . Yes, I would agree."

"I have your consent, then?" Cole asked.

Sir Caleb bowed his head. "I will speak to Sir Gavin about it myself."

Cole nodded his head in return, thrilled at what seemed like a victory as great as any battle won. "Thank you very much, Sir Caleb."

CHAPTER EIGHTEEN
MISTEL

MISTEL COULDN'T STOP SMILING.

She also couldn't sleep.

She lay in bed, overcome with all that had happened. What a glorious day! Singing with Cole. Kissing Cole. The commission of two songs, one to be sung at Achan's wedding.

She was going to sing a song she wrote at the future king's wedding!

She could die happy this moment.

Well, not just yet. After the wedding, of course.

Writing songs would give her plenty of time to spend with Cole—hopefully give her ample opportunity to convince him to join her band. She touched her lips and wished for a few more kisses like the one they'd shared earlier today.

Then she remembered the other blessings the day had brought. Dining in the castle great hall. Getting measured for two new dresses. This gloriously clean feather bed in her own room in Castle Armonguard.

Cetheria, thank you.

A nagging flutter in her stomach reminded her of the task

ahead. She could easily write about Lady Averella, but how in all Er'Rets was she to write a song about Sir Gavin, Sir Caleb, and some other old knight? Mistel had no idea what to say about them.

She needed a theme.

Strength and focus. Courage. Refusing to give up. Steadfastness and determination. Endurance. Don't lose heart. Don't lose hope. Persevere.

All good words and phrases. A place to start, anyway. Maybe something about teamwork, too, since it was a group of men working together in their search for truth.

She lay in the dark, thinking about what it meant to want something so much that you couldn't breathe. That every waking moment was fixed on that purpose, yet you were alone but for two close friends. Comrades. The entire world set against you.

Like a storm,
Flood waters high and overflowing.
Comes the world
With its story so convincing.
Stay the course
When all seems overwhelming.
You know the truth
Revealed will be a blessing.

Oh, how she wished she had something to write with before she forgot all of that.

Get up.

The thought prompted Mistel to climb out of bed and light a candle.

Wait. Why was she up?

The song! Oh, yes. She must find something to write with before she lost the words.

Get dressed.

Another errant thought, but it made perfect sense. She couldn't go out in her bedclothes. She pulled on her dress, put on her shoes, and laced them.

Where was she going at this hour?

To find a maid and ask for something to write with. The soon-to-be-king had commissioned *two* songs, and she wanted to capture her ideas. Surely someone would help her.

She walked out the door. A flickering candle on a distant wall sconce lit the corridor dimly. Mistel saw no sign of anyone, maid or guard. She started down the stairs, the soles of her shoes whispering over the stone steps.

She reached the ground floor and met a maid carrying a bucket. "Good evening, miss," the maid said. "Can I help you with anything?"

Mistel's lips parted, poised to request parchment and ink, yet her voice betrayed her, uttering words she hadn't intended. "No, thank you," she heard herself say. "I'm going out. Need some air." The words felt foreign on her tongue.

Ignoring the bewildered maid, Mistel pressed forward, her steps faltering as she struggled against an unseen force compelling her onwards.

A spike of pain shot through her head. Her pulse quickened, hammering in her ears like the beat of a distant drum.

Desperately, she concentrated hard on stopping her feet. Her efforts were met with some sort of magical resistance, her voice reduced to a feeble moan as she grappled with the invisible opposition.

Stop it! she thought—opened her mouth to try and say it aloud.

No words fer yeh tonight. A man's voice. In her head. *Jest keep walking.*

Mistel's breath caught in her throat as her body moved forward against her will. Her muscles ached with the effort of fighting. With a desperate cry, she clawed at the wood of a nearby doorframe in a futile attempt to anchor herself. Despite her frantic struggle, she found herself dragged inexorably forward. One of her fingernails snapped, leaving behind a streak of blood on the rough surface of the stone wall.

No matter how hard Mistel tried, she couldn't defy the unseen phenomenon that forced her out of the castle keep and into the dark night.

CHAPTER NINETEEN
COLE

A GOOD MOOD INSPIRED CONFIDENCE. Cole rose early the next morning and headed down to breakfast in the great hall. He ate his fill and talked with Brien, and later Kurtz, who was late, as usual.

Cole couldn't help noticing that Kurtz had removed the bandage around his neck, revealing a reddened trail of puckered pink skin across his collarbone. He'd also bathed, combed his shoulder-length blond hair into a ponytail, and trimmed his reddish beard short.

"You meet someone?" Cole asked.

Kurtz's brow sank as he sipped from his mug. "No, I just wanted to look my best for the new boss, eh?"

Cole hadn't expected such an answer. "Oh, well, thank you."

Kurtz grunted and took another drink. "Thought you said the girl was coming with us."

"She is." Cole had been bursting to tell Kurtz about kissing Mistel, but he wasn't about to do so with Brien here.

At that moment, members of Tsaftown's Fighting Fifteen entered the hall, and Cole caught sight of Mistel's ginger hair in the center of the group. "Here she comes." He stood, unsurprised that she had befriended the fabled warriors, yet his stomach flipped at the idea that she might replace him with someone stronger and—

The group parted to walk single file down the center aisle, revealing Jol Quimby as the redhead, not Mistel.

Kurtz chuckled as the Tsaftown men took over an empty table. "Girl grew a fine beard, she did. Can't wait to hear your poem about that."

Brien snorted and glanced away, shoulders shaking in silent laughter.

"Funny." Cole sat down and continued eating his breakfast, his face burning at his blunder.

"Where do we start today, boss?" Kurtz asked.

"At the tenement house in room 1K," Cole said. "That's where Akina Sessit lived. We're looking for clues as to Miss Sessit's whereabouts or the location where she does her purification rituals."

Cole continued to catch Kurtz up on the investigation. When Mistel still hadn't come, he sent Lucia to fetch her. They'd finished their breakfast when the maid returned alone.

"Her room is empty, sir," Lucia said.

Odd. She'd been so excited last night. Unless Cole had misread her.

He *could* have. He'd never been good with people. He recalled her face last night as she'd gazed at Achan—the inadequacy he'd felt in comparison and how their duet had swept it all away. No. He hadn't misunderstood.

She might be in trouble. That seemed an overreaction, even to Cole, yet he couldn't deny the sense of unease clouding his thoughts.

"Brien, see if you can find her in the common areas of the castle and bailey. Miss Lucia, please take Master Kurtz and me to Mistel's room."

They left the great hall and headed for the stairs. Each step Cole climbed brought on a new imagined catastrophe for Mistel. She had eaten something poisonous. She had fallen down the stairs or off the pier. She had run into a foul ravager or a murderer or even a common thief, who had, in his fear of being captured, wounded Mistel in some way.

She had been killed by effigy magic.

"What do you expect to find?" Kurtz asked as they climbed the stairs.

"Evidence of foul play," Cole said, praying he would find no carved statue in her room.

"What makes you think anyone would harm her?" Kurtz asked.

"Not showing up this morning is out of character for Miss Wepp," Cole said. "And we still don't know who killed her roommate or why."

But when they reached Mistel's room, the only mysterious thing Cole found was a guttered candle.

Sir Caleb's warning the previous night sprang to mind, and Cole's gut clenched at the idea that Mistel might have nefarious intentions within these walls. Perhaps *she* had killed her roommate and had come to Cole, hoping he would move her into the castle so she could harm Achan or, as Sir Caleb had suggested, maneuver the prince into a compromising situation.

The thought stung, then galvanized him, and he turned and ran from the room.

Kurtz chased after him. "Where are we going now?"

"To check on the prince."

"Check him for what? Fleas?"

Mistel's chamber was on the western arc, so it took some time to reach the southern arc. They were still running when they came upon Sir Caleb in the corridor outside the royal apartments.

"Is something on fire?" Sir Caleb asked.

Cole caught his breath. "Is the prince well?"

"He's having breakfast with Sir Eagan and Lady Averella in Tomek Hall," Sir Caleb said.

"Can you check?" Cole panted, trying to calm his racing heart.

"If you insist." Sir Caleb's eyes lost focus. Whether he was simply speaking to someone or looking out through another person's eyes, Cole had no idea. He only hoped the report would be good.

Kurtz Chazir.

Cole lowered his shields and glanced at Kurtz. "What?"

What are you worried about? Kurtz asked.

"I want to make sure that..." No, Cole couldn't speak that fear. Not yet. Not even to Kurtz.

Sir Caleb blinked, and he refocused on Cole. "The prince is well," he said.

Cole exhaled a long sigh. "Good. That's very good."

"Yes," Sir Caleb said, "we are all celebrating that the prince may break his fast wherever it pleases him. Why the concern?"

"Mistel—" Cole paused to correct himself. "Miss Wepp is missing."

"Ah." Sir Caleb pursed his lips. "I'll confess, I did hope I was wrong about her."

Cole clamped his jaw, fighting the urge to point out to Sir Caleb that the fact that Mistel was not lingering outside the prince's chambers at this moment proved her innocent of any wrongdoing. Didn't it?

"Brien is asking the staff if anyone has seen her," he said.

"I am glad to hear it," Sir Caleb said. "Keep me updated."

"Yes, sir."

As they made their way downstairs, Cole dragged his feet. His thoughts bounced between concern for Mistel's safety and worry that she had played him like a tabor drum.

"Hey," Kurtz said from behind him as Cole trudged onward. "Caleb likes being right. And while there's a mystery here, to be sure, it doesn't mean Caleb has it all figured out, eh?"

The words lightened Cole's mood somewhat. "I kissed her." The confession came easy with his back to Kurtz.

"Heh hay! Now we're making progress."

"And the prince asked us to work together and write a song for his wedding."

"That has you down because. . . ?"

Cole paused on the landing between the third and second floors and waited for Kurtz to catch up. "She seemed. . . overly pleased about it. While I agree that Sir Caleb's accusation of outright treachery is unfounded, something is amiss. Unless, of course, I'm mistaken. Which I very well could be."

"Bah! You're a good judge of character," Kurtz said. "You believed in me when no one else did. If this girl was a trickster, you'd know."

The compliment didn't sit right. Far too often, Cole had been tricked into trusting people who only meant to use or abuse him. "I've always thought I'm best with animals."

"To be sure. But being soft spoken and bashful has nothing to do with your ability to see through the charades of others to their core. You know a villain when you see one, and if you say Mistel Wepp is no villain, then I believe you."

Kurtz's validation of his intuition felt good. "Thank you."

They found Brien waiting in the great hall. "A maid saw the girl leave the castle last night at around half past two in the morning," he said. "She wanted to get some air."

Cole's nerves fizzled. "But why leave the castle? The gardens have plenty of air."

Kurtz scratched at the scar on his neck. "Good point."

"Plus, it doesn't bode well that she didn't return," Cole added.

"Indeed," Kurtz said. "You're right about that too, you are."

While Cole felt like he might lose his breakfast, he couldn't attend to two problems at once. He gathered three guards and sent them out to look for Mistel. "The rest of us will continue the investigation and see if it might unearth some hints as to Miss Wepp's whereabouts."

Kurtz slapped Cole's shoulder. "It's a good plan, it is."

Cole wouldn't label any of this *good*, but it was the best he could do. He, Kurtz, Trizo, and Brien fetched their horses from the stables and rode over to the tenement house.

Back in room 1K, they went over everything as if combing hair for fleas. The effigies and plans to use them during the prince's wedding had been left with Prince Oren, but Cole had the men search for other signs of witchcraft—any clues that might lead them to Akina, the location where she purified her effigies, or anything remotely related to Mistel Wepp.

They found jars and pouches containing various herbs, plants, and incense; a collection of cauldrons and mortars and pestles; dozens of incense cones and resins; and enough candles to fill a chandler's shop.

In the corner of the room sat a wooden altar etched with rune carvings and covered with half-melted candles. A statue of Magon mounted on the wall above stared down on Cole with fierce arrogance.

Cole prized off the wooden lid of a large glazed pot sitting on the floor beside the altar. Inside, he found a swath of wet linen covering a huge ball of moist clay and several individually wrapped clay effigies with no distinctive gender or features.

"If she can make her own effigies from clay, why use wooden ones?" Cole asked.

"Magosian mages prefer substances that were once living," Kurtz said.

"How do you know?" Cole asked.

Kurtz winked. "I loved my share of witches when I was stationed on the Wall."

"Of course you did." Cole should have known.

"They go wild for dead animals and insects," Kurtz said. "Love plants. Blood too. It's downright ghastly at times, the things witches collect."

Cole grimaced as he imagined a mage mashing blood into bits of insects and bone. "So, wood is better than clay because it was once a tree?"

"That's right," Kurtz said. "Something about different energies to connect with a life force or some such nonsense."

"Ah." Not nonsense at all, but dangerous and darkly evil. "Substances that were once living must be more conducive to channeling magic," Cole said.

"That sounds like something a witch would say, it does."

"And wood can be burned with all traces of evidence gone," Brien said.

"Except the effigy found in Miss Wepp's apartment had fallen out of the fire," Cole said.

"Perhaps that was Arman's doing," Trizo said. "Protecting his chosen king."

"Perhaps." Cole hoped Arman would protect Mistel too.

"Look here, sir." Brien stood at the sideboard, where a small stack of scrolls lined a shelf. "These aren't in the king's tongue."

Cole met him there and inspected the writing, which was a series of simple pictures and symbols. "More runes."

Kurtz peered over Cole's shoulder. "I can't read any of them, so don't ask."

"I'll take them to the castle scribe." Cole gathered the scrolls. Beneath them on the shelf, he found a packet of paper. The familiar stamp of Saren Perroy's shop sent a tingle up his arms. He opened the packet and smelled the powdery contents. "What do you make of this?" He handed it to Kurtz.

Kurtz took the packet and grinned down at the substance, sniffed it. "That's cloudweed," he said. "Lovely hallucinogen." He slid the packet toward his pocket. "Might I keep this?"

"No, you may not." Cole snatched it back. "It's evidence from our favorite apothecary."

"Bah, you're no fun, Master Investigator. So, what next? Pay this apothecary a visit?"

Cole thought about it. "As I see it, we have one goal: finding Akina Sessit. I believe she is the mage who killed Edera Duwal."

"Would she attack Miss Wepp too?" Kurtz asked.

Cole's stomach twisted. "I don't know. Perhaps."

"But her plan was to attack the prince and Lady Averella at their wedding," Brien said. "We found out about that, so she's likely abandoned the idea."

"True," Cole said, "but I'm not willing to risk the prince's life on what's *likely*. And if Miss Wepp learned something about all this, she could be in danger as well. Kurtz, you and Brien find Osrik Nath and bring him to the castle for questioning. Trizo and I will visit the apothecary. Our goal is still to find Akina Sessit or where she completes her Magosian purification rituals. Someone in such a place might know her. Meet back at the long-room near the armory. Go."

Cole and Trizo dismounted outside the apothecary shop in the Crescent. As they approached the door, two people exited the building and another went inside.

"Busy day," Trizo said, holding open the door.

Inside, the shop was packed with customers. Master Perroy stood at his table, filling an order. The pink-faced balding man looked up and met Cole's gaze. His eyes widened, but he went back to his work, dicing onion into a mixture.

Cole approached the table, and the fumes stung his eyes. "Master Perroy, I need a word."

"I don't suppose you can wait in line like everyone else." Perroy scraped the onion into a jar and fixed a lid on top. "As you can see, I'm a bit busy."

Cole withdrew the packet of cloudweed from his pocket. "I could close your shop and have you arrested for withholding information from a royal investigation."

The chatter in the line ceased at Cole's statement.

The apothecary glanced at the packet and sighed heavily. "There is nothing to worry about," he told his customers as he passed the jar to the first man in line. "A copper and ten."

The customer grimaced but finally paid and left the shop.

Perroy dropped the coins into his apron pocket. "I beg your pardon," he said to the next customer. "These soldiers from the castle require a moment of my time. I'll be right with you." He gestured to the back of the shop. "If you don't mind, I'd like a bit more privacy."

Cole followed him to the corner of the shop, around the back side of the stairs, where the customers couldn't see them. He handed over the packet of cloudweed.

"We found this in the home of the woman suspected of killing Miss Duwal," Cole said. "I have not come to question the sale of illegal substances. But if you do not tell me everything you know about this woman, I will close your shop in the name of Gidon Hadar and make sure you never do business in Armonguard again."

Perroy handed back the packet. "As you can see, I do not write my customers' names on my products, just my own, which I now realize is quite foolish. What is this woman called?"

"Akina Sessit."

Perroy hung his head. "Ah."

"I believe she is a Magosian priestess," Cole said. "Considering how vehemently you despise them, I'm surprised you would do business with her."

"She sells fanciful love potions to fools," Perroy said. "I had no idea she practiced witchcraft."

"Where can we find her?" Cole asked.

"How should I know? I don't keep record of my customers' home addresses."

The bell on the door jangled, announcing yet another customer. "How often does she come into your shop?" Cole asked.

"About once a week," Perroy said. "Though I haven't seen her in at least that long."

"Sir!" The concern in Trizo's tone drew Cole's attention to where he pointed at the entrance.

Mistel. She stood just inside, her gaze pinched, her hands fidgeting. Swaths of mud and dirt had soiled the front of her dress and one side of her face, as if she'd taken a nosedive into a pigsty.

Cole ran to her. "Mistel! Thank Arman. Are you well? I've been searching for you."

She glanced at him and looked away as if she didn't know him. "Mistel?"

She pushed past Cole through the crowd to the counter. "I require a tonic of hemlock. Right away."

"There's a line, you know," said the man waiting at the front.

Perroy's brow sank. "I'm sorry, miss, but I do not make such tonics."

"Nightshade, then?" Mistel glanced up to the sprigs hanging over the table. "Some fresh leaves will do. Hurry!"

Cole joined Mistel at the counter and gripped her arm above the elbow. "Mistel, why do you seek such poisons?"

She jerked away from him and bumped into another customer.

Cole grabbed her arms to steady her, looked into those green eyes and found them changed, frantic. Had she ingested some sort of hallucinogen? Cloudweed, perhaps? Or something more sinister? A rush of ice filled his chest, threatened to drown him, yet he forced himself to speak in a calming voice, as if talking to a spooked horse. "Easy. . . you're okay."

"Let go." Mistel tried to twist away and, when she could not, let loose an ear-splitting scream. "Help!"

Cole did his best to keep hold of her, but she scratched his face. The shock distracted him enough that she pulled away. She shoved through the crowd, and Cole followed, his heart racing, his stomach clenched. On the stoop outside the door, Mistel collided with a man trying to enter and fell.

"Don't touch her," Cole said, falling upon his strategy for settling a bucking horse. "Give her space, but don't let her get away either."

Mistel pushed back to her feet. Trizo stepped in her path, and Cole closed in behind. When Mistel spun away from Trizo, she ran straight into Cole's arms.

He caught her and held tight. "Mistel, please."

"No!" She let loose a gut-wrenching scream and fought against his hold.

Please, Arman. Help us. "I'm not going to hurt you, Mistel. I just want to talk."

Suddenly, as if someone had blown out the flame that gave her life, she went limp.

Cole lunged to keep her from falling and ended up on his knees, one arm circling her waist, the other cradling her shoulders and neck. He swallowed past the tightness in his throat and turned her face to his. She stared at nothing, her expression glassy. He slid his trembling fingers to her neck, found a pulse. Good. . . Then he froze as everything clicked into place. Cole had seen this before with Dewin Sessit.

"Help me get her on my horse!" he yelled. "If we don't move fast, we'll lose her forever."

Trizo stepped forward and crouched on Mistel's other side. "What happened, sir?"

"Miss Wepp has been stormed."

CHAPTER TWENTY
MISTEL

MISTEL SAT ON HER KNEES ON THE street, trying to get her bearings.

"Mistel? Can you hear me?"

Cole knelt a few paces away, holding a woman in his arms, touching her face. At the desperate concern in his voice, Mistel's chest tightened, and a sharp, uncomfortable sting flared up inside her.

She drew aside her skirt to avoid stepping on it and pushed up to her feet, wanting to get a better look at this damsel with hair the same color as hers.

With the same face.

"Help me get her on my horse," Cole yelled. "If we don't move fast, we'll lose her forever."

Someone stepped through Mistel from behind.

Through her.

"What happened, sir?" A Kingsguard. Master Trizo.

Mistel didn't hear Cole's reply as her heart jolted into a sprint. She pressed her hands against her stomach.

Through her stomach.

She cried out. How could this be? Was she dead?

Cole and Trizo lifted her body—*the other body*—to Cole's horse. Cole swung up behind her and took hold of her limp form.

What was happening? Mistel didn't understand. Cole kicked his horse, and the animal shot off down the street. Trizo mounted his horse and followed.

Mistel drifted after them. Stopped. Stared down at her legs. Moved one, then the other.

She was capable of walking, yet drifting seemed faster.

She fixed her gaze on the retreating horses. The next thing she knew, she was shooting through the air like an arrow and passed them right by.

How strange.

This is no place for you.

That voice. The one from her head.

Mistel slowed and cast her gaze around the crowd. "Where are you?" she asked.

Right here.

She saw him. The stranger from the great hall who had followed her in the Crescent. He flew at her from among the people roaming the streets and shoved her with such force that she tumbled, head over heels, right through the wall of a building.

Everything went dark.

Certain now that she was dreaming, she tried to regain control of her body. A little concentration was all it took, and she stopped tumbling. Thankfully, she no longer heard the man's voice in her mind, forcing her to obey, though she did have a sudden urge to see the clouds.

She began floating up, right through the ceiling and into another dark room. Six floors passed before she exited through the roof. Such a view of the Crescent from this height! There sat the castle on the little island at the northwestern corner of the massive lake. So pretty.

She drifted toward the stronghold, and pain shot through her temples. She could only think of one word: clouds.

She looked up, and sure enough, fat and fluffy clouds drifted overhead, almost too slowly for her to notice their movement. Mistel headed toward them.

What a lovely dream.

CHAPTER TWENTY-ONE
COLE

FOR THE SECOND TIME IN AS MANY days, Cole rode Cherix with Mistel in his arms. Seeing her fall had nearly shattered him. He had no way to help her—no magic. He tried to remain calm, remembering that Achan had brought Lady Averella back from the Veil by talking to her.

So Cole spoke to Mistel and sang whatever songs came to mind, but she didn't seem to hear a word.

Then, as they passed through the castle gates, her eyes fell closed.

He shook her. "Mistel? Can you hear me?"

She did not respond.

Cole rode all the way to the keep, handed Mistel down to Trizo, and dismounted. "Stable our horses," he told a guard, then to Trizo, "Give her to me."

Trizo offered a slight smile. "All right, sir. Where are we taking her?"

"To the prince."

As Trizo, a highly trained Kingsguard soldier, passed Mistel into Cole's arms, Cole knew he was being a fool. Trizo was twice as strong as Cole, and five flights of stairs was a long way to go.

Still, the moment Cole had a solid grip on Mistel, he carried her inside. He took the first flight of stairs with ease, but by the time he turned the landing to the second floor, his chest was so tight he could barely breathe.

"Help," he said to Trizo.

The Kingsguard took Mistel from Cole, who was able to catch his breath as they climbed the second flight of stairs. On the landing that led to level three, Trizo stopped.

"Might I make a suggestion, sir?" His panting breath returned a shred of dignity to Cole.

"Certainly," Cole said.

"We do this together," Trizo said. "Slide your arm behind her back and grip my shoulder."

Cole did so, frowning as he tried to understand what they were going to do, but once he had a firm hold on Trizo's shoulder, the man moved his hand from Mistel's side and clenched Cole's shoulder.

"Now find my wrist beneath her knees," Trizo said. "Together, we make her a decent chair."

Once Cole had clasped Trizo's wrist, they shifted Mistel's weight between them and turned in tandem to start up the third flight.

In this manner, they carried Mistel all the way up to the prince's wing on the fifth floor. At Achan's door, Cole waited for Trizo to get a good hold on Mistel's legs, then let go long enough to knock.

He knocked again—heard sounds inside. When no one answered his third knock, he opened the door and found the room filled with carpenters.

"Has anyone seen the prince?" he called.

"Hasn't been here all day," one man said.

Cole's heart pulsed with an urgency to find someone who could help. He made sure Trizo had a hold on Mistel, then ran ahead. "I'll try Sir Caleb's room."

Cole ran down the hall to Sir Caleb's quarters, but no one answered there, either. As he stood outside, beating his fist on the door, Sir Caleb appeared at the end of the hallway.

"Sir Caleb!" Cole cried.

The man strode toward them, his frizzy blond hair bouncing. "Is that who I think it is?"

"Mistel is hurt," Cole said. "Stormed, I think."

"Gracious me, bring her into the queen's closet." Sir Caleb scurried ahead of them and held open the door.

Cole ran inside the queen's former room, where he found an array of furniture covered with white sheets and a man attacking one of the walls with a sledgehammer.

"Where is the prince?" Cole asked.

"He and Lady Averella and their chaperones have gone out on the lake," Sir Caleb said. "I don't expect them back for hours." He pulled a sheet off a longchair. "Place her here."

Trizo set Mistel down, then Cole repositioned her head so that it rested on the arm of the chair.

"Time for a respite, if you would be so kind," Sir Caleb told the carpenter.

"But I've barely pulled one nail," the man said.

"As you can see, we are in the midst of an urgent matter and need quiet," Sir Caleb said. "Inform those in the prince's chambers to cease working also. Return after midday to see if we've finished."

The man set down his hammer. "As you wish, sir."

Cole knelt beside the settee and took hold of Mistel's hand. "Can you help her?"

"I don't know," Sir Caleb said. "Tell me what happened, as quickly as possible."

Cole relayed Mistel's strange behavior, how she'd asked for poisons, fought him, and suddenly lost consciousness. "Do you think I'm right? Has she been stormed?"

Sir Caleb dragged another sheet off a chair and sat down, balling the fabric in his lap. "It certainly sounds that way. I'll go in and have a look. Keep talking to her. It can help."

Sir Caleb closed his eyes, and Cole turned his attention back to Mistel. He hadn't missed Sir Caleb's careful words. He'd said, *"It* can *help."* Not that it would.

That wasn't good enough. Cole needed to save her. "Mistel." He squeezed her hand. "It's time to work on our song. I refuse to write it without you."

It didn't sit right with Cole that Achan wasn't here to help. The prince was the most powerful bloodvoicer in all Er'Rets. But just because Cole had never seen Sir Caleb go into the Veil didn't mean he couldn't. Right?

"What are they doing to the queen's chambers?" Trizo asked.

"The prince wants both rooms remodeled into one," Cole said. "Part of this will enlarge the king's chambers, the rest will become the queen's dressing room."

"He's a romantic," Trizo said. "And you right alongside him, Master Cole. I heard you singing all the way back, even though you could barely breathe."

"Mistel likes music." In fact, "Trizo, would you fetch the lute from my room?"

A slow smile stretched across his face. "Give her a concert. Good idea." He ran off.

Cole would do anything to help Mistel's soul back inside her body. He wished he had the ability to bloodvoice, but he didn't. He wasn't strong enough to carry her up the stairs on his own, had no magic, and if he were a better investigator, he'd likely have found the killer by now, and Mistel never would have been attacked.

"I don't see her around the castle." Sir Caleb had returned. "Any bloodvoicers been to that apothecary's shop?"

Cole stiffened. "Bazmark. And Brien."

Sir Caleb jerked his head in a quick nod. "I'll call them to help."

There were far better options, in Cole's opinion. "The prince knows Mistel best. Kurtz has met her as well. I sent him to fetch a suspect."

But Sir Caleb had already closed his eyes.

Trizo returned with the lute. Cole moved to sit beside Mistel's legs. He started with "The Pawn Our King" then went right into "Light of the World."

Mistel didn't move. Not one muscle.

Please, Arman, help her.

Cole had never in his life prayed to Arman until the Battle of Reshon Gate. Since then, he felt like he was petitioning the Father God almost daily.

But why should Arman help him? What had he ever done in Arman's name but beg and carry a flag like a coward?

Save Mistel, Arman. Not for me but for everyone else. All of Er'Rets needs her songs.

CHAPTER TWENTY-TWO
MISTEL

ISTEL ENJOYED EXPLORING THE clouds. Flying through them made her damp, so she wove her way around them instead. When she eventually grew bored and went back down near the ground, she found herself above a forest with no sign of civilization. She drifted for quite some time until she saw movement in the sky ahead.

A man.

She waved. "Hello!"

He drifted closer, and she realized with the turn of her stomach that she knew him. It was the giant black-bearded sergeant who liked to stare at her.

Suddenly, he appeared right beside her.

Mistel screamed and shot away.

"Wait!" the sergeant called. "I'm here to help you."

"You did this to me!" She soared toward a cluster of clouds as quickly as she could.

He appeared right in front of her.

She screamed again and turned around.

"I did *not* do this to you," he yelled.

Hadn't he? Her heart beat so fast she couldn't think. She slid behind a puffy cloud and came to a stop. She thought back to the man with the greasy hair and realized he wasn't the sergeant after all. Yet he looked at her in the same way. Into her soul.

"She's here, but she's afraid of me," the sergeant said.

"Can you blame her?" Another man's voice. Authoritative. "After what you've done?"

What *had* he done? Mistel wanted to peek around the cloud, but she was afraid of being seen.

"Miss Wepp?" the other man called out. "It's Sir Caleb. Can you hear me?"

Sir Caleb? He disliked her. Mistel didn't dare answer.

"Magic has ripped your soul from your body," Sir Caleb said. "Your friend, Cole Tanniyn, sent us to help you."

Cole had sent them?

"You don't have to travel actual distance in the Veil," he added. "If you concentrate on where you'd like to go, you can move from one place to another with a thought."

What if they came closer? Or, like that man had said, moved right to where she hid? The sergeant had done exactly that, she now realized, when he'd appeared in front of her before.

What had that man said? Concentrate on where she'd like to go?

She wanted to see Cole.

She closed her eyes, thought about his freckled face. She could hear him now, singing.

> *"Where water meets sky, on vast ocean waves,*
> *A lost man adrift, above a watery grave.*
> *To the skies he prays, 'I have a son, a wife!'*
> *'Oh Arman, how I'll serve you if you only save my life.'"*

Mistel opened her eyes to the most puzzling scene. Cole sat on a fancy longchair, playing his lute and singing beside the sleeping body of another Mistel.

> *"Then from the ocean deep where the dead ships lie,*
> *Comes a serpentine tanniyn with scales the colors of the sky,*
> *He sweeps the sailor up upon a back filled with spines.*
> *And carries him to a shore of rocks up which the sailor*
> *climbs."*

How could Mistel be in two places at once?

She took in the room, saw Sir Caleb asleep in a chair and Trizo standing near the door.

"She's here."

At the sound of the sergeant's voice, Mistel spun, saw him standing by the window with a second Sir Caleb. Not standing. Floating. She glanced back to where the first Sir Caleb slept in the chair.

Two Mistels. Two Sir Calebs.

"Very good, Miss Wepp," the floating Sir Caleb said. "You found your way back."

"There are two of us," she said. And thankfully, only one of the sergeant.

"Because our souls have left our bodies," Sir Caleb said. "Would you like to go back where you belong?"

Mistel floated toward the longchair and peered down on her own face. "How do I do it?"

"The same way you arrived here," Sir Caleb said. "Concentrate."

Mistel imagined herself back inside, well, herself. She had the strangest sensation of the music shifting. Before it had come from her side. Now it drifted above.

She found herself lying on the longchair, Cole sitting beside her and still singing about a man who had broken his promise to Arman.

"Such a sad song," she said.

Cole startled, and the music came to a dissonant end. "Thank Arman." He leaned forward like he might embrace her but instead clasped her hand and squeezed. "You gave me quite—us. You gave us quite a fright."

Sir Caleb approached and smiled down on her. "Indeed, you did, and while I am sure you are weary, we must first ask you some questions."

"I'm not tired." Mistel pushed herself up. Cole stood so she could move her feet to the floor, then he sat beside her again.

"Will you tell us what happened?" Sir Caleb asked.

"Last night when I was in bed, I got up." That sounded ridiculous. "I didn't want to, but I left the castle and walked toward the lake. I wanted to walk right into the lake, but I knew I didn't. That it was madness. Please don't think me mad."

"Someone was controlling your mind," Sir Caleb said. "It's called—"

"Did you see him?" Cole asked.

Sir Caleb nudged Cole. "Don't interrupt. Please, finish your story, Miss Wepp, then we'll ask our questions."

Mistel wanted to tell Cole about the greasy-haired man, but she obeyed Sir Caleb. "I refused to walk into the lake, and my head hurt so badly I screamed. I fought it—that dark voice. He persisted for quite some time but eventually released his hold on me. But when I tried to enter the castle again, he came back. He forced me to walk to a nearby farm, made me climb over a fence. I fought him and fell in the mud. There was a bull, but thankfully, it was asleep. When the voice gave up again, I walked back toward Armonguard."

She paused, rubbed her eyes, suddenly exhausted when she'd had so much energy moments ago. She looked from Sir Caleb to Cole, and the concern she saw in Cole's expression inspired her to keep going.

"It was daylight when I attempted to return to the castle," she said, "but when I got close, he came back and compelled me to walk into the city. I lacked the strength to resist and made it all the way to the apothecary's shop in the Crescent. That's where I saw you." She glanced at Cole. "He forbade me from speaking to you. He controlled my words and my actions. Urged me to find poison."

Cole took hold of her hand.

She scooted close to him. "He wanted to kill me." Her words came out in a whisper.

"Yes," Cole said. "The question is why."

Someone knocked on the door. Trizo let in a little boy with huge brown eyes and a face almost sweeter than Cole's. He had black fingertips, like he'd been playing with ink.

"Yes, Matthias?" Sir Caleb said.

"Kurtz is downstairs with a man for Cole," the boy said.

"Osrik Nath," Cole said. "I'm hoping he'll help me find Akina Sessit."

"Tell Kurtz that Cole will be down in a moment," Sir Caleb said, and Matthias scampered out the door. "Go on, Miss Wepp."

Let's see… where was she? "The man made me fight until Cole caught me, then he knocked me out of myself. Someone walked through me. It scared me so badly I almost missed Cole leaving with my body. I chased after him, but the man came back and pushed me inside a building."

"Can you describe him?" Cole asked.

As if she could forget. "He was tall with a narrow, almost bony face. Had a strange accent. Greasy black hair and a scar right here." She drew a line down through her top lip.

Cole jumped to his feet, his lute forgotten on the end of the chair. "That's Atul Shakran! I *did* see him."

"So it would seem," Sir Caleb said. "Now we know why Miss Wepp was lost in this part of the castle. He must have been controlling her, looking for the prince."

"I saw him in the Crescent yesterday," Mistel said. "I thought he was following me. And later he tried to join me for lunch in the great hall."

"He's been inside the castle?" Sir Caleb paced to the window.

Cole combed both hands through his hair, leaving it standing in deep furrows. "What do we do?"

Sir Caleb walked back. "While we don't know that Atul is connected with Miss Duwal's death, he certainly harbors a grudge against the prince. I'll pass his description to the guards at each gate and call forth a squadron of bloodvoicers to guard the castle. I'll also speak with the duchess and Sir Eagan about this. Prince Oren and Sir Gavin should be told as well."

"Not the prince?" Cole asked. "Don't you think he'd want to know?"

"I've already mentioned some mischief with local mantics. And I'll tell him Atul was spotted in the castle. But I'm not going to jump to further conclusions without evidence. Miss Wepp, I'll need your promise of discretion."

"Certainly, sir," she said.

"Thank you," Sir Caleb said. "How is the hunt for the mantic coming along, Cole?"

"I have men searching for her. We found a clue that led us back to the apothecary, where we found Miss Wepp. I sent Kurtz to fetch a man who knows her. That's who is downstairs now."

"Go," Sir Caleb said. "Miss Wepp will be safe here. I'll teach her to shield." He directed the rest of his words to Mistel. "Shielding your mind will keep bloodvoicers from hearing your thoughts or controlling you."

That would be a relief. "I would like that. Thank you."

"Hang onto my lute?" Cole asked her. "I'll get it from you later."

She pulled the instrument onto her lap and grinned. "You promise?"

"Oh, for pity's sake, go, Cole," Sir Caleb said.

"Yes, sir." But on Cole's face bloomed the widest smile Mistel had ever seen. It balled up his cheeks and cut deep grooves around the edges of his mouth.

Well, it might not be a belly laugh, but Mistel had made Cole smile after all. Mission accomplished.

CHAPTER TWENTY-THREE
COLE

Cole wanted answers. Now. His gut told him Atul was responsible for Edera Duwal's death and the plan to assassinate Achan and Lady Averella. He only needed proof.

He changed into a clean Kingsguard cloak—a shield against insecurity and inexperience as he prepared to confront the one man who continually stood in the way of solving this murder—then put on his belt and sword, wanting to look official. He went downstairs and headed for the long-room.

In the hallway off the foyer, he met Bazmark walking toward him. Cole tensed but maintained his determined stride. Unfortunately, the man slowed as Cole approached.

"Master Tanniyn," he said. "Can I have a word?"

"I'm on my way to a meeting," Cole said, not eager to speak with this man.

"I'll walk with you." Bazmark turned with Cole and kept pace beside him. "I'm, uh, sorry for provoking you the other day."

Could this be real? Cole continued walking, trying to keep his expression blank.

"I didn't see why Sir Caleb would put you in charge of this investigation when I was perfectly capable. And the girl…" Bazmark grimaced. "Well, to be honest, I was jealous that she fancied you. The better you fared with both the investigation and the girl, the more it annoyed me, and I got carried away, I did."

Cole's face flamed. The idea that this bloodvoicing warrior could possibly envy him—and over Mistel too. "I'm no one to be jealous of," he said.

"And that," Bazmark said. "Not a drop of pride in you. It's downright sickening, it is." He stopped and raised his hands, palms out as if wanting to take back those last words. "I just needed to apologize right and proper like, and I have done."

That statement gave Cole the feeling that Achan was behind this display of remorse. Regardless, Cole could appreciate how difficult it must have been for Bazmark to have said all that, and so honestly too.

"Thank you, Bazmark," Cole said, tapping his foot. He wanted to be done with this awkward moment so that he could question Osrik Nath. What might Achan say to such an apology? "I appreciate your honesty. And for helping Sir Caleb find Miss Wepp in the Veil."

"Good. Yes. Thanks." Bazmark nodded, stepped backward in the opposite direction. "I'll, uh, leave you to your investigation, then. I'm sure you'll have the knots untied soon."

"I hope so," Cole said.

With that, Bazmark walked away, leaving Cole slightly mystified by the entire ordeal. He snapped to his senses and took off in the opposite direction, toward where Osrik Nath awaited.

Cole replayed Bazmark's apology over and over in his mind as he walked the rest of the way. By the time he strode past Kurtz into the long-room, he had worked himself up into a nervous wreck. Why a man's apology should so affect him, he didn't know.

Osrik Nath stood just inside the door, and Cole wasted no

more time. "Master Nath," he said. "Describe your relationship with Akina Sessit."

"Don't know her," Nath said.

"Wasn't she with you the night Edera Duwal was killed?"

"Oh, *Akina*. Thought you said something else."

Cole folded his arms. "Take your time. I'm in no hurry."

"Gods, you're an annoying little pimple, you know that?"

Kurtz grabbed the front of Nath's shirt and pushed him against the wall, holding him the same way Nath had held Cole outside the castle a few days ago. "You'll show respect to this man, is that clear?"

"Certainly," Nath said, "though someday someone's going to catch him without any of his watchdogs around to save his sorry hide."

Curse Cole's countless inequities. That he had no strategy to stand up to such a bully except a clean cloak and to act like Sir Caleb seemed wretchedly cruel. Yet he persisted. "Is Akina Sessit currently staying with you?"

"No, she's not."

"When was the last time you saw her?"

"The night the girl was killed. She was at the club."

"What was she doing there?"

Nath shrugged. "What she normally does. Sells cloudweed."

So, the woman purchased cloudweed from Saren Perroy, then resold it, likely to make a profit. "Have you had any recent conflicts with Miss Sessit?"

"No."

"Were you aware of any relationship between her and Miss Duwal?"

"No, but you said she lives in my building with her brother. Could be they met there."

"Are you romantically involved with Miss Sessit?"

"I am not."

"Do you know if she's romantically involved with someone else?"

Nath thought about it. "Come to think of it, I've seen her with a skinny guy. Looks like he could use about ten baths."

"Does this man have a scar on his face?" Cole asked.

Nath cocked his head to the side. "Actually, yeah. Right down his lip."

Ahh… Connecting Atul Shakran to Akina changed everything. "Is Miss Sessit a Magosian priestess?"

Nath glanced away, fidgeting with the cuff of his shirt. "What? I don't think so."

Cole tried a different tactic. "Are you aware of any locations in the city where a Magosian priestess might conduct rituals?"

Nath scoffed, still avoiding eye contact. "The temples, maybe? You're asking the wrong man."

Cole doubted that very much. "Purchasing cloudweed is an arrestable offense," he said. "I'm sure Kurtz would enjoy taking you to the dungeon."

"Okay, okay. From what I hear, they don't gather at the temples. They have special altars and rotate through them. Something about the moon, I think. They put signals in windows around town to let others know what place and time."

Cole had seen runes in the windows of shops in the Crescent. He'd heard enough. "Master Chazir, escort Master Nath from the castle, then meet me in the scribe's chambers."

Ink flowed freely from the crown's quill.

Cole and Kurtz stood in the scribe's office, nestled deep within the stone walls of the castle. Cole had never seen a library, but he suspected one might look like this. The walls were covered with shelves filled with leather-bound books and scrolls. Cole stood with Kurtz before a sturdy oak desk covered with inkwells, quill pens, and the scrolls marked with runes that they'd found in Akina Sessit's home.

Behind the desk sat Master Tilman, the head scribe, a pear-shaped man with a crop of straight white hair and a magnifying lens on a chain around his neck. At his side stood his apprentice, Mertyn Albrek, a pale, slight young man with a trim rectangular mustache and tidy dark-brown hair.

The faint scent of ink permeated the chamber, mingling with the musty aroma of ancient tomes. It made Cole long to sit and write songs that would change the world.

"I, too, have seen such runes around the Crescent," Master Tilman said, "but I never once suspected they corresponded to ritual meeting places. This is a fascinating discovery."

"How are such altars different from the temple?" Cole asked the scribe.

"The temples are influenced by the ancient Rôb faith, where followers worshiped their five chosen gods," Master Tilman said. "While the Magosian temples you see throughout Er'Rets celebrate Magon and Tenma, altars hearken back to the ancient Kabaran religion."

Cole wasn't familiar with the Kabaran religion. "What's that?"

"Mertyn?" Master Tilman gestured to his apprentice. "Would you do the honors?"

"Yes, sir," Mertyn said. "The Kabaran faith goes back to before the Kinsman and Magonian people came to Er'Rets. Believers traveled between five altars. Each had a rune carved into the base of the Magon pole to depict both its order in the rotation and the required sacrifice for worship."

Cole shivered at the word *sacrifice*. "Do you know where these altars are?"

"No," Master Tilman said. "But I know the location of the temple. Someone there might know." He spread a large roll of parchment on his desk, which turned out to be a map. "The temple is here." He tapped the crest of a long and circular road.

"I think that's where Trizo went last time," Cole told Kurtz. "The Magosian ring."

"I guess it's time we all go, eh?"

Yes, it looked like Cole was going to have to visit the Magosian ring after all. "Master Tilman, did you learn anything of value from the runes we found in the tenement?"

"Mertyn and I have enjoyed translating them," Master Tilman said. "They're praises to Magon, the goddess of magic. I suspect they were being used to teach another to draw them."

Cole didn't like the sound of that. "You mean to say that our priestess has an apprentice?"

"It would appear so, yes," the scribe said.

Wonderful. "Thank you for your help, Master Tilman." Cole glanced at Kurtz. "It's time to find Akina Sessit."

Cole, Kurtz, Trizo, and Brien ate a quick lunch, changed into plain clothes—yet kept their weapons—and rode packhorses to the Magosian ring of the Crescent. It felt like passing into another world. Buildings had been constructed of mud bricks and reeds. The air smelled of fish, spices, and incense. And the music… Ethereal, twangy melodies resonated as hauntingly beautiful voices crooned out lyrics in a foreign tongue. Cole had never heard anything like it.

They passed through a market. Bright colored fabrics were printed with motifs rather than the solid silks and linens sold at the island market. Weapons were spears, knives, and crude axes. And the idols were all female: Magon, Tenma, and Yobatha. Cole didn't see one carving or painting or puppet of Achan or Lady

Averella. Hawkers called out to passersby, and while Cole didn't understand them, he recognized the tone of an offered bargain.

Since Trizo spoke Magosian, he led the way. As they neared the temple, music caught Cole's ear. It had a slower, sacred tone and dozens of voices. He also picked out some kind of a flute.

Though the temple was constructed of the same base materials as the other buildings, it rose majestically from the muddy road, out of place among so many huts. Intricate runes adorned its red painted walls.

Cole and his men dismounted and ascended a grand staircase to a massive gate guarded by five priestesses in white robes.

While Trizo asked the women about Akina Sessit, Cole readied himself in case they needed to force their way inside. The priestesses, however, waved them through.

"They don't know her," Trizo said. "But we're welcome to look around."

Inside, the smell of incense and blood made Cole queasy. Flickering flames from candles and braziers cast dancing shadows on seductive statues of Magon and Tenma. Trizo spoke to yet another priestess, and this one waved them to follow her deeper into the temple.

"She said they do effigy cleansing in the courtyard," Trizo said.

Cole perked up, curious what he might see inside.

The priestess led them into an inner courtyard garden blooming with bright flowers. In the center of the garden, a shallow stone basin had been built into the ground. Coals burned inside it, and all around its outer edge, women knelt and sang.

The priestess spoke to Trizo, who translated. "This is the potter's pit. It's purified daily with sacrifice."

"Sacrifice of what?" Cole asked.

"Animals," Trizo said. "Usually a bird but sometimes a lamb."

A familiar old woman dropped a wax effigy into the purification pit. Cole had seen those deep-set eyes and gnarled hands before in the island marketplace.

"What is she saying?" Cole asked.

Trizo translated, "Dissolve, melt, drip ever away. This wax was burned—maybe *melted*?—by fire, so shall the, uh, accused or guilty be burned by fire."

Achan would *not* like that so many were worshiping other gods in this place.

When the ceremony ended, the old priestess came over to greet them.

"I am Madam Vinzen," she said in heavily accented Kinsman. "Why seek you Akina?"

Cole thrilled that someone had recognized the name. "She has valuable knowledge that may help me solve a crime."

Madam Vinzen folded her arms. "Explain to me this crime."

"A young woman was killed with effigy magic," Cole said. "She was a close friend of Dewin Sessit, Akina's brother. Dewin is a carver, and we believe someone either convinced him to carve an effigy of the deceased or stole a carving Dewin had made for himself."

"Have you spoken to Dewin about this?" Madam Vinzen asked.

"We cannot," Cole said. "When we found him, he had been stormed by a powerful bloodvoicer."

Madam Vinzen coughed. Or perhaps that had been a gasp. "Akina is *not* a bloodvoicer."

"No, but we suspect she has a friend named Atul Shakran," Cole said. "He's a powerful bloodvoicer. If we don't find him soon, Dewin will die."

Madam Vinzen turned away. When she looked back, her eyes were red and moist. "Akina and Dewin are my children."

Ohh. . . Cole glanced at Kurtz.

"Didn't see that coming, eh?" Kurtz said.

Neither had Cole. "Do you know where we can find her?"

"For several days, I have not spoken to her," Madam Vinzen said. "She has joined the Chartom."

"Which is?" Cole asked.

"A Magosian sect," Madam Vinzen said. "Fanatics who call themselves orthodox. They look down on our temples. Claim we have strayed from the ancient ways."

"How have you strayed?" Cole asked.

"No longer do we take spirit-summoning elixirs to worship," Madam Vinzen said. "And no longer do we sacrifice humans."

"They oppose *that*?" Kurtz said.

"That and the Kinsman line of succession," Madam Vinzen said. "You're right that Akina has befriended a bloodvoicer. They plot against the crown. My son wanted no part of it, but she must have convinced Dewin to help her, and that villain harmed my son!"

"Do you know where she might be?" Cole asked.

The weight of her frustration spilled out in a sigh. "She lives within a Chartom altar camp in the forest."

"Could you give me directions?" Cole asked.

"Not for you or for your future king," she growled. "But I will do it to avenge my son."

Cole could only imagine how difficult it must be for this woman to feel like she was betraying her children. "It's not yet too late for Dewin, madam," Cole said. "You will do him good if you come to the castle. Hearing a familiar voice can help a person return from the Veil."

The old woman narrowed her eyes. "Your future king serves Arman. It's no secret that he despises all other gods. How can I be assured that he will not arrest me if I enter his domain?"

"I cannot assure you of anything," Cole said, "except that Gidon Hadar is a fair man. You have been a help to him today, and I have invited you to the castle as my guest. He will take all of that into consideration."

Madam Vinzen nodded. "Very well. I will come first thing in the morning."

With Madam Vinzen's help, Cole sketched a map to the altar camp onto fresh parchment. He asked Kurtz to bloodvoice an update to Sir Caleb, then the four of them set off.

As they made their way into the forest northwest of the city, Kurtz said, "You did good today, Cole. Questioning Osrik and that old woman."

Cole twisted in Bart's saddle to see Kurtz's face. "Really? I felt good about the conversation with Madam Vinzen, but not with Master Nath."

"Naw, you had him scared. That's why he got mean."

Cole scoffed. "He's always mean."

"I missed you questioning Nath?" Brien said. "I do like watching that man squirm."

More like Cole had been the one squirming. He wanted to tell Kurtz about Bazmark's apology, but not in front of the others.

"Next time, grab the butt of your sword," Kurtz said, "like you're thinking about using it. Looks menacing, it does."

"I can't imagine anything I do will ever look menacing," Cole mumbled.

Trizo laughed. "A sword thrust at a man's chest is menacing coming from anyone, you included, sir."

Sir... "You're good men, all of you," Cole said. "I'm grateful for your help these past few days."

Cole's temple smarted like someone had flicked their forefinger against the side of his head. *Sir Caleb Agros.*

"Sir Caleb is bloodvoicing me." He lowered his shields. *Yes, sir? Stop for a moment and let me see this map,* Sir Caleb said.

Cole reined Bart to a halt in a stretch of sunlight and held the map so Sir Caleb could get a good view through Cole's eyes. He tried not to squirm, despite how invasive it felt when another person used his body like a spyglass.

Give me a minute to sketch this out, Sir Caleb said. *Remind me who is with you?*

"Kurtz, Brien, and Trizo."

That's not much manpower, and Kurtz and Brien are not bloodvoice warriors.

Cole's stomach twisted. "Magosians don't bloodvoice."

Do you know how to defend yourself against magical attacks? Besides, Atul Shakran might be with them.

The surrounding forest seemed so peaceful. "Shall we return to the castle? Wait for reinforcements?"

No, we need to find that woman. You're still about a half hour out from their camp. I'll recruit some help. I'm done with the map. Let me know when you've arrived.

"Yes, sir." Cole rolled the map and tucked it into his pocket.

"Well?" Trizo asked.

"Sir Caleb thinks we'll have to fight magic."

"He going to help us?" Brien asked.

"He said he would."

"Nothing to worry about, then, eh?" Kurtz grinned, his dimples digging deep above his trim beard.

Cole took a deep breath. "Right."

A short time later, Cole caught sight of white canvas tents through the trees and called a halt. "Kurtz, tell Sir Caleb we've arrived." He dismounted and tied Bart to a nearby tree. The piebald tossed his head, upset about something.

"He's not answering," Kurtz said.

"Brien?" Cole locked eyes on the other bloodvoicer in the group. "Can you reach him?"

"I can't reach Brien, either," Kurtz said.

Cole spun around. "What? How?"

Kurtz slipped off his horse and tipped back his head to the sky. "It's foggy," he said.

Cole glanced at the grey sky. "So?"

"So, I'm thinking there's a reason no Kinsmen have ever found any of these camps. They've hidden them with magic."

Cole gazed at the tents through the trees. "They can do that?"

"They can do a lot of things," Trizo said, coming to stand beside Cole. "Mages have a host of salts and powders and potions to aid in their schemes."

"I'm sorry, sir," Brien said, still on his horse. "I can't get through to anyone."

Cole clenched his jaw as he again regarded the tents. "Magic."

They would have to go back until Kurtz or Brien could voice Sir Caleb.

Or go it alone.

Achan's and Lady Averella's lives were on the line.

Cole approached the clearing to get a better view. Ten dingy white tents faced each other in two rows of five. A trampled, grassy path ran between them. At one end, a red tent sat on a hillock. On the other end, what looked like a bronze flagpole ran into the sky from a circular stone altar. Instead of a flag on top, it carried the bronze figure of a woman.

"That's a Magon pole, that is," Kurtz said.

A shiver tickled Cole's arms. Ancient mythology, come to life. "They shouldn't know we're coming," he said. Kurtz and Trizo were the strongest swordsmen. Cole preferred to keep Kurtz with him, but he needed Trizo's ability to translate. "Trizo and I will walk in all pleasant-like, just looking for our friend Akina. Kurtz and Brien, you go around back of the tents and see what you can find. Keep an eye on us, too, if you can. In case we need you."

That decided, they parted ways. Cole and Trizo stepped out from the cover of the trees and slowly approached the altar. When they reached it, Cole examined the deep grooves of a rune gouged into the surface of the circular stone, stained with blood and black feathers. Rectangular with hashes for legs and a head, it resembled an animal.

"Disturbing, isn't it?" Trizo said.

A raven fluttered down and landed on the altar.

Not a raven. A gowzal, which was like a raven but had the head of a rat.

"Not as disturbing as *that*." Cole backed slowly away from the demon bird.

"*Nâtash mikan!*" a woman yelled.

Cole met Trizo's gaze, and they turned in unison to regard a young woman wearing a dress made entirely of animal pelts that ended above her knees, exposing bare legs and feet. She had sun-tanned skin, and her golden-brown hair had been tied up in a variety of knots adorned with feathers and bones.

On her forehead, drawn in what looked to be blood, was a square with a longer vertical line drawn through its center.

Cole fought the urge to reach for his sword. *Arman, be with us.*

Trizo nodded to the woman. "She said to get out of here."

"Hi." Cole patted his chest as he approached her. "I'm Cole. I'm trying to find Akina Sessit. Is she, uh, home?"

The woman swung her arm, gesturing toward the forest. "*Âzal mikan!*"

"Be gone," Trizo translated.

"Akina went that way?" As Cole pointed in the direction they'd come from and feigned ignorance, he caught sight of three more gowzals on the altar behind them.

Not good.

The woman growled. "You not come to here."

Trizo hmphed. "Looks like she speaks a little Kinsman."

"Yes. You Kinsmans not to be here," she said. "Not to be welcomed."

Cole and Trizo exchanged glances. This was off to a great start.

"We don't want any trouble," Cole said, knowing full well he was asking for it. "We need to speak with Akina Sessit. We were told she lives here."

"Who told you this?" Another woman in a similar dress of furs stepped out from one of the white tents. She wore the same rune painted onto her forehead. She had olive-green skin and a nose like Dewin Sessit's. A gowzal sat on her shoulder, its black eyes watching Cole.

This had to be Akina. Her Kinsman was better than the first woman's, but her voice held a far more threatening tone.

Looking behind both women, Cole caught sight of Kurtz and Brien sneaking out of one of the white tents and into the red one. Cole should stall a bit. Try to give them more time.

He glanced at Trizo. "Was it the old man selling foxtails who said to come here?"

Trizo shook his head. "The woman with the incense that smelled like lotus flowers."

"I thought that was sandalwood." Cole sighed and shrugged apologetically. "It doesn't matter who told us. What's important is we've found you. Akina, right? We'd like to ask you a quick question, then we'll be on our way."

"*Hitkayem le'ashan*!" Akina thrust out her hand. The gowzal on her shoulder turned to green smoke that blasted Cole and Trizo off their feet.

Cole landed hard on his back, his heart thumping wildly in his ears. He fully expected to flash to the Battle of Armonguard, but he was still here, staring at bits of black feathers floating between him and the grey sky.

One thing was certain. There was no way in all Er'Rets he was going to be able to arrest that woman.

"I'll handle this, Akina." A man's voice.

Cole pushed himself to an upright position and locked eyes on the speaker. Oily black hair and beard, scar slashed across his upper lip, and four gowzals, two perched on each shoulder.

Atul Shakran.

CHAPTER TWENTY-FOUR
COLE

"Cole, Cole, Cole." Atul sneered. "Fool boy. Yeh should'a stayed 'n Mitspah where yeh belong. Jest 'cause that stray prince don't know 'is place don't mean yeh should follow 'im."

Cole scrambled to his feet, heart racing, and set his hand on the hilt of his sword, as Kurtz had suggested. "I'll follow him anywhere."

"Oh, that's bravely said, but it don't look like yer stray prince feels the same way. Yeh come to a Magosian camp with one man teh back yeh up? What exactly is yer plan?"

Cole glanced at Trizo, then shifted his focus behind his friend to the altar now covered in gowzals.

Atul laughed. "Yer weak, boy. Pathetic. Watch a real man work." Atul melted where he stood, leaving nothing behind but a squirming pile of gowzals.

Cole cried out as pressure filled his skull and his body seized. Curse his folly. He'd forgotten to shield his mind.

Trizo's brow furrowed as he watched Cole. "You all right?"

Kinda empty 'n this head of yers, Atul said as he forced Cole to raise his arm, study his hand, and take a few steps forward. "Nice boots." This time Atul spoke aloud through Cole's voice. "Think I'll take these when I'm done with yeh."

"Sir?" Trizo said.

Cole shrank inside himself, trying to remember the lecture Sir Caleb had given Achan after he'd taken control of Polk. Cole could recall nothing said of defending against such an attack, only that using one's bloodvoicing magic to control another was wrong.

Atul pulled Cole's sword and swung it around a few times. "That stray prince *does* have good taste 'n weapons."

Cole concentrated, trying to sense Atul inside him long enough to push him out, but he felt only pressure, as if someone had smothered him in a blanket made of rocks.

"Let's dispatch yer man, shall we?" Atul lunged at Trizo, who leaped back and quickly drew his sword. "Least he's fast. I hope he don't kill yeh. That'd be tragic."

Atul, having full control over Cole's mind and body, attacked Trizo, forcing the Kingsguard into a duel. Cole had never moved so fast in swordplay—had never been able to keep up with Trizo. He spun, lunged, and swiped his blade, pushing Trizo back across the grassy clearing.

Arman, please help me. But Cole had no idea if the Father God heard his pleas or not.

Trizo wasn't wearing armor, so when Atul slashed Cole's sword over Trizo's arm, it cut through his cloak and tunic and brought forth a hiss of pain. Trizo didn't falter, though. Not until Atul cut him again, this time across the thigh.

Trizo stumbled, and Atul spun Cole's body in reverse, bringing up his arm. He bashed the back of his elbow against Trizo's face, and the Kingsguard went down. He dropped his sword, and Atul kicked it away.

No! There must be some way Cole could fight against Atul. He wished he had a connection to Arman like Achan had. The way

Achan could talk to Arman and receive an answer. How he'd sung to him and reached the minds of every soul in Er'Rets.

Of course, Cole *could* sing. That much he could do. With all his strength, he sang the lyrics of "Light of the World" with his thoughts.

> *Er'Rets was lost in the darkness within.*
> *The Light of the world is Câan!*
> *Like sunshine at noonday His glory shone in.*
> *The Light of the world is Câan!*

Atul grunted. "Must yeh sing *that* song?" He kicked Trizo, rolling him onto his back, then paced around him, glaring as Trizo breathed heavily and winced. Atul scraped the tip of Cole's sword from the hollow of Trizo's throat, down the front of his chest, and over the Hadar crest on his Kingsguard cloak. Trizo cradled his head with one arm and his bleeding leg with the other.

Cole sang faster.

> *No darkness have we who in Arman abide.*
> *The Light of the world is Câan!*
> *We walk in the light when we follow our Guide.*
> *The Light of the world is Câan!*

As Cole sang through the third verse, something inside his mind loosened. Feeling began to return to his limbs. When Atul drew back to stab Trizo though the heart, Cole fought and held back his arm.

Let go, yeh fool, Atul said to Cole's mind. *Yeh can't fight me, so don't bother tryin'.*

The words were lies. Cole could feel his body even more now, and when he sang the final verse, he heard his voice, singing aloud audibly.

*"No need of sunlight in Shamayim we're told.
The Light of the world is Câan!
For Câan is the Light in the city of gold.
The Light of the world is Câan!"*

Cole flung his arm back with a feral cry, and his sword flew from his grasp. He panted, looking around for Atul, but he found no sign of the man, not in his head or in the clearing.

Cole took in Trizo, writhing on the ground, and stepped toward him. "Trizo? It's me. I'm back."

"If Atul has failed," a woman said, "I will end you myself. That boy is no king of mine."

Cole stopped short, his attention drawn to Akina, hands raised above her head, mumbling words of magic under her breath. He knew he was about to die like Silvo Hamartano, disintegrated into dust.

Until he spotted Kurtz.

Akina thrust her hands forward and roared foreign words. *"Sabab bay—"* But before she could finish her spell, Kurtz bashed her over the back of the head with the pommel of his sword. The woman crumpled like a doll without a puppeteer. Her gowzals squawked and flew away.

To her left, Brien tackled the first woman and secured her hands behind her back. "I don't have any âleh!" he yelled.

"She's not a bloodvoicer," Kurtz called back. "Gag her so she can't speak magic to the demon birds."

"Praise Arman," Cole whispered, shocked that the Father God had heard him—helped him. That they had survived. He knelt at Trizo's side. "You all right? Trizo?"

The man groaned and opened one eye. "Next time, Kurtz goes with you."

Five women had been in the altar camp. Kurtz and Brien had subdued three in their tents before coming out to take down the last two. A quick search revealed a wagon and two horses, which Kurtz and Brien hooked up to haul the prisoners back.

Long before they came within sight of Armonguard, Kurtz's and Brien's bloodvoicing abilities returned, and Sir Caleb seized the moment to demand a report, then lecture Cole.

Why would you go in without help?

"I had three trained soldiers with me," Cole said. "One who could speak Magosian."

It was foolish.

Cole strangled Bart's reins and replied as calmly and logically as he could. "We accomplished what we set out to do, Sir Caleb. Akina Sessit is our prisoner."

Sir Caleb didn't answer, and the sound of the horses' hooves in the forest rose around Cole, so peaceful, so at odds with his rapid pulse.

You did very well, Cole, Sir Caleb finally said. *What of Atul?*

The relief Cole felt at hearing those words made his throat tight, so he answered in his mind, the way he should have done from the start. *I don't think he was ever physically present. Akina conjured his likeness from gowzals while he attacked through the Veil.*

Well, I'm very impressed that you managed to force him out.

Cole scrubbed his hands over his face and swallowed past the lump in his throat. *Thank you, sir. Arman helped me.*

Though the words felt strange coming from Cole, he knew they were true, and he'd never been more grateful.

CHAPTER TWENTY-FIVE
MISTEL

MISTEL WAS SITTING UP IN BED, TUCKED under a thick quilt and propped up by four pillows, when a *tap*, *tap* on her door lifted her eyes from the parchment she'd been writing on.

A knock at the door was filled with possibility.

Please, oh, please let it be him.

She called out "Enter!" hoping with every breath that a cute, freckled squire would be the one to walk through that door.

Instead, Lucia peeked inside. "Is now a good time for visitors, miss?" the maid asked. "I have Master Tanniyn here to see you."

Wish granted! Mistel pushed her writing aside, pinched her cheeks, and combed her fingers through her curls. "Now is perfect. Please send him in."

Lucia slipped into the room, followed by Cole, dashing in a blue tunic and brown leather vest. When Lucia remained, Mistel realized he'd brought a chaperone. Always such a gentleman.

"You look comfortable." Cole's gaze panned the room, and he walked straight for his lute, which Mistel had left on her sideboard.

"*You* look like a hero," she said. "I heard you caught the mantic woman."

"We did. It was all rather terrifying." Cole picked up the lute as if he might start playing a song that very moment. Instead, he ran his fingers lightly over the strings and body, petting the instrument like one might a cat.

"It will likely make a fantastic song," Mistel said.

"Is music all you think about?" he asked.

Mistel gestured to the lute. "I could ask you the same."

Cole chuckled and grinned that dazzling wide smile. "A fair point." He moved her chair near the bed, sat down, and strummed a few chords. "We need to work on our songs."

With Lucia watching? Mistel suddenly didn't much care for chaperones. "After you tell me about fighting those mantics. I've been dying to hear what happened."

"All right." So Cole told her the story. "It wasn't my first encounter with gowzals," he said, "but it was the first time I watched them transform before my eyes."

How frightening that must have been. Cole had endured so much to discover Edera's killer, which had deepened Mistel's admiration for him even more. "What about Akina? Has she confessed?"

"She has not, but we've pieced together the truth from the other Magosian women. She and Atul were plotting with the Chartom mantics against the prince. One day, Dewin and Edera walked in on them making plans. Akina threatened to kill Edera if Dewin didn't carve effigies of the prince and Lady Averella. Atul doubted the effigy magic's power and made her practice on Edera. When Dewin learned Edera had been killed, he tried going to the prince, but Atul stormed him."

Mistel had listened with rapt attention until the part when Akina had killed Edera. The weight of it all struck her suddenly. Killed for knowing the wrong person. Mistel had been strong all this time, but now that she knew the truth, the senseless murder of her friend overwhelmed her. Even though the killer had been caught, Mistel would never see her friend again.

Cole's gaze softened. He took her hand and squeezed.

She squeezed back, grateful for his friendship and the warmth of his touch when he could have been killed, cold and dead like Edera.

"It's over," he said.

"It's not over at all! That man is still out there. He wants Achan and Lady Averella dead. Now he wants to kill you too." Mistel sniffled and met eyes so filled with concern that they pushed her over the edge. She began to sob, mortified that Lucia was here to witness it.

"Oh, Mistel." Cole moved to the edge of her bed and tucked his arm around Mistel. He pulled her close and stroked her hair. When her tears finally faded, he said, "Enough about me. How have you been?"

She laughed. "Bored to the point of weeping. Do tell me I can leave my room now."

"That's up to Sir Caleb."

"Who hates me. I'm no good at shielding my mind. He said I need to know how for once I'm no longer living in the castle." Which likely meant she would have to leave soon.

"I can help you practice later," Cole said. "Right now, we should work on the songs. The wedding is just over a week away, and we need at least one ready to perform."

"Won't they postpone?" Mistel asked. "Given the circumstances?"

"They all feel that calling off the wedding would let the enemy win."

"Achan and Lady Averella agree?"

Cole grimaced. "They haven't been told the whole of it. Duchess Amal said she will take full blame if they're angry, but she doesn't believe they would postpone, even if they knew. She said they have been through enough this past year and deserve to enjoy their wedding celebration without fear that an assassin might be lurking around every corner."

That sounded nice, but surely that hideous man would try to attack. "Aren't Prince Oren and Sir Caleb worried?" Mistel asked.

"Sir Caleb tries not to let on how worried he is," Cole said. "But Prince Oren is relieved. With the witches unable to attack, he finds little threat against Achan since he's a much more powerful bloodvoicer than Atul."

What Mistel really wanted to know was, would Arman continue to protect Cole from that nasty bloodvoicer? She was about to ask, when Lucia coughed, drawing their attention to where she stood by the door.

Cole moved back to the chair, positioned his lute on his lap, and strummed a few chords. "Feel like writing another famous song?"

Mistel pushed aside her fears for the time being. She could not wait for him to hear what she had written so far. "I hope you don't mind that I started without you," she said. "I've had little else do to."

"Why would I mind? You're an exceptional lyricist."

Oh, she could get used to this young man in her life, saying such kind things. She tidied the parchment on her bed, then returned the sentiment. "A compliment like that coming from such a talented musician. . . It's enough to make a girl blush."

"You think me talented?"

"Very much. If only my band had someone as gifted as you."

"Burch is a fine lutist."

"Yes, but he doesn't sing. Not like you. Or create melodies that bring words to life."

"We do sound good together." Cole held her gaze. "And I *would* like to sing with you more often."

"I know Rispen and Burch would enjoy accompanying us." She

felt certain she almost had him. "If only your responsibilities with the prince weren't so great."

He twisted his lips, but a grin slipped through. "I'd have to get permission from the prince, and there might be times when I couldn't be there because of my responsibilities. But I would be honored to sing with you and your friends, assuming they won't mind."

Mistel hadn't asked them yet, so she forced a smile. "Absolutely! Cole, I'm so excited." She gripped his hand. "We are going to have such fun."

He chuckled and gestured to the pages on her lap. "When are you going to show me what you've written on all this parchment?"

She pointed to the top of her sideboard. "Grab those other sheets off the shelf, please, and I'll show you what I have."

Chapter Twenty-Six
Mistel

O N THE DAY OF THE WEDDING, MISTEL donned her new cobalt-blue dress and hurried to meet Cole in the temple garden. So many extra guards roamed the castle that Mistel couldn't imagine how that hunx Atul could weasel his way inside. She found Cole standing amidst the lush flowers with the little boy with the blackened fingertips.

"You look very pretty," Cole said. "Doesn't she, Matthias?"

The boy turned his huge brown eyes on her and nodded. Lands, what a sweetie.

Their praise thrilled Mistel to the tips of her toes. "Thank you, both," she said. "Are you nervous?"

Cole shook his head and offered his arm. "After what I went through in the past few weeks, singing with you feels like a reward."

Mistel grabbed hold and increased his reward with a kiss on the cheek that made Cole blush and Matthias giggle. She couldn't help chuckling herself. She liked the effect she had on Cole Tanniyn.

Cole led them into the temple gardens, where flowers bloomed abundantly and filled the air with sweetness. As Mistel settled into a seat beside Cole and Matthias in the front row, a sense of gratitude overwhelmed her. A few weeks ago, she never could have imagined she'd be attending a royal wedding, let alone performing at it.

Achan, his knightly friends, and Noam Fox—a mutual friend from Sitna—took their places at the front of the garden beneath a white pergola draped in flowers and vines. Achan wore an ensemble of blue velvet and silk that reminded Mistel of the bolt she had so admired in the island market.

No sign of the bride yet. Achan drew something from his pocket and ate it.

"What's he doing?" Mistel asked Cole.

"Mentha leaves," Cole said. "He likes to chew them."

How odd.

A door in the back banged open, and everyone stood for the bride. The band began to play a plodding dirge in a minor key. Mistel had never heard anything more depressing for a wedding.

"What is that music?" she whispered to Cole, who winced and shook his head.

Simply dreadful.

Sir Eagan escorted Lady Averella forward. The future queen wore a stunning gown of blue brocade with a fitted bodice, long sleeves, and a full skirt. Every bit of the fabric was embroidered with pearls and gold thread. A matching cape lined in gold satin flowed off her shoulders and dragged behind her on the stone path of the garden. On her head, she wore a gold circlet studded with sapphires and rubies that held in place a lace veil so thick it obscured her face.

Mistel had never seen a more breathtaking gown, though if she had been in Lady Averella's slippers, she would have insisted on a thinner veil. How could Achan be certain who was behind that curtain? Yet he grinned at his bride.

"He seems rather amused," Mistel said.

"They're likely voicing each other," Cole said, "making jokes about the music and their clothing. They do that often."

Yes… Mistel gathered Cole was right. She supposed that made up for the fact that Achan couldn't see Lady Averella's face. "You know a lot about them."

"The prince, I know," he said. "Lady Averella left shortly after the prince took me on."

Fascinating. Mistel could not wait to hear every story Cole had experienced since coming to know the prince. For that matter, she couldn't help wondering about his life before then too. She wanted to know him better.

The wedding began, and Mistel found it the most beautiful event she had ever seen. Not only the garden setting but the poetic vows about stars and stones and promises of love.

When it ended, she clung to Cole's arm as he led her into the great hall, which had been rearranged and decorated with almost as many flowers as the garden. Mistel picked at her food, annoyed that her unsteady stomach kept her from enjoying such a feast. Courses of venison, fish, roasted quail, and various stewed vegetables and breads and custards filled the table, and she did nothing more than taste one or two. She dared not touch the custard for fear it would affect her voice. She watched Cole enjoy the meal, marveling that he didn't seem the least bit nervous.

What if Mistel forgot the words? What if Cole played a sour chord or broke a lute string? What if the audience didn't like the song? Worse, what if the future king and queen disliked it?

Cole suddenly stood and set his hand on her shoulder. "Sir Caleb says it's time. He's asked us to open with 'The Pawn Our King,' then sing 'The Sparrow that Was a She.'"

Mistel nodded and pushed to her feet. She moved through the crowd behind Cole, her mind distant and her steps unsteady, as if she were floating rather than walking. Somehow, she managed to climb the steps to the dais and walk to the center, stopping just a few paces from where Achan sat with his bride.

From the platform, Mistel took in the hundreds of spectators and thought she might faint dead away. What a difference from the dozen or so that she usually sang to on the wharf green.

Mistel took a deep breath, hoping to calm her nerves, but one strum of Cole's lute snapped her into her role as a performer. She marveled at how this boy brought out the best in her, and rewarded him with a smile.

Cole played "The Pawn Our King" in the key of G to give Mistel the lead, and she belted it out with gusto, thrilled when the audience sang heartily along.

When they finished, Cole waited for the applause to die out completely before he strummed a lively prelude to "The Sparrow that Was a She." Mistel started them off.

> *"In the walls of Castle Granton tucked inside a vineyard*
>   *fair,*
> *Lived the Lady Averella with long flowing raven hair.*
> *The False Prince invaded to force a marriage union,*
> *To the temple fled the lady hoping to cause confusion.*
>
> *She gave up her freedom and put on a mask.*
> *A boy named Vrell Sparrow, should anyone ask.*
> *To apprentice as a healer was her only task,*
> *The Sparrow that was a she."*

The song captivated the audience and brought a rosy hue to Lady Averella's face and a gleaming smile to Achan's.

When Mistel and Cole sang the final note, a soft moment of near silence fell before the entire great hall leaped to their feet in applause. Achan seemed more pleased than anyone else, grinning wildly at his bride. Mistel knew they had done very well indeed.

Cole embraced Mistel and swung her in a circle. "You were incredible. Thank you."

"Me? You wrote it too," she said.

He laughed and squeezed her hand. "*We* wrote it."

A juggler moved onto the dais and started his act. Cole and Mistel returned to their table, and Mistel was finally able to eat. She had just finished her last bite of custard when Cole stood up.

"Is that Madam Vinzen?"

Mistel turned to see an old woman with a long walking stick creeping between the tables. "Doesn't she sell trinkets in the marketplace?"

"She's walking oddly," he said.

Why this interest in an old woman? "Is she? How can you tell?"

"I…excuse me a moment." Cole walked toward Madam Vinzen.

Of all the nonsense! Mistel got up and followed Cole.

"Madam Vinzen," she heard him say. "I was pleased to hear Dewin made a full recovery."

Dewin Sessit? Was this woman somehow connected to Edera's murder?

The woman's eye twitched. She stepped stiffly around Cole and continued on. Cole followed her to the back wall, where she set her walking stick against a trellis threaded with roses and gardenias. Was she going to pick some flowers? But no. She turned and hobbled back across the room, leaving her stick behind.

Mistel didn't like the way she moved, as if every step pained her. Could she have a rheumatism?

Cole intercepted the woman. "Madam Vinzen," he said. "Who invited you to the reception?"

"Get away from me!" she cried, forehead wrinkled, as if pleading.

Mistel recognized that desperate look and gasped. Atul! "I think she's being controlled with magic."

This put a furrow in Cole's brow. He glanced toward the nearest doors, where two soldiers stood talking. "Guards!" The two men perked up and instantly headed toward them.

The old woman saw them coming and said, "Leave me be!"

"She's not herself," Cole said to the guards. "Someone is controlling her."

Mistel scanned the great hall, seeking out that greasy-haired, bloodvoicing hunx.

The guards grabbed the old woman's arms, and she fought them, slapping and squirming and kicking. Mistel's heart went out to her. She knew what it felt like to have that horrible man inside her head.

Then, just like Mistel had, the woman collapsed.

"Oh!" Mistel cried out, thankful the guards caught the poor dear before she hit the floor.

"He's stormed her." Cole grabbed Mistel's hands, and suddenly he was looking into her eyes. "I need you to find Sir Caleb. Quickly. Tell him what happened. He must get the prince and Lady Averella to safety, then come find me."

She ignored the goosebumps prickling up her arms. "But where are you going?"

"To find Atul. Hurry, Mistel. Go!"

Mistel ran, pushing through the crowd on her way to the dais. Please, please let her not be too late.

CHAPTER TWENTY-SEVEN
COLE

COLE FOLLOWED THE PATH BACK through the tables Madam Vinzen had come from, which led to an entrance. Had she let someone inside? He questioned the guards there, but they had seen nothing peculiar.

The crowd burst into laughter at a man and his dancing dog, who were performing on the dais. The prince and Lady Averella were still there.

Hurry, Mistel.

Cole went back the other way, tracing the route the old woman had taken to the back wall where she'd left her. . .

The walking stick was gone.

This discovery raised the hairs on Cole's arms. He paced along the wall, down to one corner and back to the opposite end, where he found a ladder tucked behind the back of the trellis. His heart leapt, and he wished yet again that he had the ability to bloodvoice.

Music picked up in the hall. People were dancing now, the seats of honor on the dais gloriously empty. He hoped that meant Sir Caleb had gotten Achan and Lady Averella to safety.

Cole gazed up at the swaths of organza and chiffon that draped between the intricate ribs and vaults of the ceiling and hid the catwalk that ran along the western wall.

Movement there. At first, he thought it was only a swaying strip of organza, until beyond the boughs, a dark shaped moved.

Oh no.

Without hesitation, Cole scrambled up the ladder to the narrow pathway of sturdy wooden planks that composed the catwalk. Iron brackets held it to the stone walls and roof, yet Cole didn't like the way it rattled beneath his steps. Every ten paces or so, boughs of organza crossed the catwalk diagonally, making it impossible to see what lay ahead.

If felt warmer up here, and the music was amplified by the curved surfaces of the arches and ribs of the ceiling, making it difficult to listen for Atul. Cole brushed another swath of organza aside, hoping someone had gotten the prince to safety. And if they had not, hoping he wouldn't be too late.

Arman, protect the prince and Lady Averella. Please don't let any harm befall them or anyone else.

He reached for his sword and realized he didn't have it with him. A pang of heat shot down his spine. How foolish to rush up here unarmed. What exactly was his plan? He could hear Sir Caleb's lecture already.

Cole was halfway across the room when he came across Madam Vinzen's walking stick, lying on the catwalk in two pieces. He crouched and found it hollow. There must have been some kind of weapon inside.

A twinge at his temples preceded the sound of Kurtz's voice in his head. *Open up, it's me.*

Cole lowered the shields around his mind. *Is the prince safe?*

Yeah, he's fine. Great new song, by the way. You and the girl sounded good together. Where are you?

On the catwalk above the great hall. I think someone is up here. It might be Atul.

Eben's breath! What's he doing?

I don't know. I can't see anything. There is too much organza and the—

"That's seven!" Achan's voice rose over the din of the crowd.

Cole's heart leaped. *Is the prince still in the great hall?* he asked.

He's stacking cakes with the minnow. They're doomed to have seven children so far. That boy has no idea how to play this game.

Get him out of here!

Make him leave his own party?

Laughter below drew Cole's attention. Sure enough, the prince and Lady Averella stood on either side of a stack of cakes. Cole ducked under the next swath of organza, and Atul came into view at the far end of the catwalk, threading a bow.

Kurtz? Atul has a bow. He's going to try and kill the prince! Get him out of the great hall.

On it.

Cole breathed deeply and fortified the shields around his mind. He grabbed one half of the walking stick and crept forward. He made it within two yards of Atul before the man saw him. Atul swung the bow toward Cole, who charged, stick swinging. Before Atul could manage to loose his arrow, the hollow walking stick smacked against Atul's ear and splintered down the side.

"Not today, boy," Atul said.

Cole swung again, but Atul caught the stick and wrenched it away. Before Cole could decide what to do next, Atul punched him. Fire lit Cole's jaw, and his head recoiled with an involuntary jerk. His face stung, and a metallic taste flooded his mouth. He dropped to his haunches on the catwalk, then dove toward Atul's legs. He wrapped his arms around them and let his momentum take them both down.

Something snapped, and the catwalk lurched. Plaster rained from above, and Cole found himself back in the Battle of Armonguard, cowering under the watchtower after the sea serpent had rammed its head through the brick wall.

No. This wasn't real. He needed to stay in the great hall. Stop Atul.

He concentrated on the lingering sting in his jaw, the taste of blood in his mouth. The ceiling of the great hall came back into view. Cole lay on the catwalk, Atul above him, bow drawn, arrow aimed down toward the crowd.

Cole kicked the bottom point of the bow. The weapon spun from Atul's grip, and the arrow fell to the catwalk. Before Atul could react, Cole swept the arrow over the catwalk's edge, then kicked the backs of Atul's legs.

Atul fell to his knees on the catwalk. He growled and fisted Cole's tunic. "Yeh weary me, boy."

As he drew back his other arm to strike, the bow slipped off his shoulder. Cole grabbed it and shoved the point of one end up into Atul's face. The man screamed, and Cole delivered a forceful kick with both feet to Atul's chest.

Atul spun along the railing and fell. Both scrambled to their feet and faced the other. They had changed places. Cole was now standing over the dais with Atul a few yards away.

Atul turned and ran.

"Guards!" Cole yelled.

He chased after Atul as fast as he dared go on the catwalk. Atul reached the back wall and grabbed for the ladder. Before he could take hold, it tipped aside and fell like a tree severed at the base.

With a sweeping glance, Cole caught sight of Mistel gazing up from below the platform. He wanted to know if help was coming, but that she hadn't left him alone bolstered his courage.

Atul, arms outstretched for the ladder, teetered off-balance, so Cole surged forward and slammed into him from behind. Gripping the man's knees, Cole lifted. Had Atul maintained his position, Cole's actions would have been useless, but Atul instinctively twisted in an attempt to defend himself. Though Cole had barely hoisted Atul off his feet, it was enough that—combined with the man's precarious balance—his back bent easily over the rail. Sensing Atul's weight shifting, Cole exerted all his strength and pushed him over.

Atul's arms flailed for purchase. One hand briefly grasped Cole's hair—ripped some out—but it was not enough. Atul plummeted over the catwalk railing. For a moment, the only sound Cole heard was Mistel's scream as she leaped aside. Then Atul's body hit the floor with a sickening thud.

CHAPTER TWENTY-EIGHT
MISTEL

IT HAD HAPPENED SO FAST. ONE MOMENT, that horrible mind stealer had been reaching for the ladder, so Mistel had pushed it over.

Then he'd attacked Cole and lost. Fallen at her feet.

She inched back from the body. The man wasn't moving, and for some reason, no one in the wedding celebration had even noticed what had gone on above their heads.

Had they not heard the ladder fall? Mistel scream? Had they missed the fact that Cole had saved the lives of Achan and Lady Averella?

"Kurtz!" Cole yelled. "Trizo! Over here!"

Mistel glanced up at the catwalk, but Cole wasn't there. Her heart wrenched, but then she saw him, climbing down the trellis on the other side of the catwalk. He jumped down the last bit, landing with a thud, and in two more steps, held her hands in his.

"Are you okay? I was afraid you'd gotten hurt."

Mistel threw her arms around his waist and hugged him. "I'm okay." And she really was. For the first time in as long as she could remember, she felt safe. Not only that, she trusted another person. Cole Tanniyn cared about her. He'd made sure she was fed, had a place to sleep and clothes to wear. He'd made music with her. . . risked his life for her.

No one had ever taken care of her before. Not like Cole.

She released him, ran her thumb over his swollen bottom lip. "What about you?"

Kurtz and Trizo arrived then and ruined the moment.

Trizo knelt beside the body, set his hand on the mind stealer's throat, and declared, "He's dead."

Mistel sighed, surprisingly deeply. She hadn't realized she had still feared that man, but she needn't be afraid any longer. Edera's killers had been brought to justice. All because of Cole Tanniyn.

CHAPTER TWENTY-NINE
COLE

IT WASN'T UNTIL AFTER THE CORONATION that Achan learned the full truth of the perilous events surrounding his wedding and called Cole to his office.

The king sat behind his desk, arms folded across his chest. "Duchess Amal has taken the full blame for having kept this conspiracy from me," he said, "and while I understand the sentiment behind it, I do not condone it and never want to be kept in the dark again. Arman will equip me for any situation that comes my way. It's not the place of anyone to make decisions for me. Have I made myself clear?"

Cole bowed his head. "Yes, sir."

"That being said, I must thank you, Cole, for saving my life and the life of my wife."

Cole instantly started shaking his head. "I didn't save any—"

"You are the one who spotted Atul Shakran here in Armonguard. I did not believe you, and I apologize."

"In all fairness, I was seeing things and—"

"No, you were right," Achan said. "Plus, you were the only one who realized he was on the catwalk at the reception. You stopped him with no help from the guards."

Cole's face grew warm. He cast his gaze to the floor. "I was merely in the right place at the right time, sir."

"Don't brush this off as nothing," Achan said. "Your humility is admirable, but it was your quick thinking and bravery that stopped Atul. Accept this truth and the credit you deserve. Your actions saved us, and for that, I am deeply grateful."

Cole wished he could melt into the floor, away from the attention that felt too focused and heavy. Yet a part of him—a small, quiet part—felt a sliver of pride. Maybe, just maybe, he wasn't as insignificant as he'd always believed.

He swallowed and met the king's eyes. "Yes, sir."

"You also solved the murder of the young woman. . . I don't recall her name."

"Edera Duwal, sir."

"Edera Duwal." Achan leaned forward and folded his arms on the desk. "This is not good, Cole, you being so heroic and clever all of a sudden."

Cole's brow pinched. "It's not?"

"No. You've shown your skills, and now I must decide whether or not to put you to use."

Just when it seemed Cole couldn't become more confused, the king topped himself.

"Have you any interest in becoming a spy?" Achan asked.

Cole stared at the king for a moment. The question was so far from anything he could have expected that he wasn't sure he'd heard it right. "A spy, sir? Me?"

"Yes, you. Join the Mârad as a spy."

Cole pictured himself tagging along with Jax mi Katt and Sir Rigil on some heroic quest. The idea seemed laughable. Perhaps they had need of someone to care for their horses. "I would need to leave Armonguard. Is that what you want?"

Achan sighed heavily. "No, Cole, I do not. You are a fine squire and a good friend. But I can't deny the idea has merit."

"I don't understand."

"You're full of surprises all of a sudden. Being a musician, being nineteen years old, being a sharp investigator, overcoming blood-voice possession." The king frowned. "You look confused. Don't you know you've done well?"

"I guess so, sir."

Achan chuckled, and it ended with a singsong sigh. "Sir Caleb cannot stop praising your exceptional notes, your meticulous attention to detail, your keen observation skills. On and on. It's endless. You're a natural, it seems, and now my uncle has this crazy notion of sending you out as a minstrel spy."

"Minstrel?"

"That would be your pretender identity. To allow you to enter places and, well, spy."

Such a thing seemed absurd. "Who would I be spying on?"

"He wants you in Tsaftown and Ice Island, to start. Apparently, you have a connection there?"

What? "I know of none, sir."

"I'm sure Prince Oren will fill you in. After that, I don't know."

Mistel sprang to mind. Making music with her. How much fun he'd had singing with her at the wedding. Matthias, Kurtz, Achan, and even Sir Caleb. These people had become Cole's family. His stomach lurched at the idea of leaving everything behind.

"Tsaftown is really far away," he said.

"There are factions forming all over Er'Rets," Achan said. "Groups like the Chartom who don't think I should be king. Some don't think there should be a king at all. While I might agree with them in theory, no one has any realistic plan for how such a thing could be feasible without madmen running wild. So, I'm to fight to keep my title, you see. Besides, Arman made it so, and he's the one really in charge, so. . . " He slapped his hands on the desktop and stood. "Sir Caleb is all for it, of course, so now you see they are against me." He circled the desk and sat on the front edge. "Not that I don't think you would do well. It's just. . . I've grown rather fond of you."

Cole's throat burned.

"What I'm getting at is," Achan said, sucking in a deep breath, "until we find out who is against me and stop them, not only will I be vulnerable, but I cannot be an effective leader. When I'm forced to spend my days dodging assassination attempts and putting out fires, it leaves little time to help people. And I want to help people, Cole."

Cole swallowed his emotions, shoved them down deep. "You would like me to do this?"

"*Like*, no. I will never admit that. But the kingdom needs you. People won't suspect someone like you. You have an honest face. You're a great actor. And you look. . . "

"Young," Cole said.

"It's more than that. You look trustworthy, safe."

Because he wasn't a warrior. "I'm not a strong swordsman, you mean."

"No, I didn't mean what I said as an insult. Pig snout. What I'm trying to say is, no one will suspect you."

Cole still didn't see how he could manage such a feat. "What if I fail?"

"I'll not send you alone. Kurtz will go too."

The tightness in Cole's chest eased. All was not lost. But. . . "Kurtz, a minstrel spy?"

"He tells me he's not a bad drummer. I'll let you be the judge of that."

Cole laughed at the idea of Kurtz beating a tabor. "But everyone knows him."

"Precisely. You see, I would not let you go alone, nor could I send you with just anyone. Prince Oren and I put our heads together, and Kurtz is the only man I trust who villains will think I don't."

"Huh?"

"We will craft the story that I dismissed him from service after the events on the Lebab Inlet. Apparently I missed some military reprimand?"

"Captain's Row," Cole said, shivering at the memory of the severe, public rebuke Sir Gavin had bestowed upon Kurtz.

"Right," Achan said. "Kurtz has agreed to pretend it made him so angry that he has deserted my army and moved on. You've always been his friend, so you will go with him. Traumatized by the dozens of times you've nearly died in my service."

Cole wasn't sure he liked that part of the story. "Kurtz agreed to this?"

"When I told him the two of you would be spies, he was quite excited, though I think he rather likes having permission to play the rogue." The king frowned, as if second-guessing his decision. "Promise me you'll keep him in line?"

As if anyone could control Kurtz Chazir. "I'll do my best, sir. How will I communicate with you?"

"Oh, I'll be checking in regularly." Achan tapped his temple. "So be sure to lower those shields when I knock. For Prince Oren as well. And you can always ask Kurtz to message either of us."

Cole exhaled a long breath, resigning himself to this idea. "When do I leave?"

"I knew you would accept. You've always been one I could count on." Achan sighed and circled back to his chair, still standing as he sorted through some parchment on his desk. "You leave tomorrow. You will travel north with Lord Livna and the Tsaftown army."

So soon? Cole caught himself staring at Achan and studied his hands. He rather liked the sound of the adventure. Of using the skills Sir Caleb, Prince Oren, and Achan saw in him. But leaving just when he'd been feeling like he might have found home? Leaving Mistel...

Yet the king awaited an answer. Cole steeled himself. "I'll be ready, sir."

Achan dropped back onto his chair. "I will miss you, my friend. What will I do without you?"

Cole thought of the many ways he might answer such a statement. "Between Sir Caleb and your wife, I'm sure you'll have plenty to keep you busy."

Achan snorted, then reached across the desk and knocked twice on the glossy surface. "You be sure and sing that new song about Vrell everywhere you go, all right? I want it ten times as famous as 'The Pawn Our King.'"

"I'll do my best," Cole said.

"You're going *where?*" Mistel stared at Cole, brow furrowed.

They were standing on a dock at the waterfront, gentle waves lapping beneath their feet. The sunlight sparkled across the water's surface, yet the sparkle in Mistel's eyes had completely vanished once Cole had told her he was leaving.

"To the north," he said, keeping his gaze on the glassy water.

"North *where?*"

"I can't say."

"Can't? Or won't?"

He clenched his jaw, then finally said, "The king asked me not to."

Mistel growled like an angry cat. "How long will you be gone?"

"A few months, I suspect," Cole said. "It's at least a three-week journey, traveling with the army and—"

"What army?"

"Tsaftown's. They're heading home, and we're going with them.

Part of the way, I mean. I'm taking my lute. I'll be playing often. The king says I must make sure all Er'Rets hears our new songs."

"Those songs were written for us to sing together."

Cole hung his head, the twist in his gut proof that playing their songs without Mistel was a betrayal. "I know, but—"

"How do you know you'll get to play?"

"That's part of my. . ." He made the mistake of glancing at her, and those gorgeous green eyes with the flecks of blue threatened to convict him. "There's not much else to do on such a long journey."

She narrowed her gaze. "You're going on a quest?"

"Me? That's ridiculous." Cole winced. He'd clearly have to work on his lying. Strange. . . He'd thought he was too good of a liar. Not today, it seemed.

Mistel sighed overly loud and dramatic. "What time are you leaving? Can you at least tell me that much? I'd like to see you off."

"We're riding north at dawn."

"You keep saying *we*. Who is *we*?"

Blazes! He stank at this. "I mean. . ." He swallowed. Eyes on the water. He could get through this. He had to. "The Tsaftown army."

"You just saved the king's life, and he repays you by banishing you?"

"He's not banishing me. It's a promotion, sort of."

"Parting you from the king is not a promotion." Mistel planted her hands on her hips. "This is Sir Caleb's doing. He doesn't want us together."

While that wouldn't surprise Cole, it wasn't the truth. "It honestly wasn't Sir Caleb's idea. He and the king were both very complimentary of our performance at the wedding."

"Were they?" Her surprised tone drew his gaze back to her. She was staring out at the water now, her eyes shifting as she took that in. "That's perfect. I'll just come with you."

Cole stared at her, his mouth gaping at the very idea. "You can't come."

"Why not? Two serving Er'Rets in song would be better than one, don't you think? Besides, we're a good team."

Cole grimaced at the idea of a mob of drunken outlaws drooling over Mistel as she sang in a crowed tavern. "We *are* a good team, yes, but I can't take you with me."

Mistel folded her arms. "Is this you trying to protect me? Because you don't have to protect me. I can take care of myself."

Not likely in a mob of drunken outlaws. "I know you can, but it's not up to me."

Mistel clenched her jaw, her mouth pinched. "I don't want to sing with just anyone. Not even with Rispen and Burch. I want to be with you."

Cole hated this. Why would Arman make him choose between the safety of his king and singing with this beautiful girl? "I know we work well together. But this particular… quest isn't something you can do."

She lowered her gaze. "Is there someone else?"

Oh yes. Mistel had plenty to fear with Kurtz as Cole's new musical partner. "That's not it at all. If it were up to me, I'd bring you." Which wasn't true. He bent the truth in hopes of making her feel better. "But it's not safe, Mistel. It's not going to happen."

She drew in a breath, her green eyes fierce. "I'm not afraid. You're the one who's always running. You ran from the Crooked Arrow. You ran from the Ebens. And now you're running from me."

Ouch. Cole clenched his jaw, his voice barely above a whisper. "I'm not running. I'm choosing to serve my king."

"Which means not choosing me."

Why did she have to take this so personally? "How can I refuse the king? Would you?"

Her features calmed into a cold mask. "You know what? Rispen, Burch, and I were doing fine before you came along. It was fun and all, but I'm better off without you."

That stabbed, but what could Cole say? He'd told her that from the start. Plus, he had no idea when he'd be back. He couldn't ask her to wait for him. They really hadn't known each other all that long. What a terribly unfortunate situation. "I'm sorry, Mistel. I'll. . ." He sighed. "I'll miss you."

"No," she snapped. "You don't get to say that. If it were true, you'd think of something to make this work. A way to stay at the castle or for me to come along." She stalked away, her steps loud on the wooden dock.

"Mistel. . ." Cole jogged to catch up.

She spun around, her hand raised between them. "Don't. Just don't." She stormed off, leaving Cole alone on the dock.

The chilled breeze rustled his hair and tunic, while inside, fierce waves battered his heart and threatened to capsize him where he stood. He watched her, not daring to even breathe until she passed out of sight around the castle wall.

Then she was gone.

It was fitting, really. Cole had never been blessed with stability in relationships. Every time he found himself getting used to a new place, something happened to turn the tables and shake up everything.

He'd always wanted someone who could see him fully. Someone with which he could be honest, spontaneous, make music. Mistel had swept into his life on a song. But he'd let himself care too much, too fast. He'd known better, yet she'd been so deeply alluring that he'd broken the rules he'd crafted to protect himself from this very thing.

Never again.

Chapter Thirty

Mistel

GOING FOR A RIDE, MISTEL?" NOAM asked. Her childhood friend was now the official royal stablemaster, promoted by Achan, of course. Noam had a long face and nose and was very thin—his fine brown tunic seemed two sizes too big.

"Yes, if it's all right," Mistel said. "I'd like to ride Bart again."

"I'm sure no one would mind."

"Could you help me saddle him? I know how, but I'm dreadfully slow."

"I'd be happy to. That's quite a hat."

Mistel lifted the brim a bit. "It keeps the sun from burning my face." She'd purchased the straw farmer's hat from the men's haberdashery in the Crescent. Turned out the shop had excellent taste in hats after all. At least for her current mission. "Also, and this may sound strange, Noam, but please humor me. Can you saddle Bart with a regular saddle? I've been learning to ride one and want to practice."

Noam frowned at her long skirt. "Are you sure?"

"Positive. Don't you know it's a trend? All the ladies want to experience what the queen did on her adventures. Everyone is saying it's more comfortable."

Noam chuckled and shook his head. "If you insist, a regular saddle it is." He carried the sidesaddle out of the stall. "You must be sorry to see Cole leave," he said, his voice softened by his distance. He reentered the stall carrying a full saddle. "The two of you got along well."

At the sound of Cole's name, Mistel's chest grew tight. She ignored it. "Oh, he'll be back soon enough." She leaned against the stall and watched as Noam readied the horse. Might he know where the army was? "When are they leaving, anyway?"

"They left at dawn," Noam said.

Mistel feigned surprise. "Oh, yes. I must have forgotten."

She hadn't. She was right on schedule.

A few minutes later, Mistel rode Bart out into the castle bailey. Last night, she had stolen a saddlebag, packed it with everything she cared about, and hidden it behind some rose bushes. She stopped now to collect it, annoyed to discover that it should have gone on before Noam affixed the saddle. She managed to drape it behind her saddle, then mounted again.

She rode out the gates and along the King's Road, pushing Bart as fast as she dared. She wasn't a strong rider and didn't want to hurt herself or the poor animal.

Mistel was finished playing games to earn a bite to eat or to help her band earn a living. She wanted something real, and what she and Cole had. . . He truly cared about her. Unfortunately, he was more concerned with trying to protect her than pleasing himself. And honestly, she loved that about him—that he made her feel safe. But they were a good team. He needed her as much as she needed him, and while she had no idea what quest he'd been sent on, she wasn't about to let him walk into danger alone.

Once she reached a forest, she stopped to remove her dress and expose the tunic and trousers beneath. She stowed her dress in the saddlebag, tied her hair up, and replaced the straw hat. Then she set out again.

She had learned a thing or two from Vrell Sparrow in writing "The Sparrow that Was a She." Mistel, too, could dress like a boy and have an adventure. She would catch up with the army and ride with them, keeping herself hidden until they'd made it far enough across Er'Rets that when she revealed herself, the knights wouldn't dare send her back.

As if any of them got to make choices for Mistel. She could travel through Er'Rets if she wanted. If she happened to stay at the same inn as Cole… if she happened to join in some of his minstrel performances… well, he would not refuse her. Not again.

BONUS EPILOGUE

Thank you for reading *Squire of Truth*. We hope you loved the story. Find out what happens next with our Bonus Epilogue, a special gift, available only to our newsletter subscribers.

This Bonus Epilogue will not be released on any retailer platform, so scan our QR code to get your free gift. You acknowledge you are becoming a Sunrise Publishing and Jill Williamson subscriber. Unsubscribe from either newsletter at any time.

After years of darkness, Eric Livna, newly appointed lord of Tsaftown, returns from the battlefield ready to properly assume his title and become a true husband and father to his family. His marriage to Lady Viola, though arranged and built on mutual duty, has lacked the warmth of true affection, but Eric is hoping to bridge the emotional distance between them.

For too long Lady Viola Livna has silently endured the injustices woven into Tsaftown's laws—laws she believes will threaten their daughter's future. Determined to forge a better path for their family, she quietly works on a plan to change things...even if it means keeping secrets from her husband.

When Eric's cousin, the ambitions Sir Fenris Yarden, stirs up division in Tsaftown and wreaks havoc on the Livnas' marriage, Eric and Viola must decide whether to let betrayal tear them apart or to unite against the forces trying to destroy them.

Together, they will need to fight not only for their city, but also for the fragile trust they've begun to rebuild—before everything they hold dear is lost forever.

CHAPTER ONE

ERIC

S OMETHING WASN'T RIGHT.

A knot soured Lord Eric Livna's gut as he rode his stallion, Guffey, in the column just behind the advance guard. This same knot had warned him of looming dangers on the eve of battle, but there was no such battle waiting at the end of this journey. The war was over. Gidon Hadar, the true king, sat on the throne and had turned back the literal Darkness that had covered half of Er'Rets for the past ten years.

Instead of battle cries, the men of the Tsaftown army laughed with one another. A gleeful bard sang the chorus of "The Pawn Our King" and had entertained them with many other anthems as they traveled the long road home.

Their route currently wove through a snowy valley in the foothills of the northern Chowmah Mountains. The noon sun cast silvery light over the frosted patchwork of trees that had once been the mighty northern forest Eric had hunted in as a youth. Darkness had marred its beauty these past ten years, but the stark whiteness revealed signs of renewal. Oak and maple trees stood tall beneath icy mantles, their trunks shedding remnants of lichen and moss. Even brittle grass peeked timidly through patches where the snow had thinned, a fragile promise of life beneath the wintry shroud.

The land was healing at last.

"Something on your mind, my lord?" Whiffs of vanilla-scented smoke tickled Eric's nose as his grey-bearded valet rode up alongside. Apparently, the pleasant weather had inspired the typically reserved Walter Blackburn to relax a bit and savor his pipe.

"Home is the only thing on my mind," Eric said. "A warm hearth, a proper meal, and a soft bed."

"And a nice pair of dry boots," Walter added, puffing on his pipe.

Eric chuckled. "If that is your wish. You may use your downtime however you see fit."

Walter leaned in toward Eric. "I hadn't wanted to say so, but your squire appears to be getting a head start on his downtime."

Eric traced Walter's gaze back toward where Derby Wenk, Eric's young squire, followed on his own horse. He was supposed to be serving as Eric's back rider, but the lad had drifted several horse lengths and was listening to one of the soldiers weave a longtale.

Not just any soldier, Eric noted. Kurtz Chazir. One of the king's men. Originally from Tsaftown, he had long ago earned a reputation for indulging in drink and female company. He had been involved in King Gidon's now legendary escape from the Ice Island prison and had served at the king's side faithfully throughout the war, sometimes heroically, other times making blunders worthy of a Captain's Row.

Apparently, there had been some falling out between the king, his former squire Cole Tanniyn, and Kurtz in the weeks following the war. The king himself had asked Eric to let the two men ride north with the Fighting Five Hundred to seek out some new endeavor.

Derby cackled as Kurtz's tale reached its climax. The lad was clearly enjoying himself at the expense of his duty. While on campaign, such a lapse in discipline would have been met with harsh rebuke. Yet with the army but two days from home after months of battling their way down and back up the length of Er'Rets, perhaps such valiant service had earned the lad a bit of latitude.

On the other hand, Eric didn't want his squire getting accustomed to being lax in his duty.

"Master Wenk!" Eric barked. "On your post."

Surprise shone in Derby's eyes as he turned away from Kurtz. The lad prodded his horse and quickly resumed his position behind Eric.

"I'm sorry, my lord."

"Chin up," Eric said. "If you hope to make the Fighting Fifteen one day, you can start by keeping vigilant. And you can't do that while staring at your boots. You'll have plenty of time to trade stories with your comrades once we reach home."

Derby forced his head up, making proper eye contact. "Of course, my lord."

Eric internally squirmed at Derby's repetition of the words "my lord." Not merely the words themselves—he'd heard them plenty over the past few months—but the reverence Derby often put in them. The title still didn't seem to fit. Like an overly snug shirt, tugging at his shoulders. Like he was borrowing the title from his father.

A sharp ache spiked in Eric's chest.

Four months ago, Esek Nathak, the false prince, had run the elder Lord Livna through with the sword. Eric's father, killed on the whim of a bloodthirsty tyrant.

There had been precious little time to grieve. Soon after, Eric and the Tsaftown army had marched south to war with the then Crown Prince Gidon Hadar. This left Eric's grieving mother and his wife, Viola, to tend to the needs of the city in his absence. Eric had no doubt they were up to the task, but he hated that he had been pried away from his family when they no doubt had needed him most.

The bard ended his performance of "The Pawn Our King" with a playful flourish which earned a round of laughter from the men. He segued seamlessly into "The Sparrow that Was a She," a new song first sung at the king's wedding that chronicled the adventures of Lady Averella as she traveled through Darkness with the then-Crown Prince.

Queen Averella now. It would take some time for Eric to get used to addressing his younger cousin by such a title.

A sharp whistle echoed from the front of the column, signaling a halt. Hooves and armor clattered as the line came to a lumbering stop. Eric pulled Guffey out of formation and galloped toward the head of the column with Walter and Derby riding close behind.

At the front of the line, Eric reined Guffey to a halt beside Captain Roxburg Demry, the commander of the army. A large clearing on the side of the road exposed the burned-out husk of a house. Beyond lay a snowy field, stretching far into the distance. Dark scorch marks marred a stone half-wall that formed a large rectangle around the perimeter of what had once been the manor house. The only structure left standing was a dilapidated shed on the back corner of the property.

"By the Three," Walter muttered. "This was Glodwood Manor."

Eric's chest tightened.

Glodwood Manor had long been a landmark for travelers of the King's Road. It wouldn't have rivaled the beautiful structures in Carmine or Armonguard, yet such an elegant home stood out in the north where most houses were built to be functional. But where the beautiful log home and barn once stood, only scorched timbers and a collapsed chimney remained. A swath of snow blanketed everything. The tragedy must have transpired months ago.

Could it have been an accident? Such an explanation didn't satisfy Eric. He eyed a strange mass covering a section of the cobblestone walkway in front of what used to be the door. A closer look, and Eric noticed that the lump wore boots.

A body.

Eric slid from Guffey's saddle and gave his squire a pat on the leg. "Come along, Derby. Get your shield and let us take a closer look."

Derby grabbed his shield off his saddlebag as he dismounted, and the pair strode through the snow toward the iron gate.

Captain Demry called after them, "My lord, what is it you mean to do?"

Eric looked back. "I merely wish to see the scene for myself."

Captain Demry's eyes narrowed. "I can send soldiers, if you want to investigate."

Eric smiled to himself. Captain Demry was a fantastic commander, but he could be paranoid when it came to Eric's safety. "Your concern is touching, but unnecessary. I'll take a quick peek, then we can carry on."

The iron hinges of the gate creaked as Eric and Derby entered the front yard. A faint stench of death touched Eric's nostrils. The fire might have been months ago, but the poor soul lying prone on the walkway couldn't have been dead for more than a week.

Eric knelt by the remains and used his gloved hand to brush a fine layer of snow off the body. The man was dressed in traveling clothes with a black sash running over one shoulder to his opposite hip. He had been run through multiple times and pinned to the ground with a series of stakes and ropes. A steel badge bearing the likeness of a wolf had been fastened to the sash, right above his heart.

"What do you make of this?" Eric asked.

Derby crouched beside Eric and gestured at the corpse. "Why'd they pin him to the ground?"

Eric traced the length of the rope with his gaze. Something about this seemed familiar, but he couldn't say exactly what.

"Here's another one." Derby pointed at a second thin rope tied across the corpse's waist. He hooked his fingers around it and gave a tug.

"Stop!" Eric seized Derby's wrist as a sudden realization came over him.

Poroo raiders.

Derby glanced at Eric, rope still in hand. "My lord, what—?"

"Take care, lad. It appears you've stumbled across a trap."

Derby's eyes went wide.

Eric had seen a snare like this years ago while hunting with his father. He reached around Derby and slipped the shield from the lad's shoulder. "Hold tight. You've only engaged the first part of the snare, but if you let go, it will fire." The trap would have been invisible in Darkness, but daylight had exposed a line of footprints trailing away from the body through the snow and into a cluster of trees some ten paces away.

"Captain Demry!" Eric called. "Have archers ready."

Demry hollered out the order, arming his bow along with the others.

Eric slid Derby's shield in front of them. In their crouched position, it might be enough to save them. "Remain absolutely still."

"I'm sorry, my lord. I didn't—"

"None of that now. Do as I say, and we'll all come through this." Eric's eyes darted to the nearby trees. The patches of underbrush that edged close to the stone wall. The run-down shed in back. Anywhere the Poroo might be hiding. Scurrying motion in the woods caught his eye.

"On my right, Captain," Eric said.

More movement. Glimpses of pale skin and furs shuffling through the underbrush. Were there four? No, five.

"More on the left," called Walter.

Eric glanced quickly to the left and counted at least three Poroo behind a snowbank. He couldn't worry about them. The bigger threat was on the right, so he'd have to trust Walter to watch their backs.

All chatter among the men had ceased. Only the creaking of the gate, buffeted by a soft wind, could be heard in the otherwise silent scene.

Eric slowly turned on the balls of his feet toward the expected direction of the strike. "Captain Demry, I'm going to spring the trap." He hunched his shoulders, making himself as small of a target as possible. "Duck your head, Derby. Then let go of the snare."

Derby's dark eyebrows shot up.

"Now!" Eric said.

The squire swallowed, lowered his head, and let go.

There was the sound of stretching leather. Then a sharp wooden snap.

As the rip cord snapped back, snow flew up from the ground and flung a wooden projectile into Eric's shield. The impact rattled his teeth and knocked him and Derby to the ground.

A chorus of angry war whoops shot up on the fringes of the forest. Footsteps scampered over the ground as a war party of fur-clad Poroo warriors charged out of the woods on Eric's left and right.

Twice as many as he had first counted.

"Loose!" Captain Demry yelled.

A collective flutter of fletchings preceded the arrival of the first volley of Tsaftown's bowmen. Several arrows met their targets, and three of the charging raiders fell.

Eric leapt to a defensive position and drew his sword. The embedded spear threw off the shield's balance, but it was far better than nothing.

Two of the raiders vaulted the stone half-wall and sprinted toward Eric and Derby. One took an arrow to the chest and fell. The other swung a massive club at Eric, who sidestepped and sliced his sword deep into the man's thigh. The Poroo stumbled and was swiftly finished off by a barrage of arrows from the bowmen.

"More beyond the sheds!" Captain Demry's voice roared over the battlefield, calling out the order. "Wroxton! Get your men to Lord Livna."

Wroxton leapt off his horse, followed by Torin Oxbow and Gunnar Gedmund. Kurtz Chazir also drew his sword and charged into the fray.

Derby still knelt on the ground, pawing at the snow. What was he doing?

"On your feet!" Eric yelled.

"I—I'm trapped!"

Eric took a closer look. The rope from the snare had cinched Derby's wrist to the ground. Eric stepped between the helpless squire and the oncoming attackers.

"Cut yourself free. Quickly." Eric slammed his shield into the next Poroo, breaking off the remnant of the wooden spear against the attacker's breastbone. The man crumpled, and Eric ended him with a swift stroke.

Wroxton and the other soldiers barreled over the half wall and joined Eric at his side.

A cry from Derby distracted Eric. The loop pulled tighter and tighter around Derby's wrist. Poroo trickery. The trap kept twisting. Derby tried to cut himself free, but now he risked slashing his wrist open in the process.

Eric traced the line of the snare to its source. The rope led into the burned timbers of the house. He slashed with his sword. The line snapped and retracted completely into the house. Finally free, Derby fell onto his backside.

"Up, and make haste!" Eric yelled.

Derby got to his feet, drew his sword, and joined the fight. The six men stood in a loose circle, ready for the next onslaught.

Horse hooves rumbled, and Jol Quimby led a trio of riders around the outer edge of the wall. The Poroo in the open scrambled away from the charge, but arrows flew from the underbrush and from behind snowdrifts in the field. Three riders in a disorganized charge were simply not enough to deter the attackers.

"Form ranks. Prepare your spears!" Captain Demry bellowed.

Yet more Poroo tore out of the woods. How many more were there?

The army could have handled the raiders easily if they were prepped for battle, but the ambush had caught them completely flat-footed. And the Poroo's evasive tactics meant that Captain Demry's men had no target to engage. The bowmen provided support at a distance, but they couldn't easily get past the fence to charge into the fray without exposing their flank.

Eric and his group would have to hold their own until Captain Demry's men could form a proper cavalry charge.

A trio of Poroo climbed over the stone wall and charged Eric's position. The tallest bore down on them with a great ax. Swift arrows slowed the two smaller attackers, but the first man charged forward, ax already swinging. Eric raised his shield and caught the ax in the wood. He wrenched the shield to the left and slashed into the man's unguarded left arm, nearly severing the limb at the elbow.

The Poroo dropped the ax. Eric swung at the raider's neck. Somehow, the one-armed man caught the killing stroke, wrapping his meaty fingers around the blade and pushing it back. He glared with bloodshot eyes and howled an ear-splitting war cry in Eric's face.

A sword strike came down on the Poroo's collarbone. Derby Wenk landed the final blow. The Poroo's grip slipped from Eric's sword. Derby slammed his shoulder into the man and knocked him to the ground. The squire quickly pivoted to stand shoulder to shoulder with Eric, and they braced for another onslaught.

"Northlanders, ho!" Captain Demry's voice called out over the din of the skirmish.

The thunder of a dozen sets of hooves shook the ground as Captain Demry rode his red warhorse at the head of a properly organized column around the outside of the stone wall. Even Walter had joined the charge, firing his bow into the heaviest group of Poroo. Quimby's trio followed in Captain Demry's wake, wielding their swords like men in a blood rage. More arrows zipped past as the cavalry charge swiftly wheeled around the back of the homestead and picked off the raiders one at a time.

Eric gazed across the battlefield. The skirmish had turned into a full retreat as the surviving Poroo made for the safety of the woods. Or at least most of them.

A solitary figure stood in the burned remains of the barn, lingering far longer than any of his compatriots. A great deal older than the majority of the Poroo who had fought today, this man leaned on a large staff adorned with bear claws and glared at Eric across the battlefield. Was that hatred in his expression? Contempt?

Eric took a measured step toward the Poroo and raised his sword in a silent challenge.

The lone Poroo retreated from the barn and disappeared amidst the snowy trees.

Eric met Derby's gaze for a moment and clapped the young man's shoulder. "Well done, Derby. Keep that up and Captain Demry will have no choice but to appoint you to the Fighting Fifteen."

Captain Demry brought his mount to a halt at the gate in front of Eric. The rest of the riders secured the perimeter of the homestead, ensuring no Poroo stragglers lingered.

"Are we clear, Captain?" Eric called.

Captain Demry tucked his bow over his shoulder. "All clear, my lord. We took a few wounds from the Poroo hiding in the trees. Nothing life-threatening. No doubt they expected a wagon train of peddlers, not the leading edge of the Fighting Five Hundred."

Eric and Derby withdrew through the gate and rejoined the scattered column.

"Are you quite satisfied with your investigation, my lord?" Walter asked.

Eric chuckled. "I believe so."

"Well, look who stumbled into a spot of bother," Wroxton said as he handed Derby the reins to his horse. "Wenkling was determined to fight the Poroo single-handedly."

"Consider yourself lucky you didn't step in a cham trap, eh, Wenkling?" Kurtz added. "That would've shortened your step in a hurry, it would."

The men laughed, and Derby's overlarge ears reddened as he climbed up on his horse again.

"But did you see the way he tackled the big brute?" Quimby said, his voice filled with admiration. "Wenkling may have stumbled into that trap, but he sure knows how to wield a blade. Saved his lordship's hide, he did."

Derby sat a little higher in the saddle after that comment.

Eric mounted Guffey and took one last look at what had once been Glodwood Manor. The fight had only left him with more questions. Too many to feel at ease.

Poroo weren't known to conduct raids this far north. Perhaps the end of Darkness had changed their hunting patterns? But why burn the farmhouse? Why mutilate a body and set a trap in the ruins? And all this happening so close to Eric's home. Too close for comfort.

"Onward!" Eric called. "To home."

The column resumed their procession toward Tsaftown. There he intended to find answers to his lingering questions.

Something wasn't right.

NOTE FROM JILL

I found myself in a strange place when I received an email from Susan May Warren in the fall of 2021 asking if I might be interested in writing more Blood of Kings books with Sunrise Publishing. I had just started my second full year of teaching fifth grade at an online school, which didn't allow me as much time to write as I liked. I had been writing stories on Kindle Vella, which I could do one morning a week. But I was dreaming about what kind of book I should write next, and I admit I hadn't yet decided what to work on.

Then came this intriguing request from Sunrise Publishing. I had always wanted to write some continuing Blood of Kings stories, and here was an amazing opportunity to do so! Saying yes was not a difficult decision.

First, I want to thank God for this amazing blessing. There are still days that I pinch myself when it all seems so incredibly unreal, just to make sure that I am, indeed, awake. This opportunity to work closely with Susan May Warren and Sunrise has been a delightful and humbling gift. But without Jesus, I would have no strength or margin to walk down this road and see where it leads. All glory and honor goes to the master storyworld builder.

Thanks to Susan May Warren and Lindsay Harrel for starting Sunrise and for their heart to mentor new writers. This experience has been one of the greatest honors of my career and such a blessing in my life.

Second, I'd like to thank some of my dear friends and readers for brainstorming with me what might be happening in Er'Rets after Darkness has been defeated. Hugs to Bethany Baldwin, Carissa Barrows, Hannah Carmichael, Phillip Devereaux, Jami Lewis, Larry Nielsen, John Otte, Shantel Pike, and Brad Williamson.

A huge thank you to every writer who auditioned for the Blood of Kings Legends series. Your heart for the characters and story-world of Er'Rets blessed me to no end! It was a joy to read your work and your ideas and one of the hardest decisions of my life to have to choose between you.

I am so grateful for Andrew Swearingen, Kelly Fernlake, and Niki Florica. It has been a true pleasure to get to know each of you and to work with you on your stories. You are talented writers, kind friends, and I can't believe I get to work with you. Thank you for setting your own projects aside to write your Blood of Kings Legends books. Thank you to your family and friends too, because I know these stories took up your time. It continues to be an honor to create stories with you.

Special thanks go to Bobbi Mash, Kimberly Titus, and Brad Williamson for being my beta readers for Squire of Truth. Your feedback made this story stronger in so many ways.

Huge gratitude goes to my Patrons whose generosity and support allow me to create all kinds of fun writing projects. I am thankful for each and every one of you: Madi Trandahl, Bethany Baldwin, Carissa Barrows, Connie H., Deena Peterson, EL, Emily Hutnyak, Jenni McKinney, Jennie Webb, Linda Samuels, Marie Lynch, Paul James, Jim Denney, Kay Freeland Chang, Danielle Birney, Darrin Hutnyak, Rachelle Sperling, and Tracie Heskett. Thanks to the Sunrise team: Susan, Lindsay, Rel, Sarah, and Essie. And to Emilie Haney for designing amazing covers, and to Megan Gerig and Katie Donovan for being top-notch editors.

And finally, to you, dear readers. Thank you for loving these characters and this world of Er'Rets and for shining light in the darkness. I am forever grateful to you all.

Jill

ABOUT THE AUTHOR

Jill Williamson is a multi-passionate creative who loves the arts. She's written over two dozen books for readers of all ages and is best known for her Blood of Kings fantasy series, two of which won Christy Awards and made VOYA magazine's Best Science Fiction, Fantasy, and Horror list. She produces films with her husband and teaches about writing at conferences.

Visit her at www.jillwilliamson.com.

Connect With Sunrise

Thank you again for reading *Squire of Truth*. We hope you enjoyed the story. If you did, would you be willing to do us a favor and leave a review? It doesn't have to be long—just a few words to help other readers know what they're getting. (But no spoilers! We don't want to wreck the fun!) Thank you again for reading!

We'd love to hear from you—not only about this story, but about any characters or stories you'd like to read in the future. Contact us at www.sunrisepublishing.com/contact.

We also have a monthly update that contains sneak peeks, reviews, upcoming releases, and fun stuff for our reader friends. Sign up at www.sunrisepublishing.com or scan our QR code.

9 781963 372588